H.C. Kingsmill Moore has spent twenty-six years in corporate broking where he has acquired a wealth of inspiration for his debut novel, the City being a rich environment for drama that seldom needs embellishment. From a medical family, Hugh studied Biology at Durham University which led to many years specialising in biotechnology company financings, the inspiration for the story in *Selection*. He lives in Berkshire with Nina, his wife of twenty years, a preparatory school headmistress, his three teenage children, and two large messy dogs.

This novel is dedicated to my beautiful wife, who inspires me daily to be the best I can be, to my late father whose integrity in all things showed me the way, and to my mother for her enduring wit and unconditional love.

SELECTION

Who chooses?
The hunter or the hunted?

H.C. Kingsmill Moore

NINE
ELMS
BOOKS

Selection
First published in 2024 by
Nine Elms Books
Unit 1g, Clapham North Arts Centre
26–32 Voltaire Road
London SW4 6DH

Email: info@nineelmsbooks.co.uk
www.nineelmsbooks.co.uk

ISBN: 978-1-910533-77-2
Epub: 978-1-910533-75-8

Copyright © H.C. Kingsmill Moore

Protected by copyright under the terms of the International Copyright Union.

The rights of H C Kingsmill Moore to be identified as the author of this work have been asserted by him in accordance with the Copyright, Designs and Patents Act, 1988. All rights reserved.

This book is sold under the condition that no part of it may be reproduced, copied, stored in a retrieval system or transmitted in any form or by any means, electronic, mechanical, photocopying, recording or otherwise without prior permission of the author.

Cover design and typesetting: Alan Cooper Design
Printed in the UK.

ACKNOWLEDGEMENTS

First and foremost, I want to thank my wife Nina for allowing me the indulgence of writing a novel, and her fastidious proof reading with her headteacher's red pen, which helped tidy up the early drafts to the point at which a publisher could possibly consider taking it on. My mother and siblings, Alexandra and David, have also provided very helpful critiques that provided essential guard rails and much-needed encouragement at important points along the way.

Technical expertise was provided by Professor Cockwell (medical), Paul Howlett (specialist military), Richard Quellyn-Roberts (technical surveillance), Pete Dunlop and Andrew Winterton (legal). Further specialist guidance has been provided by friends who wish not to be named, but have provided accuracy in areas where I have no firsthand experience. A particular thank you to Peta Broadfoot who painstakingly edited this debut novel and made the experience enjoyable against the odds. And of course to Anthony Weldon, my publisher, who saw a diamond in the rough and was prepared to work with me to make it shine.

CHAPTER 1

'Be lucky, Seb', said the prison officer as he handed him his possessions in a clear plastic bag. 'And for Christ's sake don't come back, you hear!'

'Thanks, Bob. I won't.'

They both said the right words, but neither with any conviction. In reality, Feltham Young Offender Institution was more criminal college than rehabilitation centre. Most of the inmates would return, and multiple times, so why would he be any different. Seb's six-month sentence for assault was his rock bottom, he hoped, but that was the full extent of his planning.

Shoulders hunched, head down, he walked out into the visitor car park and a dreary November day. He half dreaded seeing his mother. He knew he'd broken her heart again, and her devotion and determination to love him no matter what were sometimes hard to take. Her battered, twenty-year-old Volvo was nowhere to be seen. Instead, a car door opened in the middle distance and a familiar grey-haired figure stepped out, striding purposefully towards him. Seb's heart sank.

'Uncle Pat. What are you doing here?'

'Hello Seb. You mother asked me to pick you up. Do you have everything?'

'This is it.' Seb held up the plastic bag with a dismissive shrug.

'Then let's get away from this God-awful place.'

No handshake offered by either party. Patrick Faber wasn't given to trivial conversation. Retired military. No wasted effort. Everything had to have a purpose. They drove away from the borstal through the endless succession of drab West London suburbs, and nothing was said for some time. It was Seb, in the end, who broke the silence.

'Where are you taking me?'

'Home, Seb. To your mother, brother and sister. But we won't be going there until we've cleared a few things up.'

Seb looked out of his window, ready for the onslaught; his uncle had long given up on trying to help him. But here he was.

Pat paused for a moment before he spoke again.

'I haven't been the uncle I should've been since your father died.'

He looked across at Seb, slouched low in his seat, and took a deep breath.

'I know you blame yourself for what happened, but you have to know it wasn't your fault.' He delivered his next words with slow, precise emphasis. 'He should have waited for help, but he tried to play the hero and he got himself killed.'

Seb tensed, his guts spasming, and clenched his fists. He'd worshipped his father.

'I was stuck on a cliff with the tide coming in. What else was he supposed to do?' he burst out.

'You were thirteen and perfectly capable of swimming to

Chapter 1

safety. As you subsequently proved I might add. He should have told you to jump into the water well clear of the rocks and swim to the beach. Scrambling over the cliffs to try and fish you off was bloody madness.'

Seb had heard enough.

'Stop the car!'

He'd just completed a custodial sentence for putting a drug dealer in coma, he could intimidate anyone. Not his uncle.

'Listen to me Seb. My brother died because he made a mistake. The best of intentions, yes. But a terrible mistake. I will not let your life be ruined any more by the decision he made on that day. He loved the very bones of you, Seb. It would absolutely destroy him to see you like this. To see you end up in a hell hole like that.'

Seb had never seen his uncle be so emotional. Pat took a moment to gather himself before he continued.

'So, I have spoken to your mother, and we've come up with a plan. Your conviction will be off your record in eighteen months. That gives you time to re-sit your A-levels next summer. And you'll do well this time. A, because you're bright and B, because you bloody well have to. The following February you'll attend the Army Officer Selection Board in Westbury. There's a preliminary assessment where you'll be put through various physical and mental tests to allow you to progress to the main board. If you commit to the process, I have no doubt that you will succeed. But I can't help you with that. It has to come from you.'

Seb shifted uncomfortably in his seat.

'Even if I agree, how could the Army take a convicted criminal?'

'I've just told you. Your conviction will be spent by

then, so you won't have to declare it. If anyone discovers it subsequently, they'll have no legal recourse to take any action against you or treat you any differently. If you pass the tests at Westbury, you'll earn a place at Sandhurst. And forty-four weeks later, God willing, your mother will have tears in her eyes as she watches you pass out as an officer in The British Army.' Another deep breath, 'And all this mess will be behind us.'

Seb was stunned into silence. He'd never even considered the Army. But then again, he'd never damn near killed a man before, and he wasn't exactly overwhelmed with career choices. Or ideas.

'It's a lot to think about it. I need time.'

'You have the forty minutes it takes to get you home to think about it. Your mother will want an answer. And she deserves one.'

Seb stared out of the window as they drove down the Great West Road towards his Berkshire home. He thought of his mother. What he'd put her though. His brother and sister, who were growing up without their beloved father just like him, but who weren't fucking up their lives like he had. But mostly he thought of his Dad.

'OK. I'll do it.'

'Good. Now let's get you home. You start again from here.'

CHAPTER 2

SAS Selection: Test Week.
Brecon Beacons, South Wales.

Can't be far now. Just keep fucking moving...

He didn't know if the words were coming out of his mouth or were just in his head. He had long since transitioned into a zombie-like state where he refused to give in to the pain, treating it like a defiant child best ignored. Seb had completed thirty-eight miles of Endurance. Four to go. His Bergen was sodden, much heavier by now than its 55lb dry weight. His rifle was gripped in his right hand in a claw-like fist, his joints rigid from seventeen hours of unbroken, unyielding slog. He hurt everywhere but had dodged the fate of half of the candidates on this brutal element of SAS Selection, whose feet, ankles or knees had failed them. Removed from the course by the Directing Staff, some protesting manically, others in abject resignation. All in physical and psychological despair. RTU. Returned to Unit. Course failed.

It was dawn. The overnight rains had given a little, but everything was still saturated. Every foot placed with anxious precision; no idea who was ahead and who was behind, the group having strung out into an extended snake several miles long within an hour or so of the start. A heavy mist foreshortened the view in every direction. Still on target for the anticipated twenty-hour cut-off. The exact time allowance was never known by the men on the course; yet more uncertainty to mess with their minds. Daylight, such as it was, began to seep through the sky, inspiring a resurgence of energy, a bit more confidence in his footing. He fixed his thoughts on to the next phases of the course, the ones he hoped he'd get to attempt, chiefly resistance to interrogation. The battery, stress positions and disorientation he was confident he could work his way through, but he had a nagging concern that he'd weary of the simulated capture environment and tell the interrogators to go fuck themselves. It was a brutal monitored exercise, but it was still obvious that that was all it was going to be. They weren't going to shoot him. He'd have to repress that knowledge, not let himself act on it.

Still on target. Left foot, right foot, left foot, right foot. Breathe and stride. Not so hard.

His right foot slipped on the wet granite. The path fell away to his right and, unbalanced by the dead weight of his Bergen, he fell forward heavily onto his right hand. Torn between maintaining his grip on his weapon and protecting himself, his body twisted unnaturally as he fell. He knew instantly. It was a sensation he'd felt before and never forgotten. His right arm was not where it should be.

'Oh, fuck fuck fuck,' he muttered under his breath, desperate to avoid drawing any attention to himself. He couldn't see any of the DS, but he knew he'd be wrong to assume they couldn't see him. He was lying face down on the path, rifle still clasped in his right hand, bloodied knuckles bearing witness to his dogged loyalty to his weapon.

He needed two hands to push himself up but only had the use of one. Painful contortions freed his left arm from the shoulder strap, which he used to unclip the chest and waist straps. With all his remaining strength, he used his one good arm to thrust his left shoulder upwards in a violent motion that was just sufficient to rotate the Bergen off his back and down the slope, but his right arm was still partially constrained by the shoulder strap and, as the pack fell away from his body, it tugged sharply on his dislocated limb. He barked in barely contained agony.

'This needs to go back in, and it needs to go back in right fucking now,' said Seb to himself fiercely, forcing down his mounting panic. His muscles would contract and start to spasm with every second that the ball was not in its socket, he knew, making it hard, and then impossible, to reposition it without expert assistance. His father had applied exactly those skills after the first time it happened on the rugby pitch, but his father wasn't here. He was going to have to get it back himself. He had to keep going.

With great care, he managed to sit up and lean forward to allow his right arm to hang without engaging muscles already stretched beyond their natural tolerance, trying to retract to their normal length but unable to. He started to punch the inside of his bicep in an upward arc, just as he'd done the last time. The result of an initiation beating during his first week inside. It had worked on that day, and his fearlessness in mending himself so brutally had discouraged future attacks.

But this time, nothing. Two minutes of battering his arm, each blow causing almost unbearable pain, and still nothing. He got to his feet and cautiously shuffled off the path to where his Bergen had come to rest, holding his bad arm with the good one like a mother cradling her baby. He bent down over the pack and looped his hands under both shoulder straps, left hand gripping his right wrist. He straddled the pack giving himself a solid broad base from which to raise both himself and the ballast.

'Sharp tugs or long steady pull…don't know.'

He was mumbling in a sort of controlled terror, but talking to himself helped. Not allowing himself any time to change his mind, he stood up sharply, the full weight of the Bergen pulling in the opposite direction of his spasming muscles. The pain was appalling, but he managed it in relative silence, bar some hyperventilation and jagged groans. His muscles were still winning. With increasing dread, he started to squat and rise jerkily, resulting in a succession of violent, agonising tugs to his shoulder, and started counting.

'One. Two. Three. Four. Five. Six…not working.'

What more to do? He started to raise himself to his full height, squatting so sharply that the pack was briefly in free fall, then snapping his legs straight before the bag hit the floor, catching the falling Bergen with his dislocated arm, increasing the effective weight to more than double the still mass.

'SEVEN. EIGHT. NINEYOUFUCK.'

Then, euphoria. With an audible squelch, his arm slipped back into its socket providing immediate relief, the muscles no longer hyperextended, the function returned. The pain soon followed, growing in intensity as the initial high from the endorphin surge faded away. He had to get moving and keep moving. He could still make it. Bloody-minded endurance in adversity. That's what he was there to

Chapter 2

prove, and he would.

He completed the forty miles in nineteen hours thirty-one minutes, the fourth candidate to complete the course. The senior DS ordered him to throw his Bergen in the back of the wagon and climb in. He was aware of being more than usually observed by the DS and the medical officer. He undid the straps and slipped the pack off his back, using his left hand to take the weight. In his state of exhaustion, the weight of the wet Bergen was too great to risk a one-armed sling into the back of the truck. He placed his rifle carefully on the ground by his feet at the back of the battered '4-tonner' and employed both arms in the task. He gripped the top of the Bergen with his left hand, supporting the bottom with his right, limiting the vertical movement of the injured limb. He managed it, if clumsily, using a violent thrust from his legs to provide the momentum that would otherwise not be required, clearly protecting his right side.

'Step over here, Faber,' snapped the DS. 'The MO wants a word.'

Oh shit.

'We heard you up there, and now you are plainly protecting your right arm. Do you want to tell me what's happened?'

Compared to the NCOs and officers running Selection, the medic had quite the bedside manner, but in absolute terms he was still a bastard.

'Hard fall, sir. Nothing permanent.'

Both true. He stood directly in front of Seb and considered him with professional concentration, first his posture, then staring directly into his eyes.

'I've read your medical file, Captain Faber. If I'm not mistaken, you dislocated your right shoulder aged thirteen and then again aged seventeen. Reconstructive surgery aged nineteen proved successful, and you passed all your medical tests in basic training. No reported sequelae.'

'That is correct sir.'

Oh shit.

'Do something for me will you, Faber? Slowly raise both arms up directly in front of you.'

I'm fucked.

'Sir?'

'Just as I said, Faber', delivered with the pomp of a detective preparing to unmask a murderer.

Seb knew full well that it was hopeless, but he tried nonetheless. He managed to keep both arms parallel until they were at ninety degrees to his body but every inch beyond that point required him to arch his back just to keep his right arm rising, decelerating the progress of his left arm to keep them synchronised.

'Captain Faber, I'm only going to ask this once. Did you dislocate your right shoulder when you fell?'

'Yes sir,' he said without hesitation.

Recurrent serious injury post reconstructive surgery. That was it. In that moment his Special Forces Selection, and army career, were over.

CHAPTER 3

After six months spent in the forlorn hope that the medical board might relent, his bags were packed. He was making the final sweep of his mess accommodation when his phone rang.

'Seb, it's Max. I heard. Jolly bad luck, but I have something to discuss with you. Are you at the barracks?'

'Yes, but whatever it is I'm not interested...'

Seb wasn't allowed to continue.

'We can discuss it face to face. Don't go anywhere.' And he hung up.

Max was a former Guards officer who had served with Seb before moving on into some nondescript City existence once his short service commission had run its course. They weren't close.

Ninety minutes after he'd put the phone down, Max arrived at Merville Barracks, Colchester, the UK home of '2 Para', The 2nd Battalion, Parachute Regiment.

'I have a man I want you to meet. William Fletcher. Ex-Royal Marines. Fucking weirdo if you ask me but he's very senior at Blount & Co and he's well known for hiring ex-Forces personnel. I called him as soon as I heard about your RTU.'

Max wasn't like Seb. Seb had been destined to serve until his mandatory retirement at fifty-five; Max was like most of the men he passed out with on short service commissions, looking for a bit of adventure after their sponsored university years, and a stepping-stone to leadership positions in commerce or finance. Seb was the only comprehensive school kid in his intake at Sandhurst, one of only two non-graduates. And to the best of his knowledge, the only one who had done time.

'What is Blount & Co?'

Seb spat out the name with distaste.

'It's a bank, Seb. The oldest merchant bank in the City.'

'Shit, Max. I've no idea what I am going to do, but I do know I don't want to sit behind a desk in a bank with a bunch of chins for the next thirty years.'

'Just meet him, Seb. You need a job, and actually plenty of us are doing alright in the City as it happens.'

'I don't want to do 'alright'!'

'Look, it isn't the Army, but nothing ever will be. On the other hand, you don't get shot at and I get paid multiples of what you could ever get here. Just look at this shit hole.'

Seb looked around at his spartan digs. Basic, but they were all he needed.

'Wouldn't it be nice for your mum to move back into the family house?' said Max.

Seb winced. His mother had been forced to let out their family home a few years after his father died. The four of them squeezed into the two-bed annexe that offered an unobstructed view of other people living in *their* house. Living the lives that belonged to his family. The legal battle to commute his attempted murder conviction to GBH gave Seb the chance of a life, but not without consequences. His father's life insurance policy paid off the mortgage on Orchard End, but the only way his mother could pay for the legal costs was to re-mortgage, and with insufficient income of her own, the only way she could keep the house was to let it out. Appalling as it was, she'd never once signalled any regret at her decision, never once complained about living in a tiny outhouse. She only ever found joy in Seb's rehabilitation and success, his second chance at life. He'd make things right for her, whatever it took.

'If I agree to meet him, what does this Fletcher bloke want me to do?'

'He runs all the equity trading and sales at the bank, so something in those areas I guess.'

'I don't know what the fuck you're talking about Max. What would I actually *do*?'

'Selling. You'd be in sales.'

'Max, apart from having no interest in doing that, what makes you think I'd be any good at it?'

'You got into Sandhurst with no degree and a criminal record. I'd say you're quite good at selling!'

Which was true enough, he supposed. Seb had had no obligation to tell the Army about his conviction, but he was incapable of telling a lie. It was one of the immutable characteristics his father had left him with.

He paced around the room, arms folded.

'Why are you helping me, Max? Why have you raced out of London to tell me all this?'

'You were a fucked-up mess when I met you. You've sorted your life out and I admire that. OK, the Army played a big part, but it doesn't have to end there.'

Seb wanted to believe it was all down to fraternity and

goodwill, but he thought otherwise. Max always had an angle on everything.

'When and where do I meet him?'

'Friday. White's. 12.30 sharp.'

'Am I supposed to know what that is?'

'You really should. Oldest gentleman's club in London, don't you know.'

'Are you a member?'

A direct question to which he already knew the answer.

'Well, no.'

'Stop your bollocks.'

He picked up a small, framed photograph from one of the three cardboard boxes that contained all his worldly possessions. A faded image of his father throwing him high into the air, arms outstretched in preparation for a safe landing. His four-year-old eyes so trusting.

'OK, Max. You can tell your Mr Fletcher I'll be there.'

CHAPTER 4

Seb arrived at White's at 12.15, punctuality being another of his father's traits he would never escape. He didn't want to appear over eager, so he walked around the block to kill time and stepped through the door at 12.30 precisely, wearing his regimental tie as Max had advised. It went against his natural instinct. He knew who he was, and who he wasn't, and didn't need any affirmation. Still, when in Rome.

White's was typical of the type of bastion of privilege which made Seb feel as if he was trespassing. He could act the part, but knew it was a performance. Most of the time it all bounced off him; he was a paratrooper after all, and officer class at that. He knew that should be enough but sometimes, in some places, it wasn't. In the dark recesses of his mind, he felt a fraud. He was shown to a reception room adjacent to the bar where he found William Fletcher, one long leg crossed over the other, in a leather armchair reading a crisp copy of The Times. He stood up to reveal the straight back, heels together posture that was unmistakably that of a soldier in Her Majesty's Armed Forces, took a moment to fold the paper neatly, and ostentatiously consulted his

Cartier dress watch.

'Bang on time. Jolly good. Let's get a drink.'

Wanker was Seb's first thought. Disingenuous, showy, manipulative. Ten seconds in and Fletcher already had ground to make up.

They ordered their drinks from the barman, who showed Fletcher a level of deference at least a hundred years out of date in Seb's view and took them into a voluminous back room that accommodated a snooker table and a couple of dozen portraits of great soldiers past.

'How do you know Max?' asked Seb, taking control of the conversation. He was determined not to treat the meeting like an interview, even though it plainly was.

'Professionally. He's a recruiter, sends me through interesting candidates from time to time. None more interesting than you Sebastian.'

'It's Seb.'

'I'm sorry?' said Fletcher. Seb's response was so unexpectedly blunt he didn't quite compute.

'My name, it's Seb. Everyone calls me Seb.'

'Understood, Seb. Well, did Max tell you much about me and Blount & Co?'

'Enough to be here.'

Seb was still bristling. He took a sip of his beer, relaxed his facial muscles to the semblance of a smile, and continued.

'I gather you served in the Royal Marines for a decade before joining the City, and that you run sales and trading. I don't yet know what you sell or trade, or how you do it. I know that the bank is very old. But I've yet to work out whether that is a good or a bad thing. And you seem to want me, but I'm not really sure why. So that's why I came to meet you today. That, and the fact that I need a job now that the Army won't have me.'

Fletcher's air of superiority slipped momentarily as he took the measure of his quarry. He bought himself some time by placing his glass on the table carefully, leaning back in his chair and crossing his legs again before answering.

'That was the most honest answer to that question I think I've ever heard. And I meet a lot of very confident people.'

Seb didn't respond, forcing Fletcher to continue.

'Yes, I was a Royal Marine commando, so we have some shared experiences, including Selection. On my floor we sell and trade equity and derivatives to make money. For today, that's all you need to know. The bank is indeed very old and that is a good thing, because longevity and history engenders trust. And I do need someone like you on my team. Someone who has overcome a lot to be here but has a bit to prove.'

Fletcher was firmly back at the helm and seemed to know about Seb's past. It wasn't a state secret, but why would he know his history, Seb wondered. Fletcher caught the eye of someone in the bar, drained his glass and stood up sharply.

'Have to run. My lunch meeting is here. My secretary will be in touch with you in the next twenty-four hours with the formal offer. We'll start you on seventy thousand and see how we go.'

It was Seb's turn to be silent. He'd just about muttered a thank you before Fletcher continued.

'Afraid guests can't be unaccompanied, so you'll have to finish your drink and I'll show you out. Silly rule, I know.'

Silly rule perhaps, but it sat very comfortably with Seb.

He swallowed the rest of his pint and followed Fletcher to the foot of the grand staircase that led up to the formal dining room, where his lunch guest was waiting. No introduction as Fletcher shook Seb's hand.

'We'll meet again soon I hope, Sebastian.'

And disengaged.

'Willy, thanks so much for coming all this way.'

Seb watched them and other aged suits climbing the stairs with stultifying uniformity. So utterly and completely *their* place.

He walked briskly down the stone steps out of the club and onto St James's Street, pulling off his tie as he sucked fresh air into his lungs, unexpectedly invigorated by the whole experience. He had just been offered a job for more than double his army wage, doing something he didn't understand by someone he didn't know, and certainly didn't like. And Fletcher had also been through Selection, but *he'd* evidently passed.

He walked two minutes round the corner to the pub he'd spotted on his earlier circuit and sucked down another pint before taking out his phone and scrolling through his recent phone calls. He hovered over the last number dialled and made the call.

CHAPTER 5

Seb's mother picked up on the second ring. After his injury and the inevitable consequences, his entire family had been on high alert. They'd seen him spiral downwards before and the thought that he might descend to those depths again terrified them.

'So how did it go?'

'Well, I think. It was all over in ten minutes. He didn't even offer me lunch.'

'That sounds a bit odd. What's he like?'

'Stiff. Pleased with himself. You know the type.'

'OK, so what did he say? How was it left? Come on! This is like trying to get blood from a stone!'

'He offered me a job. Some sort of salesman. I'm still getting my head around it.'

'That is amazing news!'

She collected herself. She was at pains to show him support, not relief.

'Well, I suppose you'll have to wait to see what he's offering before you give him an answer.'

'I know what he's offering. It's ridiculous. I'd have been a full colonel before I got what he's just offered me.'

'Well it's a different world up there. Your father and I never had any exposure to it, but I'd grab it with both hands of I were you.'

She tried to sound like someone giving dispassionate, sensible advice rather than his desperate mother. But she was, utterly desperate. Desperate for him to find something worthwhile, a new path to consume his energy. She couldn't bear to see him lose all the ground he'd gained all over again.

'Don't worry, Mum, I probably will. I just need to tie up a few loose ends first.'

He finished the call and immediately dialled again. 'Max, I think we need to talk, don't you?'

CHAPTER 6

'How much money will you make from this?'

Max was caught fast in Seb's glare over the beer barrel table. He'd been floating around Mayfair nervously for some time in anticipation of his call.

'Yes, well, I was going to tell you about that. Since you ask, fourteen thousand pounds, twenty percent of first year's salary. Market rate. Oh, and you're bloody welcome by the way!'

He clinked his glass against Seb's stationary pint pot resting on the table.

'Fair enough, I suppose. But before we start popping corks, I need to know what made you put me forward to Fletcher? You and I haven't spoken in years, Max, and from what I remember we weren't that close when we did.'

Seb eyeballed him. It would have taken someone more sophisticated than Max to lie under that gaze.

'Well the truth of it is that Fletcher called me.'

'He called you and said what?'

'He said he had heard that a good soldier needed a job. He asked if I knew you and could I persuade you to meet him. Easiest fee I've ever made, actually. If you don't act like a total pillock and turn him down, that is.'

'And seventy grand. Is that normal? I'm pretty sure my dad didn't get that as a consultant orthopaedic surgeon.'

'It's the right level for your age, not your experience. Blounts is one of the few City employers that place any real value on military experience.'

'How many other ex-military types have you placed in the City?'

'Half a dozen, I should think. Two of them at Blounts.'

'And how many have started on seventy grand?'

'Just one. If he doesn't bugger it up!'

CHAPTER 7

Seb started at Blounts two weeks after his meeting with Fletcher. In the intervening period the bank had made him aware of a rental flat on very reasonable terms at the cheap end of Chelsea, otherwise known as Earls Court. The landlord was apparently a retired Blounts' board member who owned a few such properties around London, let out to new bank employees needing a base in a hurry. The rent would be deducted directly from his pay cheque each month.

He reported to reception at 8am as requested and was met by a bouncy, heavily made-up young woman with a bold handshake and a spring in her step.

'Seb, I'm Jaz, the desk assistant. Let's get you upstairs and settled in.'

She led the way to the escalator and up to the first floor, almost all of which was dedicated to one single open space. Like many other investment banks, Blounts (pronounced Blunts, for no logical reason save to make foreigners look foolish) had a trading floor roughly the size of a football pitch. European Equities occupied the North-West corner, compass points being relevant in such a vast space.

Seb was led to a seat in the middle of two banks of six desks. He took in the attention, and conspicuous inattention, of the men and women surrounding him. The Pan-European Equity Sales team was a harlequin set of over-tailored telesales people. They clearly shared many fundamental characteristics, and yet no two were truly alike.

Jaz proceeded to make the introductions.

'That's Vicky.'

The strikingly pretty blonde was deep in conversation with a client and only managed a raised hand to acknowledge Seb's presence. She was urgently riffling through some papers on her desk, seemingly trying to find information to support whatever point she was trying to make.

Jaz walked Seb further down the desk.

'And this is lovely Penny.'

The smiling thirty-something brunette leapt up to greet him.

'Nice to meet you, Seb. Get yourself settled and then I'll take you for coffee and tell you everything you need to know.'

Penny spoke with a refined American accent and a ready warmth. Kind, Seb thought.

'And this is Paul.'

'Great to meet ya, Seb,' said Paul in a strong Dublin accent.

He shook Seb's hand competitively. They were physically well matched, but based on his effusive greeting, Seb felt he was more likely to be friend than foe.

The next person in line couldn't have been more of a contrast physically. Even in his generously heeled loafers, his bald head was not more than chin height to Seb. But his

Chapter 7

physicality wasn't what defined O C-B. Seb had overheard him on the phone when he first walked onto the floor. He spoke with such eloquence and melody that the effect was quite hypnotic.

'O C-B, say hello to our new boy. Seb, this is Oliver.'

'Oliver Charrington-Brown, lovely to meet you Seb. I hope I can tempt you out for a jolly good lunch later this week.'

Before Seb could respond to the invitation, a gruff man, who had up to that point been head down buried deep in conversation, popped up.

'No, he won't be tempted to the pub by you Oliver. He's here to work and, as I might point out, so are you.'

He made his own introduction.

'Charles Bathurst. Head of Sales. We would normally have met by now, but William seemed very convinced of your credentials without input from me, so here you are.'

He didn't sound too pleased about having been circumvented.

'Stick close to me and do as you're told,' he continued, 'and you should be alright. It's nothing like the Army though. No loyalty either way, you'll see. This lot will be off to another bank if they're offered more money and Lord knows the bank will shoot you with no warning and no remorse if your face doesn't fit. Bloody dreadful business. Can't build anything without loyalty.'

There was a lot of noise coming from desks in the middle of the trading floor.

'What happens over there?'

'They're the traders. Different sort of chaps. No education, but all the brains in the world. Let me do a quick introduction but they're busy so let's be sharp about it.'

Bathurst walked him briskly over to the noisy hub at the heart of the trading floor. Hostile glances followed him. The desks were adorned with football paraphernalia, West Ham and Millwall being heavily represented. Their occupants all looked dressed for a night in the pub rather than a day in the City.

'Charlie, sorry to bother you, this is our new boy, Seb.'

Seb bridled at the classification.

'Seb, Charlie is the head of trading. You'll get to know him well if all goes to plan.'

After a few keystrokes and a scan of the six screens he had in front of him, Charlie stood up to greet Seb.

'Pleased to meet you, Seb. Which firm have they pinched you from?'

'The Army actually.'

'Oh OK, first job on Civvy Street?'

'I suppose it is.'

One of Charlie's screens started to ping and flash red.

'I've got to get this. Nice to meet you. Good luck.'

Seb was escorted out of the trading area as quickly as he'd been trotted into it but nonetheless caught a sotto voce comment, loud enough to know it was clearly intended for his ears.

'Another brainless army boy to wet nurse. Add him to the pile.'

Bathurst, who at sixty-one was already quite deaf, possibly didn't hear it. He certainly didn't react if he had.

Seb shortened his steps and let his boss walk off, already lost in his own thoughts and oblivious to external stimuli. He span back and walked directly to the source of the comment. Not hard to identify as all eyes were focusing on him. A short, fat man in a Ralf Lauren Polo shirt three sizes

Chapter 7

too small for him.

'Hi. I'm Seb.'

The fat man stayed seated and swivelled around to face Seb head on.

'This is my first day,' said Seb. 'No idea whether I'll be any good, but then neither do you because you don't know me. But I hope that'll change. I hope to learn a lot from you and your mates here.'

Charlie shouted over an order.

'Tony, you dozy sod! Hit the bid on those Glaxo! It's drifting.'

The fat man wheeled around and banged away at his keyboard to remedy the situation. Task completed, he span round to face Seb.

'You've only been here five minutes and already cost us a hundred grand. Nice start.'

Seb leant in and peered at the screens.

'Twenty-two thousand one hundred.'

'You what?'

'You lost twenty-two thousand one hundred pounds on that trade. I saw the Glaxo price on Charlie's screen. You just sold a hundred and thirty thousand shares at £12.50. They were £12.67 a minute ago. But I'll get out of your way. Good to meet you, Tony.'

Seb walked away with the astonished focus of the entire bank of traders boring holes in the back of his head. He caught Charlie's eye, and his baffled expression.

'Darts,' said Seb with a grin as he passed his desk. 'Misspent youth. Made me half decent at sums though.'

CHAPTER 8

12 months later

Seb slumped into a corner booth at the Cheapside branch of Costa Coffee. His first annual performance review was in half an hour, and he was trying to decide whether he could even be bothered to turn up to it. He'd been a very fast learner. Max had been right: Seb could sell. In a world of half-truths and obfuscation, his honesty was an arresting novelty and it worked. He was given responsibility for clients the day he passed his securities exam, responsibility for entire transactions after only three months and his early run in with Tony had earned him the respect of the traders. His precocious success at selling equities made him less popular on the sales desk, but he was getting noticed.

He scanned the room. A smartly dressed woman in her mid-forties sat to his left, weeping. She was being comforted by a friend who was stroking her arm while trying to find words to stem the flow. For some time her efforts were in vain. Death of a parent? No. Not traumatic enough for a middle-aged woman to be crying in public over. Death of a child? No. The inescapable horror and despair from that

Chapter 8

tragedy had no place in a coffee shop. That grief can barely get dressed in the morning. Her husband leaving her for another woman? Almost certainly.

A couple in their late thirties holding hands furtively under the table, both wearing wedding rings. Married, but not to each other, and good luck to them.

A lump of a man with a booming ocker Australian accent at a table in the middle of the room was ostentatiously holding court. From his brash demeanour and nationality, almost certainly the CEO of a mining company, was Seb's instant judgment. Leaning back, legs spread, anchored to the chair with one arm, waving the other about to emphasise some point. The main point being 'for Christ's sake look at me'.

'And I told him stick it up his arse and like it...Oh yeah he listened...not like he had much fuckin' choice.' His words achieved the required cooing and homage from his young audience.

Seb drew his thoughts back to the present. He'd made his decision. The coffee shop was full of bullshit, the whole bloody City was drowning in it. The dot-com bubble had burst spectacularly, and that fantasy was over. God, he'd only been at it for a year, but it was more than enough. He had to get out, and he needed to get on with it.

He made his way back to the office with a renewed sense of purpose, cutting through Masons Avenue, one of the City's myriad of ancient, labyrinthine passages only navigable by foot. He passed The Old Doctor Butler's Head, a fifteenth century inn, already filling up with its florid, corpulent clientele. That would not be him.

He strode through the revolving door into the opulent marbled atrium of Blount & Co, where he'd clocked in at

06.45 every day since leaving the Army, sat down at his desk and started to wade through the dozens of pointless emails accumulated in the forty-five minutes he'd been out of the office.

'Hey Seb, Fletcher and Simpson are after you. It looked…important,' said Paul mischievously.

Seb nodded without taking his gaze of his screens. His review should have been with Bathurst, being his immediate boss. But Fletcher and Mark Simpson were after him, the Heads of Equity and Investment Banking. Not something he had anticipated.

'Fancy a glass, Bertie?'

No one other than Ollie C-B called Seb Bertie. Why on earth would they? But Seb quite liked it.

'Very possibly.'

Seb didn't expand. He picked up his telephone and dialled.

'Hi, William. You wanted me?'

CHAPTER 9

He peeled off his headset and made his way to Fletcher's office, a large glass box overlooking London Wall.

As he approached, he caught sight of Simpson sitting at the table in one corner of the generous space. Mark Simpson was the complete caricature of a British investment banker. The shoes, half brogues from Church's. The bespoke suit from *his* Savile Row tailor. The double cuff shirts from Turnbull & Asser of Jermyn Street. The tie, Hermès. Always Hermès. Unwaveringly, imposingly smart. His ilk were fighting a rear-guard action against the new breed of young, multilingual, over-educated young Turks. In Seb's experience, the ability to speak multiple languages generally meant that you were incapable of being funny in any of them.

'Morning, William,' said Seb.

'Come in. And shut the door,' replied Fletcher with unexpected impatience.

'Mark,' Seb offered his greeting with a nod of his head.

'Hello Sebastian. Do take a seat.'

Fletcher picked up a folder from his desk and walked over to the table where Seb and Mark Simpson were both now sitting.

'I'll get straight to it. William and I have both admired the way you've approached the challenges you've been tasked with since you joined us,' said Simpson.

Seb gave an appreciative smile but was starting to feel slightly apprehensive about the direction they might be going in.

'You've worked bloody hard, Seb, and handled everything we've thrown at you. With precious little help from that lot out there, I might add. You continue to impress me and my colleagues on the sixth floor and, more importantly, our clients are talking you up.'

Seb had barely had a nod in the corridor from Simpson in twelve months, so this unforeseen tribute was mildly disconcerting.

'After you closed the placing for Exgen last month, the Chairman gave me a call. He was seriously impressed Seb, seriously impressed, and he wants your services again. I don't know whether you know but he is also Chairman of Free State Biotech, a private South African business developing drugs from tribal remedies. They've spent a decade chasing around Africa investigating every jungle juice that the locals claim has some therapeutic effect.'

There was a knock on the door and Saki, the senior biotech analyst, was beckoned into the room.

'Right on cue, Saki. You can give Sebastian the technical guff.'

'Hey Seb. Where had you got to?'

Saki was a second-generation British Indian, a North London boy to the core and an inveterate one-eyed Arsenal fan.

'South African biotech company hunting for tribal

Chapter 9

remedies,' said Seb.

'Cool. Right, as you know, you can't patent a plant, so they need to demonstrate that the isolated active ingredient contained in the plant is efficacious in the extracted, purified form. And they need to be able to make it.'

'Got it.'

Seb did get it. His A level retakes were in Biology, Chemistry and Physics, somewhat inspired by his medical heritage, and he'd got A grades in all three.

'They have tried a bunch of times to replicate the observed and reported effect of various indigenous remedies but thus far all their drug candidates have failed. They now have something more encouraging to show us. Hoodia Gordonii, a cactus indigenous to the Kalahari Desert. The San people have been chewing on this plant for thousands of years before setting out on hunting trips. It acts as an appetite suppressant and prevents hunters consuming their prey before they can return to their villages to feed their families.'

'Does it work?'

'There was an un-blinded trial within the San community that demonstrated that the isolated, purified active extract worked as well as the raw plant extracts.'

'Sounds suspiciously like bollocks to me, Saki.'

His blunt response took everyone by surprise, which felt good. He was going to be resigning in a matter of hours and relished the licence it gave him to say it how it was. Saki chuckled nervously and picked up the thread again.

'I thought that at first, but it is the first positive efficacy data ever seen for a patented isolated active ingredient of Hoodia, and we know Hoodia works.'

Seb maintained his exasperated expression. An IPO of

an African biotech company, with no history of success and no tangible assets, in a market that was in catastrophic freefall. He hadn't failed yet but there had to be a first time.

'That *cannot* be the data you are expecting to float the company with!'

'Of course it bloody isn't,' snapped Fletcher, who had been watching Seb's reaction to the pitch with growing irritation. 'Carry on, Saki!' he barked.

'OK, so, they are now recruiting a multi-centre, double blind placebo controlled Phase 2 proof of concept trial. Here's a copy of the company's presentation and my one-page note covering the product and the potential market applications. The diet market is worth two billion dollars in supplements and diet foods. The supplements don't, and can't, make any clinical claims and are therefore sold for tuppence a bucket. Anything that is proven to reduce appetite will be frikkin' massive. On my numbers, a clinically proven appetite suppressant would have annual peak sales of over five billion dollars.'

This was now sounding a whole lot more interesting.

'When do they expect to get the data?'

'Best guess, end of Q2 next year. They want us to go and kick the tyres down there early in the New Year, and if all goes well, list them on AIM when they have the positive result.'

It was time for Fletcher to re-enter the debate.

'The issue we have is that the San People Community Foundation have recently been granted rights over the raw ingredient.'

'Why is that a problem?' asked Seb.

'The problem is, Seb, no pharmaceutical company can possibly do a deal with FS Biotech until these rights are crystallized into a formal licensing deal between FSB and the San,' replied Fletcher.

'Still not sure I see the problem.'

Seb was being deliberately obtuse. He had nothing to lose.

'Well let me spell it out for you then. Our client needs to acquire the rights on sensible terms and has asked for our help to do it.'

'You mean give the San as little as possible.'

'That's exactly what I mean. Does that upset you Seb?'

Simpson stepped in before Seb could respond.

'That'll do for now. Let's get on.'

Both Seb and Saki took the cue but just as Seb reached the door he was summoned back.

'Thanks Saki. Seb, hold on minute.'

Saki flashed Seb a quizzical look, and Seb's shoulders and eyebrows rose in agreement to show he had no idea what they wanted him, and only him, to hear.

'Shut the door and sit down.'

Simpson was brisk, and uncompromising.

'Seb, you should know that the CEO, Richard Barnard, is someone we have some material concerns about. Our Risk and Compliance teams have been pouring over his documented history, but they haven't found anything concrete to worry us so far.'

An unexpected tangent. Seb's interest was piqued.

'But just because they can't find it, it doesn't mean it doesn't exist,' said Seb.

'Quite. The bank has to make money, but we simply can't survive another scandal after the Asian situation. We have to be sure of him one way or the other. So, I want you to take extra care in observing Barnard. Take notes. Be watchful. Sniff about where you can, but you mustn't arouse his suspicion. You may wonder why I'm handing you this extra layer of responsibility. Well, your former CO is an old chum of mine as it happens, and he speaks very highly of you. Thinks you're made of tough stuff, like a challenge and all that. Well, here it is.'

Seb fought the grin that threatened to break across his face.

'I can do that Mark, but can I ask where your 'material concerns' come from?'

'You don't need to know,' said Fletcher, sharply.

'Quite right, for now. We'll tell you more as and when needed. I should forewarn you that he has a reputation as an intellectual bully. Unpleasant bastard, actually. Don't let him wrong foot you. He doesn't suffer fools, and he'll go out of his way to make you look like one.'

From which Seb concluded that Simpson had himself been wrong footed and made to look a fool.

'OK, where to from here?'

'Sunningdale,' said Simpson. 'You and William are playing golf with Barnard and his finance director on Thursday morning. You play don't you Seb? Rather assumed.'

'Played a bit as a kid.'

'With my Dad', was how that sentence finished in his head.

CHAPTER 10

Seb had back-to-back client meetings after he left Fletcher's office, and he day-dreamt through them all. He was determined that this new project wouldn't change anything. He was still going to leave, but it might just make his remaining time at the bank less painful while he plotted his next course, and he might just hold off from resigning until he knew what that course was.

He got back to his desk at 17:40. Everyone on the sales desk apart from Bathurst, who had a stubborn compunction to be the first to arrive and the last to leave, had left for the evening. His military doctrine was largely wasted on his wards, but for all his institutional gruffness Bathurst was a decent man. As such, he would never rise to any real level of seniority or accumulate any great wealth.

Looking down the corridor, Seb could see Fletcher sitting at his desk in his glass walled office. He was on the phone but was still scanning the trading floor noting activity, inactivity, presence and absence. Fletcher was the man they all feared. He was the man who doled out the carrots and it was he who applied the stick or, more commonly, the axe.

'What did you come back for? Every other bugger's in

the pub,' grumbled Bathurst.

'I need to write up some notes. Decent meetings actually. Should get some lumpy orders.'

Bathurst stopped listening halfway through Seb's response. He didn't get involved in Seb's biotech deals. Builders' merchants and Midlands based engineers were more his thing.

'Righto then. That's me for the evening. See you tomorrow, Seb.'

'Evening, Charles.'

Seb sat at his screen and typed 'Richard Barnard Free State Biotech' into his browser. The homepage of the FS Biotech corporate website popped up with a photo of an unsmiling Barnard sitting at the head of a grand mahogany board table, exuding alpha dominance from every pixel. His biography noted his 'breadth of experience as a serial CEO in multiple geographies and industries'. No names of companies he worked for, nor the geographies, nor the industries. His military service was also referenced which, given that all able-bodied white South African men were required to do national service, seemed a pretty strange thing to single out in a career spanning almost four decades.

Seb scrolled down the search results for 'Richard Barnard', a process that wasn't helped by a scandalous US senator and an author of populist scientific literature both sharing the same name. On page three of the search results, he found a link to a news article in April 1993 concerning a company called Sanderson Medical Ltd. The article talked about a failed clinical trial for a cardiovascular stent 'as a result of a major adverse event'. An unexpected death, to be more accurate. It went on to state that 'an unnamed

Chapter 10

private individual' invested an unspecified amount of money to rescue the company, and this coincided with the appointment of a new CEO, one Richard Barnard. Then came a name he wasn't expecting to see. Chris Gardener. A fairly common name, but the Finance Director of a biotech company? It had to be. Chris Gardener was now the Chairman of one of Seb's largest clients, Viprotab Pharma, a company that made rattlesnake anti-venom, and did rather well out of it. He dug out Chris's card from the pile in his desk drawer and dialled his mobile number.

'Chris, Seb, sorry to bother you. Can you speak?'

'Ah Seb, yes of course, what is it?'

'Actually, a pretty random question. Does the name Richard Barnard mean anything to you?'

Chris drew a long deep breath before responding.

'Richard Barnard.' He repeated the name back slowly, each syllable laden with feeling. 'Yes, yes it does.'

'Don't suppose I can buy you a drink and pick your brains. You in town tonight?'

'I am as it happens. Come and join me at the club. I'm walking in now so shall we say 7pm?'

CHAPTER 11

Chris Gardener's club was The Reform, one of the grand collection of gentleman's clubs on Pall Mall. Seb climbed the steps to the entrance atrium and gave the name of his host to the porter.

'Mr Gardener is waiting for you in the library, Mr Faber. Turn right and walk to the end of the corridor.'

The porter proudly pointed out that the club had just taken down the dust covers and scaffolding after a multi-million-pound restoration project. As he walked through the columned marble hall, Seb noted that a redecoration project had, bizarrely, managed to make the place look and feel even more antiquated than before. Somewhat at odds with the club's name, he thought.

The scent was an evocative blend of antique leather-bound books and firewood, the sound of the creaking, two-hundred-year-old oak floorboards adding to the general effect. Gardener was sitting in one of two leather wingback chairs in front of an open fire on the far side of the vast room. He leapt up and greeted Seb like an old comrade, despite the fact they had only known each other for eight months. It was amazing how quickly a bond was created when he made money for someone.

'I've got a bottle of the club claret on the go. Alright for you?'

'Perfect. Thanks for meeting me at short notice,'

'My pleasure Seb, but I have to say right off the bat that the name Richard Barnard is one I never thought I would hear again. Hoped I wouldn't hear again.'

He stared intensely into the fire for a moment before he spoke again.

'Sanderson Medical was developing a new cardiovascular stent with our proprietary biocompatible coating. It was supposed to reduce post-operative thrombosis and did in all the animal studies. We'd just signed a hundred-million-dollar joint development agreement with J&J, but then it all went wrong. We had a death in the Phase 1 safety study, which obviously torpedoed our plans to float.'

'Not the best result for that patient either,' said Seb.

'Sure. But it quickly became clear to the clinical team that the patient had died of a massive aortic aneurysm on the golf course. Completely unlinked to the stent.'

The corners of Chris's mouth rose just a fraction.

'He five putted on the first green apparently,' he said.

'That would do for me,' said Seb.

They burst into explosive laughter, triggering much ruffling of broadsheets and disapproving harrumphs. Chris returned straight-faced to the matter in hand.

'I can't actually confirm the five putts, but the aneurism was unequivocal. Our stent had nothing to do with the death. But as you know, under the strict protocol of the trial, it had to be halted and investigated. That's when things started to get strange. We were introduced to a man called Ivo Karvonen, a hugely wealthy Finnish private investor. I only met him once, but I was instantly wary.'

'Why?'

'Well, he didn't say much and seemed terribly eager to part with his money. Red flags I know, but I was fighting for the company. Thirty-five jobs. Thirty-five families depending on the salaries we were paying.'

'How much did he invest?'

'Twenty million pounds in senior ranking liquidation preference shares. It covered all our costs for two years. More than enough time to complete the inquiry and re-run the trial.'

'OK, but where does Barnard fit it?'

'Barnard's appointment as CEO was the sole condition of Karvonen's investment. He had no experience in the healthcare sector, but it was the only offer of investment on the table so we had to do it. I should have pushed back, but I had another job offer lined up so decided to just walk away. And to be honest, Barnard scared me. It seems ridiculous, I know, but he looked capable of anything.'

'What do you mean?'

'I mean he physically intimidated me. He used to bang on about his military background and if even half of it was true, he did some dark things in his youth.'

'Probably bollocks,' said Seb. 'The guys that blabber on about it tend to have seen very little action. What happened after you left?'

'They restarted the trial with the new money and there was a second death. That time it wasn't unrelated to our product. Years later it was traced back to a manufacturing fault. The wrong balance of ingredients in the stent coating mix. Operator error. The result was that the coating actually accelerated thrombosis. Fatally so. The company was mothballed and eventually the platform and patents were sold to J&J for five million pounds. Two percent of the value of the company at its peak.'

'So, what happened to Barnard, and Karvonen's investment?'

'They both vanished. Literally without a trace. Barnard left work on a Friday evening and didn't show on the Monday. All his meetings were still in his diary. His office was still full of his things, just not him.'

'I can sort of understand why he might have fled the scene, but your Finn was due the full five million sale proceeds wasn't he?

'He was. We tried everything to contact him, SFA, the police, even the Foreign Office. It was like he never existed.'

'What happened to his five million quid then?'

'His holding was via an offshore trust in Cayman. A trustee made contact with us with all the required documentation, and we transferred the money.'

Chris took a long tug on his claret and fixed his eyes on the dancing flames, completely lost in his thoughts. Then snapped back into the room.

'And you say that Barnard has surfaced. What on earth is he doing now?'

'He's back running another biotech company. A South African venture that has hopes of developing an appetite suppressant from a plant-derived tribal remedy. We're lined up to list it in London next year.'

'Jesus. Does it check out?'

'That's what I am being asked to find out, with a particular emphasis on your friend Barnard.'

'He's no friend of mine. Find out what you can but be very careful, Seb. In my opinion, he's a very dangerous man.'

Seb doubted he was, but politely acknowledged the advice anyway.

'One other question Chris. Who introduced you to Karvonen?'

'Lord, it was a long time ago, let me think.' He stared into the middle distance while he retraced more steps. 'Oh yes. Funnily enough I think it was William, William Fletcher.'

CHAPTER 12

05.32. Boom. Seb's morning ordinance was Capital FM, the powerful mix of pop music and Chris Tarrant's forced badinage more than sufficient to wake the dead. Thrust into consciousness by Spiller's ever so bouncy *Groovejet*, Seb went through his morning routine without conscious thought. Showered, shaved, dressed he was out the door by 06.05. Fifteen minutes earlier than usual because he was having to resort to the tube, his Vespa left in the City, having foreseen that the evening would probably develop as previous ones had with Chris Gardener.

Adrenaline was still firing round his body after the dramas of the previous day. He strode the six minutes up to Earls Court station with new verve, bought his copy of the Financial Times at the news stand, taking the vendor somewhat by surprise with an uncharacteristically ebullient greeting, and made his way down to the platform. A District Line train arrived moments later, and he plonked himself down on one of the half-dozen available seats. At that time of the morning, the carriage was generally filled with an assortment of City slickers and tradesmen, Papworth brief cases and spirit levels in tow, all sharing the journey in silent, harmonious resignation.

Seb set about wading through the arid content of the pink pages while trying to avoid contacting his neighbours with his elbows as he wrestled the broadsheet to a manageable size. He didn't lift his head until the train stopped at Victoria, as ever a chaotic exchange of humanity with the weary strap-hangers joining from their Home County dormitory towns. The tube pulled away, and he lowered his paper and looked up. Sitting directly opposite him was an olive-skinned girl in her mid-twenties with shoulder-length, wavy brown hair. Her slightly upturned top lip formed a perfect Cupid's bow, and she had a gentle dusting of freckles on her nose and cheeks. She was reading a battered copy of a French novel and had an ethnic fabric bag resting at her feet, with a ring binder file poking out of it. She wore a chunky blue jumper and a nautical style six button coat. Faded ripped jeans and Converse trainers completed the look. Funky chic. Her head was bowed as she focused on the dog-eared pages of her book, a few strands of hair falling in-front of her face, drawing Seb's eyes back to her mouth. Her age, clothes and general demeanour suggested that she was a student, probably post grad, although the early hour of the day suggested otherwise. Another lock of her hair fell in front of her eyes, which prompted her to throw her head back, and in doing so, glance up at Seb. It was too late to look away. He offered a half smile, and she held his gaze a fraction of a second longer than she needed to, before she returned her attention to her book. But just a few seconds later, after reading a few more lines - or perhaps not? - she raised her eyes to glance up at Seb, who was so transfixed that their eyes met again. And she smiled. Briefly, almost imperceptibly, but she smiled.

Chapter 12

Between Earls Court and St James's Park he had fallen in love, and it would all be over as quickly as it had started unless he did something, but he couldn't seem to think, act or speak. As the tube approached Embankment, she put her book in the fabric bag, stood up and walked to the door, at no point looking at Seb. The train screeched to a halt, the doors slid open, and she stepped out. He did nothing. He stayed put, glued to his seat. She turned right and walked towards the exit. As she passed the seat she had just vacated, she decisively turned her head ninety degrees and looked directly at Seb, this time not smiling, the subtle expression on her face seeming to ask a question. Then she was gone.

Ping, ping, ping. The doors were closing. Finally, Seb's body reconnected with his brain. He leapt up and bolted for the door. His path was clear, but the pace he needed to get out of the carriage before the doors closed resulted in a speed incompatible with that of the passengers who'd exited ahead of him. Essentially, he jumped on the back of an extremely startled joiner. Seb looked up to see whether the girl had witnessed it, but he couldn't see her. The burly tradesman had no time to react. Seb leapt up, offered a quick but sincere apology and strode off in pursuit.

He took the stairs two at a time, in haste but not yet frantic. As he reached the exit barriers, he saw her turning left out of the ticket hall, pulling on a white woollen beanie as she set off towards The Strand. Seb was now facing a pressing issue. If he did catch up with her, what the bloody hell was he going to do? What the bloody hell was he going to say? As she approached the crowded thoroughfare, he saw her again. The green man was flashing at the traffic lights and she crossed over, heading North, in the direction of Covent Garden. Seb arrived at the crossing ten seconds later, just as the light turned red. He walked straight into the road without breaking stride, one eye on the white beanie and one on the oncoming vehicles. As he was about to reach the other side, a motorcycle courier on a battered old bike shot out from behind a bus, heading directly for Seb's left flank. He leapt five feet in the air and narrowly avoided the courier, but not the pavement, landing in a staggered forward roll, with his right arm and shoulder taking most of the impact, his suit and shirt torn at the elbow and a graze weeping blood into the frayed fabric. The sight of someone falling in public always draws enormous attention. Add to that the screech of brakes, the biker hurling expletives at Seb and the bus driver hurling more measured abuse at the biker, and it was quite a rumpus. A circle of faces soon surrounded him as he lay on the pavement taking stock. All eyes bar the one pair that mattered. After checking all his key joints to establish their ongoing usefulness, he got up, assisted by multiple anonymous hands, thanked the kind people for their concern, and strode up to Covent Garden in the rough direction she'd been heading.

The incident had cost him at least thirty seconds, and hope was fading. He got to the junction of Bedford Street and Henrietta Street and scanned in every direction. There was no sign of her. He thought about running but it was just as likely he'd be running away from her as towards her. It was futile, she was gone. He was already late, and as much as he wanted to spend the rest of the day combing the streets looking for her, he had to get to work. With huge reluctance he hailed a cab, climbed in and set off, feeling a bit foolish and a lot sad.

'Stop!' he yelled at the cabbie.

There she was, behind the glass frontage of a street café.

Chapter 12

He emptied the contents of his trouser pocket onto the cabbie's tray and jumped out without another word. The café was half-full of builders eating their full Englishes with three-sugar teas, but she wasn't there. She'd gone. Again. A large Mediterranean-looking man addressed him from behind the counter, just as he was beginning to wonder whether he'd really seen her at all.

'Take a seat sir. The waitress will be with you in a minute.'

Seb looked around the room, completely at a loss as to what to do next, but just before he was forced to make some form of decision, a door marked 'Private' at the back of the café opened to reveal the girl, his girl, tying a white apron round her waist. Behind her, her hat and coat on a hook, headphones dangling out of her coat pocket. She hadn't ignored the kerfuffle. She hadn't heard it. She walked out to the middle of the room and immediately saw Seb, whose face broke into the most natural smile in the world. They ignored the café manager, and everything else, as they slowly approached each other. She looked at his torn suit and the blood-stained shirt beneath.

'Jesus, you're hurt!'

An Irish accent, with a just a hint of something else running through it.

'I'm OK, just a bit of a mess.

'Christ alive. You looked like you were in quite the mad rush to get off the tube.'

Before he could answer the proprietor bellowed from behind the counter. 'Sophia, give the customer table three and clear table six.'

Sophia. Just perfect.

She gestured to a table in the corner and walked him to it.

'Let me get you a coffee…'

'Seb'

'Let me get you a coffee, Seb.'

With an intoxicating smile, she passed on the order to her boss and served another table. A minute later she returned and placed the coffee in a takeaway cup on the table.

'Am I leaving?'

'Sure you are. I've work to do and so do you. And you'll be wanting your bill.'

She jotted something down on her pad, tore off a leaf and handed it to him.

Sophia - 07774 545678

The coffee is on me (well the fat bloke behind me actually!) x

'Now go to work, mister. I've to get on with mine.'

With a swish of her apron, she was off to attend to other customers. Seb watched her for a moment as she moved around the café like a dancer, navigating the room with effortless grace. He slipped out while she was taking an order from a table of police officers but couldn't stop himself from looking back at her through the window. She was standing with her shoulders facing her customers, pad and pen in hand. Then, knowingly, she turned around and fixed her eyes on Seb's. It had begun.

CHAPTER 13

He walked into the office just as the morning meeting was finishing, catching Fletcher's eye from thirty feet as he stepped out of the lift, but nevertheless walking boldly and unapologetically to his desk.

'Late one with Chris Gardener,' he announced to anyone who cared.

Vicky Seager looked in horror at his dishevelled state, but Seb jumped in just before she did.

'Tripped over running to the tube.'

He was only twenty minutes late, and he'd been out with one of the bank's important clients, but the code was simple: *out with the boys, in with the men*. On this morning he couldn't have cared less. His head was spinning with the events of the previous day and now with the meteoric effects of his morning. He tried to go about his daily routine, but it was hopeless. The thought of calling fund managers to try and sell them something was laughable. He flipped between daydreaming about Sophia and ferreting about the internet to find out more about Barnard and his benefactor Karvonen. So compelling were both activities that the day passed by in a blur and was entirely unproductive. The internet searches came up with nothing new on either party. The only interesting fact was that for rich and influential people, Barnard and Karvonen had disproportionately small online footprints. It took effort and specialist knowledge to achieve that.

He spent much of the afternoon mentally preparing for the only call that mattered and left the office immediately after the market close, riding his Vespa straight home. Convinced though he was that something with such an auspicious start couldn't fall at the first hurdle, it was still a worryingly possible outcome.

Would you like to meet for a drink?
No thanks.

Final as death. His pulse quickened as he punched in her number and, suddenly aware of his breathing, he took three deep lungfuls of air and pressed dial. She answered after two rings.

'Hi, it's Seb…from this morning…in the café.' A stuttering start.

'Seb, yes, hi.' For someone who'd handed over her number not twelve hours earlier, she seemed oddly surprised to hear from him. 'I wasn't expecting to hear from you quite so soon. Aren't you meant to leave it a day, or two before calling a girl?'

Too keen. Bollocks.

'Possibly, but I couldn't take the risk of some other bloke chasing you off public transport and getting your number, so here I am.'

Sophia laughed, tickled by the idea that no man could resist her.

'It doesn't happen every day I have to tell you.'

'Well, now that it has, would you like to meet for a drink?'

Chapter 13

'You are quite the direct fella, aren't you, Sebastian.' The use of his full Christian name felt like a playful way of her taking control of the situation. And he liked it.

'Why not. Jeez, I'd be a bit a cow if I said no after your performance this morning, now wouldn't I!'

Seb suggested that they meet on Wednesday night at a pub in South Kensington. He also took the precaution of booking a table at a nearby restaurant but kept that to himself. To suggest a drink was casual, unthreatening, and easy enough for either party to extricate themselves from if it started to go south. And as they had only marginally more shared history than a blind date, a venue with a bit of bustle felt like a good place to start.

He got to the pub ten minutes early, settled himself at a corner table with a copy of The Standard and watched the door like a hawk. Managing exits and entry points was something he had some experience of and as such he chose a table that gave him good clear views of both back and side doors. He quickly established a pattern, reading a line in the paper, looking up to the right, looking over to the left, then looking down to read the same line of the newspaper he'd just read, repeated with the precision of a metronome. This pattern was only interrupted when the doors were swung open and a punter entered the premises which caused Seb to place his weight on the balls of his feet and an alarming escalation of his heart rate.

At twenty to eight, after several false starts with assorted other brunettes setting the hares running, she walked in. It was a chilly October evening, and like most of the other women who had walked in from the cold, Sophia was wrapped up snuggly in a hat and scarf, with only the top half of her face exposed. And yet it was unmistakably her.

She pulled off her hat and met Seb halfway between the table and the bar. He hadn't bought a drink for himself while he waited, partly to avoid looking impatient, partly to make their first drink together just that. Together. He kissed her on both cheeks, but as he drew away, she leant in for a third kiss, catching him off guard and leaving her hanging.

'Sorry, it's three where I come from.'

'Ireland?' he asked, confused.

'South of France.'

'There's a story there,' said Seb as he leant forward to complete the triple 'bise'.

She sat down while he went to the bar and got them their drinks. By the time he returned, she'd deposited her winter layers on a nearby stool. Underneath, she was wearing a white, long-sleeve plunge-necked t-shirt and an olive-green cashmere V-neck jumper. A simple silver chain with a small silver crucifix rested sacrilegiously between her breasts. Her faded blue jeans gave definition to her long slim legs. On her feet she wore brown, laced ankle boots with a two-inch heel. Unselfconsciously cool.

'So, I guess at least one of your parents is Irish.'

'My mum. She's from Cork and my dad from southwest France. But tell me now, what you did this morning. Do you put on that sort of performance for all the girls?'

Seb gave the question the respect it deserved and took a few moments to respond.

'No. That would be the first time I've chased a girl off a train to get her number.'

'I've to say it was a first for me too. I don't know whether I should be more flattered or scared,' said Sophia.

'Oh yes you do,' replied Seb, summoning all the unthreatening charm he could muster.

Chapter 13

They were both suddenly aware that the pace of the conversation was getting away from them and dropped the intensity down a few gears with some entry level *what do you do's.*

Sophia was doing a post graduate diploma in fashion at Central St Martins and had taken on shifts here and there in the café to help pay her rent. Seb gave a perfunctory precis of his enforced journey from the Army into the City. That took them to the bottom of their glasses.

'Would you like to have dinner? I booked us a table at a place I know nearby. A French restaurant, actually.'

'How very presumptuous!' said Sophia rather seductively. 'Sure, I'd like that Seb. Where are you taking me?'

Seb's suggested destination was approved somewhat disconcertingly with a barely muffled chuckle. La Bouchée was, admittedly, something of a clichéd first date restaurant. Lit with volcanic red candles erupting out of wine bottles, the walls adorned with Moulin Rouge and Folies Bergère posters, the waiters with suspiciously strong French accents. But it was popular for a reason; it led to plenty of second dates.

Sophia re-robed, and they walked the hundred yards to the restaurant. Both were greeted, rather embarrassingly, like old friends by the manager.

'Sorry. I haven't been very imaginative with this choice,' said Seb.

'Nonsense. I love it here. You did just fine,' reassured Sophia.

They squeezed themselves into their seats in a restaurant where intimacy was guaranteed, but privacy emphatically wasn't. They crammed the tables so closely together that your lateral neighbour was a foot nearer than the date opposite you, which made for a huge amount of exaggerated forward leaning and plenty of effort ignoring the sometime superior entertainment on your flanks.

Seb chose 'l'escargots' to start, aware of but unabashed by the cliché, and Sophia went for the French onion soup. He selected a bottle of Pouilly-Fumé that arrived in moments and was theatrically uncorked by the frenetic young waiter.

'So, how did your parents meet?' asked Seb.

He topped up their glasses and settled in for the story. Her mother had met her father on an extended post-university graduation holiday in the summer of 1972. The description of her mother meeting him was deliberate, her mother being the instigator.

Her 'Papa' was doing a summer job at his family wine business. Her mother, an English Literature graduate from University College Cork, was doing a backpacking trip round France, financed by the few francs she and her best friend could earn picking grapes. They had a whirlwind romance and, much to the dismay of both families, married six months later in the medieval church in Castelnau de Montmiral, a hilltop 'bastide' in The Tarn region of southern France.

'What a story. Almost Shakespearean. Your mum sounds like a very passionate lady.'

'Oh, that she is. Be careful now. They say I'm my mother's daughter!'

She flushed with embarrassment the moment the words left her lips, but her blushes were quickly calmed by Seb's burst of laughter.

'And the wine farm is still home?'

'Yes. Papa inherited the land and the farmhouse. He's

worked his fingers to the bone for thirty years to build the business up and provide for us.'

'What an amazing place to grow up. Sounds totally idyllic.'

Just as his own childhood was meant to be.

'I guess it was, but it's a very hard life. You're completely tied to the land. We never had summer holidays, not one, but I can't complain. Our summers were beautiful.'

She described them with sepia-tinted nostalgia, the images peppered with little details that brought her childhood to life. The smell of the vines after a thunderstorm. Her Papa's huge leathery hands on her face as he kissed her goodnight. Every night, without fail. The excitement of new young men helping with the harvest each summer. The sadness of the goodbyes. And her mother, the bond that made it all work. Always busy, the doors to the house always open. Food, wine and love dispensed with Celtic passion.

'What happens in the winter? Not much I should imagine.'

'When do you think the wine is made, Brains?'

'I thought it pretty much made itself.'

'For Christ's sake don't say that to Papa.'

'Oh! So when am I meeting him?' said Seb, revelling in the hole she'd dug for herself.

'Oh! Piss off,' she snapped back, scrunching up her face in playful exasperation.

The waiter arrived to clear their starters and they both took pleasure in the brief silence. She was so utterly beautiful. So keen of mind. He wanted to reach out and hold her hand. Not now, not yet. He tried to keep his cool.

'With an Irish mum and a good Catholic family, I guess

you have a houseful of siblings you've left behind.'

'You'd think, but no. Just me.'

Sophia explained that her mother had had great difficulty conceiving and then, after two years of trying when hope was but all but lost, Sophia appeared. They were not blessed again, but they told Sophia all the time that she was all they could want. She was their world. Which made the decision to enrol at Central St Martins a very difficult one.

'It can't have been easy for your parents.'

'Dad was pretty gutted. And he worries about me being in London. He worried if I went out in Toulouse when I was at Uni there, so this is really hard for him.'

'Worried about meeting men like me?'

'Too right, but Mum is quite the opposite. She lives for adventure. She was practically pushing me out the door to have some adventures of my own.'

Their main courses arrived, for Seb the 'authentic paysanne' Coq au Vin, served in a brass saucepan for maximum impact. Seb had never ordered anything else there. Sophia, however, dismissed it as being overly wet, saying with confidence that she made a better one. She chose the lamb chops Saignant, and the conversation ebbed and flowed naturally, increasingly relaxed and pleasurable.

Seb listened intently as Sophia gave him a bullet point summary of her new life in London. She shared a second floor flat in Pimlico with Tilly, one of the girls on her course. Tilly was tall and willowy with a beaky nose and enormous brain, who had apparently broken her parents' hearts by turning down a place at Oxford to read History in favour of fashion at St Martins. But he was already thinking about the logistics if the evening were to have some longevity, and his thoughts drifted to Pimlico. The river to the south, Chelsea

Chapter 13

to the West, Belgravia to the North and Westminster to the East. It should be a prime location, but it wasn't. It was an enclave of transience; flat shares, bolt holes, midweek dormitory apartments. No time for a community, no soul, at a permanent discount to its lofty neighbours. For those who stayed for just a year or two in the tiny Victorian conversion flats in vast four-story buildings, it worked well enough.

Sophia talked passionately about fashion, not dazzled by the glamour but the amazing creativity of the kaleidoscope of personalities she was meeting and working with. Seb, knowing nothing of this world, was only half convinced.

'Sounds great. It does, really. But how will you make money?'

'Jesus, you sound like my father!'

Seb shrugged his shoulders, smiled defiantly, and let the question stand.

'I've no great wish to make a fortune, but if you mean how will I make a living, I have a plan. But I haven't even told my parents all the details so I'm sure as hell not telling you!'

'Very sensible. I'd only nick the idea and do it myself. I'm looking for a career change as it happens.'

'You can come and work for me if you play your cards right.'

All she was prepared to divulge was that she hoped to create a brand, more street than couture, and open shops in the major cultural centres, travelling the world seeking inspiration.

Seb, in contrast, summed up his life in a few sentences, with some cavernous omissions. Normal childhood. University deemed a waste of time and adventure sought in the Army. Injury on a training exercise that forced him to get a normal job. He gave a brief explanation of his job and an even briefer sketch of the new biotech project he was working on, with its added extra dimension.

'That sounds quite dangerous. Do you know what you're getting in to?'

'Not really. But I doubt it will be very exciting.'

'Did they ask you because you are a tough military man. Incorruptible to the last?'

'I think they asked me because they could see that I was bored out of my mind and this might make me want to stay.'

'And will it?'

'Not a chance. Anyway, I have a career in fashion to look forward to now.'

'So, you do. Anyway, that's enough about me, tell me about your family. I want to hear all about the Fabers of Berkshire. What do your mum and dad do?'

He knew it was coming. He had been here many times before.

'Dad was a surgeon and Mum was a nurse.'

'How cool. Are they retired?'

'Mum stopped working when me and my sister arrived on the same day.'

'You've a twin sister!?'

'I do, and a younger brother.'

He was delaying the inevitable. Better to just get it done.

'And Dad died in an accident when I was thirteen.'

Sophia put her glass down and moved her right hand to his but fell short of making contact with it.

'That's horrible. I'm so, so sorry to hear that.'

'It was a long time ago.' It was like yesterday. 'Tough for my mum, but we survived.'

Chapter 13

He could tell she wanted to ask what happened. Everyone did. But Seb's rigidly closed expression didn't permit it. He changed the tempo and described his experiences growing up in a Home County village with farms but no real farmers. His very ambitious twin sister with her professional tuba playing husband, trying to manage her life as a barrister while bringing up two young kids. His maverick younger brother, a PR man who could make anyone look and, more importantly, feel good. And, of course, his mother, who had held them together with such strength against such adversity.

'She sounds like an amazing woman,' said Sophia.

'She is. I hope you get to meet her some time,' said Seb, it being his turn to accidentally accelerate their courtship.

Sophia described how her own small family had been augmented with the labourers that worked on the estate for as long as she could remember. She talked about her cousins. One set of French and four sets of Irish.

'My French cousins basically hate us because Papa inherited all the land when both his parents were still alive. Very unusual in France. Complicated legal stuff that I've stayed well out of, but the upshot is that my uncle's family are consumed with envy. Sad really.'

She didn't expand, but it was clear that it was an unresolved issue.

As they made inroads into their second bottle of the evening, inhibitions started to crumble. The most pertinent question, their respective relationship status, was mercifully straightforward. Both single. Neither felt any need to delve into each other's romantic pasts, a minefield best avoided.

As the evening progressed, he probed and she teased. Seb risked increasingly prolonged looks and was rewarded with roguish glances from Sophia. Smiles and gestures unaccompanied by speech. Comfortable, alluring silences. Sophia's delicate right hand was resting on the table. Long slender fingers with a simple silver band on her third finger. As he laughed at her description of her 'fou' cousins, Seb extended his left hand and softly held the tips of her fingers in his hand. She gently clasped his, moving her thumb as softly as a butterfly over his fingertips. He was aroused beyond belief. They held each other's gaze for a few seconds before the moment was shattered by the waiter bowling in and thrusting pudding menus under their noses.

Too full of rich French food, they resisted the offer and Seb asked for the bill. He paid it, declining Sophia's quite insistent demand to go Dutch, and they gathered themselves and made for the door. He didn't want the night to end, and neither did she. Just as Seb was trying to think of a suitable venue to naturally prolong the evening, Sophia locked arms with him and strode boldly down Old Brompton Road towards Chelsea.

'Let's just walk. I love to walk the streets at night,' said Sophia.

'Do you now?'

They both acknowledged her cheeky double entendre with dancing eyes and big grins. And so they walked. They walked through the stucco fronted streets and crescents of South Kensington, stopping to gaze into the lavishly decorated drawing rooms with their Louis XVI décors. Down to the funky bustle of the Fulham Road, stopping to comment on some of the independent boutiques' window displays. Past the cinema, the pubs and the hospital until abruptly, and without fanfare, Sophia steered Seb into a cobbled mews, stood squarely in front of him and pulled him close by his lapels.

'Isn't it about time you kissed me?' she said, with friendly authority.

They kissed delicately, but with a passion that blocked out everything around them. After a minute they broke away and just held each other in silence.

'Now take me to your flat and make love to me. It's just round the corner if I'm not mistaken.'

He looked at her in a state of bewilderment.

'You are utterly extraordinary.'

She was suddenly unsure of herself.

'Oh God, is that good, or not?'

'Very good.'

A few minutes later they stood in his sitting room undressing each other, item by item, giggling at the challenges and un-sexiness of the removal of laced boots and tight jeans, until they stood opposite each other with just their underwear covering their nakedness. Seb held her close and kissed her deeply, reaching for the clasp of her black lace bra, gently caressing her breasts while she simultaneously slipped her fingers inside the waist band of his boxer shorts and eased them down, careful to make space to accommodate his arousal. Seb slowly slid her lacy knickers down past her bottom and they fell to her feet. The reciprocal unveiling was both scary and intoxicating. She had such natural beauty. Her freckled nose, the softness of her skin, her shoulders, breasts, hips and bottom. Features so beautiful in isolation, achieving orchestral crescendo when he looked at her standing naked in his flat.

The blinds were open, and they risked being seen by the occupants of flats across the street. It didn't inhibit Sophia, but Seb wasn't given to exhibitionism and didn't want to share her with anyone. He led her to the bedroom, leaving the pile of clothes behind them. They stood by the bed pulling each other close, excitement giving ground to frenzy with every delicate touch. Wind whistled through the Victorian sash windows. Sophia jumped under the covers and Seb slid in next to her. They kissed and explored each other's bodies with their fingertips and their mouths, careful not to rush or overstimulate, their desire mounting almost unbearably. As he lay prone on her body, he propped himself up in a press-up position and fixed Sophia in an intense gaze.

'Do you, err, what I mean is can we…?'

'Jesus, you're lying naked on top of me man, so you've done the hard bit. And no, I'm not on the pill. Makes me crazy, well crazier.'

'OK, well I have something I think.'

He started to rifle though his bedside table in something of a panic. After a few noisy moments he pulled out a dusty unopened box with all the joy of a child pulling out a fat bag of sweets from a lucky dip.

'So, you thought this would happen?' she responded, with mock offence.

'I thought it may happen at some point with someone. I've had these for a while'.

'Well, we better use mine then. I'm too young to be a mum.'

A mantra her sexually liberated mother had drummed into her. Never promiscuous, always prepared. She reached into her bag and pulled out the small foil sachet, removed the condom, and instead of handing it to Seb, reached down and tantalisingly rolled it onto him. It was almost too much for him to bear.

Chapter 13

They needed both packets in the end, and a few more besides. After several hours of frenzied activity, both greedy and wonderfully generous, they collapsed and lay in silence just looking at each other, their legs entwined. Drained. Spent. And plunged into deep hypnotic sleep.

Seb woke shortly after 3am, intolerably hot and dangerously thirsty. He walked to the kitchen and poured two tall glasses of water. Still tingling all over. Still visibly aroused. They drank their water, kissed and made love once more.

An indeterminate time later they woke to shards of light hitting them through the narrow gap in the curtains.

Birdsong? Fucking birdsong?!

His clock screamed 07.56 at him with its bright green digital display. A 09.00 rendezvous at Sunningdale Golf Club was now barely achievable. He ran through the shower and shaved in three minutes flat. He dressed at warp speed, chased around the flat to hunt down his phone and wallet and keys, and returned to the bedroom to find Sophia sitting up in bed wearing a t-shirt she had liberated from his drawer. He crawled onto the bed and kissed her.

'This has been lovely,' said Seb.

'I should certainly hope so, now off you go to your golf, mister. You can call me later if you like.'

'You know, I just might.'

And he ran out the door as high as kite.

CHAPTER 14

The dashboard's digital display read 08.55 as he screeched to a halt in front of the wrought iron electric gates separating the members of Sunningdale Golf Club from the mere aspirants.

He punched in the security code he'd been texted by Fletcher, and parked next to the line of Porsches, Aston Martins and Bentleys that the more arriviste section of the membership tended to favour. As he took his clubs out of his own ten-year-old VW Golf, a black S Class Mercedes pulled into the car park and came to rest in one of the spaces reserved for committee members.

The driver's door opened, and a black man of astonishing scale stepped out. He looked around with dead eyes, scanning the car park for any signs of threat before opening the rear passenger door to allow a rangy silver-haired man to step out. Richard Barnard cut an impressive figure himself but was dwarfed by the physical mass of his driver. The giant wore a blue single-breasted suit over a black polo-neck. His head was clean shaven and there appeared to be some sort of marking on one side of his face. He plucked his employer's clubs out of the car with one hand and carried

Chapter 14

them to the caddy master's hut, all the while attracting open mouthed gasps from people who traded on having seen it all.

Richard Barnard walked into the clubhouse and Seb followed promptly. As was his wont, William Fletcher had arrived early and by the time Seb got to the changing room Barnard and Fletcher were already greeting each other with a vigorous and prolonged handshake. It was more than the exaggerated effervescence of the British upper classes. They clearly had history.

'Ah, here he is. Richard, I would like you to meet Seb Faber.'

'Very good to meet you, Mr Barnard. Thanks for inviting me to your club.'

'My pleasure, Sebastian. William has told me a lot about you. It would seem that you are the man of the moment at Blounts.'

When Sophia used his full name, he liked it. When Barnard used it, he did not. But now wasn't the time to object.

'Are we being joined by your colleague?' asked Seb, gesturing towards the car.

'Come now, Sebastian, does he look like he's here to play golf? No, my Finance Director, Johan Smith will be here any moment. I hope,' he said, looking down at his watch impatiently.

He spoke with the sort of imperial South African accent that the Boers went to war to eradicate, his words delivered at a measured pace slow enough to demand patience from the listener. It was clearly deliberate, and Seb was instantly irritated by being expected to accommodate such studied arrogance. But accommodate it he would, for now.

Barnard was imposingly tall and long limbed, and moved with the long, languid strides of a man not to be hurried. His thick silver hair crowned a tanned face, high of cheekbone, with arresting bright blue eyes; a man used to attracting attention whenever he walked into a room. As they set off towards the putting green, someone trotted up behind them with his golf bag bouncing up and down on his shoulder.

'Richard, I am *so* sorry I'm late. The traffic out of London was terrible.'

A short, round, balding man, he almost genuflected when he addressed his boss, his every movement betraying his unease. Johan Smith, evidently. Barnard gave him a withering look and gestured to the locker room, and he scuttled off to get himself ready.

He returned minutes later, sweat pouring off him, his glasses sliding down his nose as he tried to get himself settled. They stood on the first tee of the Old Course and accepted Barnard's decree that they would play a four-ball match, and it was to be England v South Africa. Barnard, with a handicap of six, was the low handicapper. Fletcher was off eight, and Smith was off a very generous twenty-four. Seb had barely played since his father died. He had his father's old clubs in his bag.

'I haven't played for a few years so why don't I play off eighteen.'

'Eighteen, Sebastian? That makes you either a very ordinary golfer or a cheat.'

Seb looked into Barnard's eyes to search for any levity or humour behind the barb. He found none, and returned even less.

'Well, we'll find out soon enough.'

Chapter 14

Barnard elected to ignore the comment and turned to Fletcher.

'The usual wager, William?'

'Of course, Richard.'

Sunningdale was well known for high stakes gambling. Whatever the 'usual wager' was, it was certain to be far more that Seb was comfortable with but there was precious little he could do about it without losing face, so he said nothing.

Barnard won the toss and teed off first. He addressed the ball like a Captain standing at the helm of his ship, commanding the ball to fly two hundred and fifty yards down the middle of the fairway. It duly obeyed.

Smith was next, and entirely predictably topped his ball, failing to get it airborne. It came to rest in the heather a hundred yards ahead of them. He made a weak self-deprecating joke and hurried off the tee box. Next up was Fletcher. William Fletcher had played cricket for the Combined Forces and clearly had a natural eye for a ball. He swept his three wood in a perfect, elegant parabolic arc and sent the ball down the right half of the fairway with draw, bringing it to rest in position 'A'.

And so to Seb. Given the events of the past twelve hours, this game of golf meant absolutely nothing to him. He grabbed his driver, teed up the ball and knocked it off. It was straight and long, his ball sailing past both Fletcher and Barnard's efforts, coming to rest just before a bunker that one of the caddies was quick to point out was a remarkable 320 yards from the tee.

'Simple enough swing, but it works,' said Barnard, gruffly.

Simple enough swing?

But it was, Seb had to concede. His muscularity and

timing meant he could just stand there and hit it. It wasn't stylish, as Barnard had declared, but it was highly effective.

They all set off down the fairway, Seb carrying his bag, the portly accountant pulling a trolley and Barnard and Fletcher with caddies. Barnard, being a white South African, was more than used to servants in all their forms and treated his caddie with barely veiled distain. Fletcher was polite enough to his man but certainly got his money's worth.

Smith arrived at his ball first and rather hurried his second shot which resulted in yet another mishit, this time into the waiting bunker 150 yards from the green. Fletcher and Barnard were a few yards from each other but with Fletcher's ball marginally longer, it was Barnard to play first. He played a sensible seven iron approach, leaving himself a simple wedge onto the green. Fletcher followed it with an almost identical shot. They all walked on to Seb's ball which was lying 225 yards from the pin.

'What will it be Seb? I dare say you could make it with a decent swish from your three wood.'

More mind games. Seb could feasibly reach the green, and that was the problem. The sensible shot was a lay-up with a nine iron, and a simple chip on, but because of his length off the tee he had put himself in more danger than if he had hit a much shorter drive. He had barely slept and was still a little drunk, and he was being closely observed. The wise choice would be to play safe and lay up. A thought, of course, he dismissed without pause.

'Not sure I need that much club, Richard,' said Seb flashing a grin as he pulled out his four iron.

He addressed the ball, and caught Fletcher hiding a rarely seen smirk behind his gloved hand. Seb gripped the

Chapter 14

club firmly, took one deep breath as he coiled his torso and, unleashing brutal force as he uncoiled, hit through the ball. He couldn't have struck it better. The four iron sent it long and high, sailing over the fairway bunker. Starting over the left edge of the green, it faded right towards the pin.

'That'll do,' said Fletcher, in a rare public expression of support.

'Might be a bit much. Perhaps should have gone for the five,' said Seb, heading off towards the green.

'This is only the first hole William, and your boy hasn't won it quite yet,' muttered Barnard.

He did win it, two putting for a birdie four, one better than Barnard. The unfortunate Smith flailed away in the fairway bunker, and after three unsuccessful attempts at extracting himself, he picked up his ball and shuffled on in a puce-faced huff.

While Seb got lucky on the first hole, it was inevitable that his washed-out state would catch up with him. Luckily Fletcher was the very definition of consistency, and the holes that Seb played no part in were evenly shared by Fletcher and Barnard, so the match remained tight throughout. On the eleventh hole, after wolfing a very welcome sausage sandwich at Sunningdale's famous halfway hut, Seb pulled his drive left into the heather, and Barnard promptly hit his ball in precisely the same direction and followed him in there. Barnard hadn't hit a single shot left all day, so the temporary esprit de corps felt contrived. They set off towards their balls, and when Barnard felt that they were sufficiently distanced from the others, he took the conversation sharply in a new direction.

'Seb, the London IPO we are planning for next year is the most important event in our company's history. We need it done right'.

Seb too changed gear in response to Barnard's bluntness.

'You do, Richard, and I think you know our firm's record in the biotech sector.'

'I do, and I also know your personal record. For a new guy fresh off the parade ground, you seem to have considerable placing power.'

So, Fletcher had been talking. A bit odd, Seb thought.

'I'm a quick learner.'

'That much is clear, but that only goes so far. I need total commitment from my broker. This deal cannot be allowed to fail.'

Barnard's words left his mouth through a curled lip, and Seb immediately bristled.

'If you get that data, we'll get you the money,' said Seb.

'If we get the data we want, anyone can get us the money. We want to hire a broker who sees the true value of our company. Do you understand me, Seb?'

He did. He had heard this pitch before. Richard Barnard was the single largest shareholder of Free State Biotech. His sixty percent stake would make him very rich indeed if Seb's clients were prepared to pay up for the shares. Barnard wanted to achieve as high an IPO price as possible and would hire the bank that told him what he wanted to hear. Not at all Seb's style, but he realised he'd best keep that to himself for now.

'If an appetite suppressant actually works then it has the potential to be the biggest drug ever approved,' he said. 'The vain will be desperate to get their hands on it, and the sick will need it. I get it, Richard, and my clients will too.'

All true, but deliberately nebulous. H57 was a drug with no clinically proven efficacy to speak of. The Hoodia cactus reportedly supressed appetite in its natural state, but even that was anecdotal and the odds of developing a successful drug at the start of a Phase 2 trial were thirty percent at best. Despite all Richard Barnard's silver haired gravitas, the potential to create a multi-billion-dollar drug was, on a risk-adjusted basis, far more likely to fail than succeed. A point which would not be wasted on Seb's institutional clients.

'I hope and trust that you are right, Seb. But this is particularly important to me, you see. I can't leave anything to chance.'

Seb couldn't see how this conversation could possibly get more bizarre. Barnard asked for a six iron from his caddy and signalled curtly for him to walk on ahead. They watched as Smith played his second shot before Barnard addressed his ball.

'I will give you three hundred thousand pounds cash for every ten-million-pound increment in value we achieve above your current base case value of one hundred and twenty million,' he said, assessing his next shot with care. 'I think this would be a fair reward for your efforts and I hope it would ensure your full commitment to achieving the right price for the current shareholders. This will be a personal arrangement between the two of us, you understand.' And deftly knocked his ball on to the front edge of the green.

Seb didn't dare make eye contact with Barnard for fear of revealing his shock. On the face of it, it was victimless. It was his job, the job of every corporate broker, to get the best possible price for their clients. But personal incentives that were paid directly to him were forbidden and broke multiple codes of practice, and probably laws. Still, three hundred thousand pounds, cash, for every ten million increment? Life changing money for him. For his mother.

'Well, that is a generous proposition.'

He sliced his next ball straight into the trees to the right of the green, clearly rattled. He didn't look at Barnard, didn't want to see his self-satisfaction.

'Yes, it is Seb, so think well on it. I would see it as complete alignment, something I place a lot of emphasis on, and I'm sure you do too. Looks like my hole, don't you think?'

This had suddenly become very sinister. It was no longer an offer he could diplomatically refuse; it was a condition of engagement. The proposal would have been easy enough to dismiss, but the threat wasn't.

He needed to speak to Fletcher, urgently, but was denied any opportunity by Barnard's constant proximity. As they stepped onto the eighteenth tee, he still hadn't had a chance to speak to him.

The match stood all square. They each hit their drives, and Seb sent his ball high and long into the heavy rough to the right of the fairway. As they approached their balls, it was clear that Barnard's ball was lying in the first cut of rough. Only by a few inches, but unambiguously so. Seb found his ball buried deep in the tall grass, nothing to do but chop it out onto the fairway and accept that par was no longer available to him. He was ten yards ahead of Barnard, so it was Barnard to play first. Seb watched as Barnard discussed club selection with his caddie with his usual supercilious manner.

'Your five iron should be spot on sir.'

The caddie had pulled the club halfway out of the bag when he was stopped short.

'No, I'll take the six.'

'I don't know, sir. This is a 170 yard uphill shot, out of the semi rough, with a left to right wind. The six iron brings

Chapter 14

the greenside bunker into play. I'd go with the five.'

Barnard span round to face his caddie.

'I've played this shot about three hundred times, so I suggest you just hand me the club I've asked for. If that doesn't offend your professional sensibilities.'

The caddie, tip in mind, conceded and put the five iron back in the bag. He pulled out the six, which was snatched out of his hand by Barnard.

'Left edge, sir.' A good piece of advice that Barnard failed to acknowledge as he walked up to his ball and stood bolt upright behind it, visualising the shot he was about to play. With the club still in his right hand, he leant forward and dragged the ball an inch to the left with the blade of his club. Out of the slight depression it had been lying in, it was now sitting proud of the grass surrounding it. It was an unconscionable act of deception for a golfer. If it was an error, you could apologise and return the ball to its original position, no harm done. In a competition, the tariff would be one penalty shot. But if not declared by the player, it would result in the forfeiture of the hole, even the match and very possibly his golf club membership, and indeed any chance of any future membership anywhere else. Indelibly branded as a cheat.

Barnard, of course, knew exactly what he was doing. Seb could see a barely suppressed grin, but just as he was deciding whether or not he gave a damn, Barnard took the decision away from him.

'That alright Seb? Just rolled into a divot.'

Completely irrelevant if not on the fairway, even when playing winter rules, which they were not. He took a deep breath and shrugged his shoulders.

'You do what you need to do, Richard.'

He was at least pleased to see he'd hit his mark. The smirk fell away from Barnard's lips just a fraction before he made a perfect strike, sending the ball just beyond the bunker his caddie had advised against flirting with. Barnard handed his club to his caddie without deigning to look at him and marched off towards the green. Seb took an almighty heave at his part-buried ball and only succeeded in propelling it yet deeper into the undergrowth, where it would remain, given that Seb had neither the interest nor energy to go digging for it.

He reached Fletcher just after he'd played his second shot. Another metronomic strike, coming to rest a few yards to the left of Barnard's ball. This was the first moment in two solid hours that he could speak to Fletcher out of Barnard's earshot.

'Richard has just tried to bribe me.'

Fletcher looked at him with dead eyes. Seb continued.

'He'll pay me, just me, three hundred grand for every ten million premium on his valuation.'

Fletcher showed no indication that this was surprising or notable information.

'OK. How did you respond?'

'I didn't really, just kind of stalled.'

'Good. I thought he would make you some sort of offer. He has a reputation for that sort of incentivisation. Nothing to worry about. We can chat about it later.'

'Nothing to worry about? Oh, and he's a brazen cheat!'

'Something else he's renowned for. This is business Seb. Just toe the line. I can trust you to do that, can't I?'

With that comment doing laps of his head, he turned to watch Barnard deftly chip up to the hole. Fletcher wasted no time in giving him the putt. A missable four-footer, and a decision that Seb should by rights have shared. Fletcher calmly addressed his ball with his lob wedge and, incongruously, skulled it through the green into the back wall of the awaiting bunker. He needed to hole his bunker shot to halve the match. He took one limp swing at the ball, and it stayed resolutely beached. Two shots that were completely inconsistent with his performance over the previous seventeen holes.

'Bad luck, Seb. Just not your day. Twelve shots weren't quite enough.'

Seb took Barnard's hand and gripped it firmly while staring into his eyes.

'Well played, Richard. Not much I could do today was there.'

'Not really,' he said a smug grin breaking across his face.

They left the green. Barnard and Fletcher, a few yards ahead, were stride for stride and shoulder to shoulder. They exchanged a comment and burst into laughter, and as they did so they turned around to glance at Seb before they walked, still in close conversation, into the clubhouse.

CHAPTER 15

Seb drove back to London wondering what the hell had just happened. None of it made sense. And then he thought about Sophia, and that did.

His phone rang in his pocket as he parked outside the flat and he whipped it out eagerly only to see 'Mum H' illuminated on the screen.

'Seb, exciting news. Harry has just called and he's coming home for the weekend! I spoke to Emily this morning and she says that with work and the kids she just can't get away. Please tell me you can come!'

Mary Faber didn't do favourites. She was always drawn to the child with the greatest immediate need. That had been Seb for far too long. But she felt her second son's absence keenly, and his occasional visits always called for the killing of a fatted calf. Seb had hoped to see Sophia on Friday, but that would have to wait.

'Sure. I'll be there. And let me speak to Emily.'

'Oh, would you. And you should call Harry because he says he has to go into the office for a few hours tomorrow. He'll need a lift.'

Seb dialled Emily's number straightaway and got her

Chapter 15

voicemail.

'Emily, what are you doing on Friday night that can't be done over the rest of the weekend? Mum's pretty upset. Call me.'

He followed up with a brief and highly efficient call with Harry who was boarding his plane at Dulles Airport, Washington DC. A few minutes later a text came through from Emily.

> I was going to be working (know what that is?) but…. the prosecution just settled! Woofuckinghoo! I'm now the world expert in bloody big rubber bands! Have texted Mum. Geoff has a concert on Sat so can't be ruined (yawn!) so he's staying here with the kids. Need a big night! 6pm Earls Ct?

Seb had been given chapter and verse on Emily's latest case from his Mum, who took huge pride in everything her children did. He had to admire the level of expertise that Emily could acquire on the most obscure subject matter you could think of in just a matter of weeks. This case had required her to become an expert in the breaking strains of bungee cords under different climatic conditions. But apparently that was now behind her and before she embarked on her next case, for one night only, she was free to go bananas.

CHAPTER 16

They all left their respective offices as soon as was acceptable and headed for Earls Court tube, Seb picking up his car en-route.

As they hit the elevated section of the M4 heading due west, the traffic began to flow, and the burdens of the city started to blow away. Given the week he'd had, this wasn't any ordinary Friday. After a cursory catch up in sibling shorthand, he turned on the radio and flicked though the pre-programmed stations until he heard the familiar drawl of Michael Stipe and belted out the chorus with abandon.

'…I'm breaking through, I'm bending spoons, I'm keeping flowers in full bloom. I'm looking for answers from the great beyond…'

Another half-dozen butchered sing-alongs and they were home. They drove past the main house, their childhood home, and peeled right down a rutted track to the annexe, where their mother's near vintage Volvo estate was parked.

Seb knew immediately that something had changed, but he couldn't work out what it was. Before he had the chance to, Harry piped up.

Chapter 16

'The tenants have taken the tree house down! What the fuck?'

Orchard End was a gloriously haphazard red brick farmhouse. As young children, it was a good space in which to be together, with enough space to be comfortably apart. It had absolutely no pretence to grandeur, the only nod to privilege being the grass tennis court on the lawn, but that had long since gone, successive tenants finding neither the time nor inclination to keep it maintained. Nevertheless, Orchard End remained what their father had been given to smilingly describing as a 'gentleman's family home'. It was a constant source of anguish to Seb that the short-term plan to let the main house had become permanent out of financial necessity. Fourteen years of scraping to get by. And it was his fault. All of it.

Before they were even out of the car, the front door swung open and their mother came rushing out to greet them.

'What the hell happened to the tree house Mum?'

'Harry, I haven't seen you in six months and that's all you can say? For heaven's sake!'

Harry swept his mother up in a giant bear hug.

'Lovely to be home. I've missed you.'

'That's better. And I've missed you, too,' she laughed, as she hugged him back. 'The truth of it is that it was twenty-two years old. The timbers were rotten and the last thing I need is a lawsuit if one of their little ones should fall out of it, so I got a man to take it down for me. That's all there is to it.'

That really wasn't all there was to it. Their father had built it in the summer of seventy-nine. He'd toiled away in the evenings and weekends for most of August and, even despite putting broken bodies back together for a living, the treehouse was pretty much his proudest achievement, apart from his family.

Nonetheless, it was hard to argue with their mother's logic, or the maths. There wasn't much money around and she steadfastly refused any contributions from the children, however robustly they were offered.

'Don't be silly,' she would say, 'I have everything I need.'

But she didn't. Not her home. Not her husband.

They dumped their bags in the hall without breaking stride in their passage to the kitchen, the table already set with an encouragingly large array of cutlery.

'Seb, you're in charge of drinks,' said Mary.

Along with carving the Sunday roast, pouring drinks was a responsibility Seb had inherited far too early.

'Any white will do for me. And to the brim. I want to see a meniscus!' said Emily. 'I can't tell you how much I need this.'

Seb already had his head in the fridge and pulled out the white wine and a four pack of Kronenbourg, handing one to Harry.

And they were off. Their mother was already well briefed on Emily's news, so she probed Harry with her usual zeal, and then it was Seb's turn.

'Now Seb, how is life in the big city?'

Seb was pregnant with news. His life, in fact, had been turned upside down, but he didn't want to talk about the Barnard situation. It would make his mother worry herself sick. And he had absolutely no wish to share anything about Sophia.

'A few things. One quite interesting deal. A South African biotech, but pretty early stage. Lots of hope, big aspirations, including their valuation.'

'What does this one do?'

'Natural appetite suppressant. Extract from a cactus found in the Kalahari.'

Mary puffed on her cigarette and leant in.

'Sounds interesting, go on.'

Seb was into his second beer, and he was fairly helpless when caught in his mother's investigative gaze. So, he expanded, but only on the unremarkable elements. The drug. The reasons for all the excitement. The due diligence they were performing to check it all out, while managing to withhold every one of the other aspects of his remarkable week.

He was saved from further inquiry by a saucepan of peas boiling over on the hob. Mary leapt up and turned the gas off, and that was the cue to serve the salmon mouse starter. And to propose the toast.

'To Dad,' said Mary.

'To Dad,' they all agreed.

The evening proceeded with its customary gusto, following the usual well-trodden path. They started out being civil. Argumentative, but polite, but that phase was short lived. With a few more drinks in them, the siblings started to make bold and provocative statements, usually only very loosely based in fact, waiting and hoping for another to bite. It was Harry's turn to throw out the bait.

'The American system of crime and punishment tells you plainly and in words of one syllable that felons reoffend. Money spent on fluffy workshops and 'learn to write your own name' lessons is entirely wasted. This is taxpayers' money that should be spent on building more prisons. And the legal system should fill them up.'

It wasn't a taboo topic. Harry knew what they all knew. Seb had been found guilty of Grievous Bodily Harm in the eyes of the law of England and Wales. But if you are stopping a drug dealer from sexually threatening your defenceless sister, different laws should apply. And a different judiciary.

'All very interesting, but we weren't talking about the US,' replied Emily.

'You weren't, I was,' said Harry. 'The statistics from every Western nation with a developed legal system will tell you exactly the same thing. Career criminals are beyond redemption.'

'You cannot genuinely believe that,' said Emily.

'I can and I do. It's infantile to take any alternate view.'

Harry was in the zone now, which Seb observed with amusement. His brother was deliberately attacking her liberal outlook, but he expected at least one other member of the family to stand with him.

'Where on earth do you get your information?' demanded Emily.

'The Washington Post, and they get theirs from the US office for National Statistics.'

'You are a vulgar, intransigent brute, Harry,' said Emily.

Seb felt a twinge of fraternal unity.

'That he may be, but he's right, you know, Emily. Once you're in the system, you pretty much stay in it. Not everyone has a family like ours.'

'One, you were only in there for six months and two, Harry's argument is entirely based on a weak journalistic reference.'

'And your information comes from...?' asked Seb.

'The Home Office. That OK for you two luddites?'

Now she must have been bluffing. She was a corporate

Chapter 16

lawyer and hadn't studied criminal law since Oxford.

'Emily, you're forgetting there's a difference between intelligence and knowledge. You can't revise your way out of this argument,' said Harry.

That was a little too close to the bone.

'Enough!' said Mary.

'So she can call me any name under the sun, and I have to just sit here and take it?' pleaded Harry.

'Basically, yes. It's called being a man, darling. You'll make a lovely one someday,' replied Mary.

'Aren't you going to back me up, Seb?'

At that moment Seb's phone buzzed in his pocket. He'd been checking it with some frequency hoping for contact from Sophia and sidled off to the corner of the room to read her message.

Nice family party Sebastian, but I need an answer.
What will it be? RB.

All the happy anticipation drained from his body as he span around to look out of the windows into the garden.

'Some girl just give you the flick?' asked Harry, grinning.

Emily read his body language quite differently.

'What's going on, Seb? Who's the text from?'

He couldn't answer.

'What is it love? You've gone quite grey.'

Seb pulled himself together.

'Probably nothing Mum. Harry, can I borrow you for a sec?'

Harry, as pissed as he was, responded immediately. Seb opened the kitchen door to the garden and shut it behind them.

'Don't freak out but there's a small chance we're being watched. I'll explain later. Just look tough and stay close.'

'Don't be ridiculous. Watched by who?'
'The South African CEO,' said Seb.
'Watched from where?'
'Somewhere out there.'
Seb pointed to the garden, and the field beyond it.
'Jesus. What a weirdo. Sure, let's check it out.'
Seb gripped Harry by the arm.
'Wait, it could be his driver.'
Harry looked at Seb with wide eyed excitement.
'Is that a problem?'

Seb thought better of providing a fuller description of the 'driver'. Seb was ex-para with all that implied, and Harry was a 17 stone, 6 foot 2 inch gorilla. Both were fit and powerfully built, but Barnard's bodyguard was a different scale of human being altogether. He didn't want to alarm Harry, though, and he thought it vanishingly unlikely that he was out there anyway.

'Not if there are two of us, come on.'

Harry read between the lines and quietly picked up a battered old cricket bat from a basket of garden toys under the log pile lean-to. Within five paces they could no longer be seen from the annexe. They slowly paced around the perimeter of the garden, straining to pick out any sound or movement in the moonless night. Harry couldn't have looked less anxious and, with all the drink in him, thought the sortie a bizarre but amusing addition to his evening. Seb felt quite differently.

After a few minutes of stalking around with nothing to report, Harry had had enough.

'Fuck this, there's no one here and I'm freezing. Let's go back in.'

'Wait a sec. For someone to see us in the kitchen they

Chapter 16

would have to be standing where we are now. You'd either have to climb a fence, come through the front gate or come through the fields. You wouldn't choose to come from the front if you wanted to stay hidden, and neither Barnard nor his driver would choose to clamber over that rickety fence if there was an alternative, so if someone has been stalking us, they'll have come through that gate. I'd like to just check it out. It'll only take a minute.'

They walked purposefully between the untamed rhododendron bushes, under the boughs of two vast horse chestnuts to the back fencing that separated their garden and the neighbouring farmer's field to the rear. The pedestrian gate was closed.

'Wild goose chase. Let's get back,' barked an impatient and thirsty Harry.

'Wait.'

Seb scanned the ground on either side of the gate, opened it, stepped through and bent down, illuminating a small area of grass with the light that his phone screen offered.

'Bollocks to this, I'm...'

'Fresh footmarks.'

They both stood stock still as they looked and listened all about them for any signs of life. They strained to see anything in the near pitch-black night, the loudest noise the thumping of their racing pulses in their ears. Then, in the far distance beyond the woodland, what sounded like laughter before the sound of a car door shutting, ignition and lights being turned on and an unseen car slowly driving off.

'What the fuck was that, Seb?'

'A bullshit attempt to scare me. We can't say anything about this when we go back inside. It would terrify Mum, and Em would spin out completely. I can manage this.'

'You sure?'

'Yes mate, I can. But thanks. Really.'

They started back for the house, shoulder to shoulder.

Harry suddenly stopped dead in his tracks.

'Shit, what do we say when we go in? They all saw your face when you got that text.'

His family were impossible to lie to. Honesty in all things wasn't just a Faber thing. It was *the* Faber thing. Seb needed to distract them with the truth. Or a truth at least.

'I know, we'll tell them I needed your advice about a girl.'

'You what! They'll never go for that.'

'Oh, I think they will.'

He briefly flashed the text message that Sophia had sent him after their night together. Not enough time for Harry to read it, but enough to see her Sophia xx…x sign off.

'Now that is *much* more interesting,' said Harry.

They tramped back into the kitchen and Harry, the cricket bat returned to the basket unnoticed, broke the news.

'You will find this very hard to believe, I know, but Sebastian Faber has a girlfriend!'

'I knew it. I just knew it. You sit right here and tell your mother every last detail,' said Mary.

'This calls for more wine,' bellowed Harry, who already had a fresh bottle in his hand.

CHAPTER 17

As much as she wanted to stay for the rest of the weekend, Emily needed to get back to her family. Seb offered to drop her at the station and Harry was hoofed out the door by his mother, who reminded him he lived four thousand miles away and seeing his hard-working sister to the station was the very least he could do. But close siblings being what they are, they coexisted in silence. Emily annotated her new brief, while simultaneously texting instructions to Geoff covering her arrival time, kids' parties and meal plans for the rest of the weekend, while Harry slumped across the back seat with half an eye open and his finger up his nose.

Seb had his eyes fixed on the road, but his mind galloped away with thoughts of Barnard. He was snapped back into the present by the sound of his phone. Before he had a chance to react, Harry had fished it out of the tray in the central console and noted the identity of the caller.

'It's Sophia, shall I answer?' said Harry.

'No, just put it back and I'll........'

Harry already had the phone to his ear.

'Sophia, hello, how are you doing?'

To most people, Harry and Seb's voices were

indistinguishable on the phone. There was a slight pause at the other end before Sophia's slightly confused reply:

'I'm fine. Seb?'

Seb jumped in.

'Sophia, *this* is Seb. That's Harry on the phone. Tell him to piss off and I'll call you back in an hour.'

'Sophia, after Seb's very gracious introduction, I feel we can speak freely. Can you please take good care of my brother, as you must have worked out by now that he's pretty much a lost cause.'

'Harry you bloody ignoramus, give it to me,' said Emily, snatching the phone out of his hand from the back seat.

'Sophia, this is Emily, Seb's big sister and I can only apologise for my baby brother Harry.'

'Oh, hi Emily, no worries. I'll call Seb back later,' said a highly confused Sophia.

'Emily, what are you doing?' said Seb.

'Nothing. Now Sophia, I know you've only just met my brother, but I hope we get to meet you soon. He's really not as bad as you might think.'

'Emily!' yelled Seb.

'I better hang up before he crashes and kills us all, but lovely to speak to you Sophia. You sound every bit as fabulous as he described. Byee.'

'Guys, what the hell was that all about?'

'Is she fit? She sounds fit,' probed Harry.

'Harry, don't be so base,' interjected Emily. 'She sounds very nice actually.'

'But she is fit, isn't she?' continued Harry.

'Harry!' bellowed Emily and Seb in perfect unison.

CHAPTER 18

Seb and Harry dragged themselves through the rest of the weekend, collapsed on sofas, not doing terribly much. Their mother continued to probe Seb about Sophia and he fed her appetite with the story of how they met, and a considerably censured version of their first date. Harry was not so easily fobbed off. Seb avoided being alone with him as much as he could but it didn't last.

'What was all that about last night ,Seb?'

He was loathe to burden Harry, or anyone else in his family, with any more problems but he couldn't lie to him. Not Harry.

'OK, I'll tell you, but I don't want Mum or Emily anywhere near this.'

Harry sat down on the arm of the sofa, his mind heading to bad places.

'Near what Seb?'

'Relax will you!'

'I'll relax when you tell me what's going on.'

Seb told his brother everything. Even down to the alarming dimensions of Barnard's bodyguard. Harry didn't rush to respond and when he did, he stood back up to look down at his big brother.

'Seb, I'm twice your size and I should be able to throw you around like a rag doll, but we both know that would never happen. Emily has the Oxford Law degree, but you tie her in knots when you're brave enough to deal with the consequences. I don't care how big that bloke is, you'll look after yourself, and you'll already have worked out all the angles and risks in getting involved in all this. But I am worried that you might be getting sucked into something messed up. Maybe this isn't the best thing for you right now.'

'What are you talking about?'

'I just think that this whole thing, all this stress could be a trigger.'

Seb had spent every day since Feltham navigating triggers. And he was having to work very hard to navigate this one.

'Look, I'm not the same guy I was back then. I drink in moderation. Unless I'm with you, of course! I haven't taken a drug since I started basic training and I haven't thrown a punch in this millennium.'

'I know. It's just…'

'Just what!'

His frazzled response was a bit too loud. Their mother's footsteps were coming from the kitchen.

'What's this? You two can't possibly be fighting.'

'Dead right, Mum. Because he couldn't possibly win,' said Harry, diffusing the situation as best he could.

'Good. Anyway, lunch is ready so come through.'

Mary returned to the kitchen and Harry started to follow her but was held fast by a firm grip on his forearm.

'Harry, I need you to know that I am OK. I need you to really know that.'

Chapter 18

Harry looked down at the hand gripping him, and Seb relaxed his grasp.

'Happy to hear you say it. That's all any of us want. You know that. Now let go of me before I toss you into that fire!'

CHAPTER 19

With distended bellies, and the usual sense of foreboding that creeps up on the employed on Sunday afternoons, Seb and Harry said their goodbyes and set off for town. The thirty-two miles were spent in near silence before Seb dropped his brother at his mansion flat in Kensington, care of his American employers, and drove the last mile to his own flat in Ifield Road. He dumped his bags, grabbed two motorbike helmets and ran out of the door. He was at Sloane Square at exactly five o'clock as they'd planned, to find Sophia, wrapped up in a scarf and mittens, sitting on the steps of the Royal Court Theatre as he pulled up on his Vespa.

'That looks ominous.' she said, as she took in the spare motorbike helmet he was raising in the air with intent.

'I thought we could go for a ride.'

'Did you now? And where are you planning to take me, because I'm sure my mother warned me about boys like you.'

'Very sound advice. I've a few ideas but is there anywhere you'd like to go?'

'Hmm, well now, I know a fun little place in Westbourne

Chapter 19

Grove. Will that contraption get us there?'

'Let's find out. Shall we?'

Sophia put the helmet on, climbed on to the scooter in one easy movement and wrapped her arms tightly around Seb's waist, pulling herself close to him. Seb took particular care as he navigated though the traffic from Chelsea to Knightsbridge, through Hyde Park to Notting Hill and, with Sophia giving instructions via hand signals, to a little basement restaurant on Westbourne Grove. It was an artisan bakery run by two bearded men in skinny jeans and white plimsolls, who clearly put great store in making every single item on the menu entirely from scratch and on site.

'Sophia, my darling!' said the slightly heavier set hipster, hugging Sophia like a long-lost sister. 'Where the fuck have you been hiding? We haven't seen you in an age.'

They were ushered towards one of the small round tin tables with their little rickety tin chairs.

'You're popular,' said Seb.

'I know, I'm big news in the cool North London set.'

She tossed her hair back to ape faux narcissism. But it was clearly the case.

'Nah. Actually, Mark was at college with me last year. After three years at fashion school he decided he'd rather bake bread.'

They ordered the freshly made potato, leek and lemon grass soup, a perfect hearty antidote to the early autumnal air they'd just been knifing through on the scooter.

'You made it to your golf on time then?' inquired Sophia.

'Just. No thanks to you!'

The oblique reference to their night together made him prickle with excitement. Sophia's mischievous grin indicated she felt the same, and they shared a moment or two of blissful reflection before Seb spoke again.

'Did you make it in to work?'

'I did indeed. I looked a bloody sight, mind.'

Seb looked at her, at how beautiful she really was.

'I very much doubt it,' he said.

She smiled, allowing the moment, before her instinctive flippancy resurfaced.

'So how was the golf? Did they find you out. Blow your cover?'

'God knows, but it was very bloody strange.'

'How so?'

Seb paused before replying, not certain quite how much he wanted to share. How much he should share.

'Actually, I'm pretty certain I was being bribed, then threatened.'

'What! That's crazy. What did he say?'

Seb related the events in full.

'What did you do? What did your boss say?'

'I told him what Barnard had said to me word for word. And then the most unnerving thing. He wasn't remotely surprised. In fact, he didn't react at all.'

'I wouldn't know whether this is normal in your world, but from the look of your face, I'd say it isn't. What's he like?'

'I'm still pretty new to the City but nothing like this has happened before, and Fletcher's straight as a die. Ex-forces, family man and very senior in the bank.'

'What exactly did he say when you told him?'

'He asked me, no, he told me to 'toe the line', and questioned whether I could be trusted. I haven't caught up with him since and I'm not sure I know what to say to him when I do.'

Sophia put her cutlery down.

Chapter 19

'How well do you know him?'

She'd changed gear, was taking control, which gave him some comfort.

'I have spent a large part of each day with him for the past year, but I can't say I know him well at all. Come to think of it, I don't think I know anyone that does. But that's not all. I got this text from Barnard on Friday night.'

He handed his phone to Sophia.

'How did he know you were at home?'

'I just don't know. Maybe he didn't. My first thought was that he or his driver cum bodyguard bloke were watching us. I took Harry with me round the garden to check it out. It was pitch black, but we found fresh footmarks leading to our back gate, and we both thought we heard male laughter. We definitely heard a car start on the lane at the perimeter of the field and drive off.'

'You don't sound very certain.'

'I was at the time, but we'd been on the sauce for a few hours by that point so, really, who knows.'

They took a moment to eat, and to take stock. Sophia broke the silence.

'What did your mother say? She must be worried sick. My parents would be doing somersaults.'

'I didn't say anything, exactly for that reason. I threw them off the scent by talking about you.'

'Did you now? They'll be thinking I'm an awful tart.'

'Hardly. I spared them the details!'

They laughed, their legs entwined beneath the rickety table, but a pulse of anxiety tore at Seb.

'What the hell am I going to do?' Seb stared up at the ceiling despondently, but his eyes eventually met Sophia's, who was waiting for his unspoken invitation to help.

'I think you know what you have to do.'

'I do?'

'Yes, I think you do. You'll do what your soul is telling you. You'll do what's right.'

The way she put it, so simply, made him fall for her even more. He leant back and crossed his arms.

'So I need to confront him then.'

'Looks like it.'

'My boss's boss.'

'Yup.'

'One of the most senior respected and revered people at Blounts.'

'If you say so.'

Seb puffed his cheeks out as the true realisation tied his stomach in knots.

'Can't I turn a blind eye to my soul just this once?'

'Eat your soup, mister, and don't ask silly questions!'

They finished up, with Sophia insisting on paying the bill.

'My turn, and that's all there is to it!'

Both the bearded proprietors hugged Sophia as she left.

'We like this one. If you get bored of him, I'm sure I could cheer him up!' said Mark in as flamboyant a stage whisper as could be imagined.

CHAPTER 20

Seb sat through the Monday morning meeting avoiding eye contact with Fletcher, trying to anticipate the multiple ways the conversation to come could possibly play out.

The meeting ended. The analysts returned to their conclave and Fletcher to his office, while the salesmen and traders hit the phones to broadcast the stories of the day.

'You OK, Bertie? You look somewhat discombobulated,' probed O C-B.

'I'm fine. Just got a few things going on.'

'Anything I can help with?'

'Not right now, but thanks.'

The desk started to hum with telephone calls of questionable value being executed by everyone on the sales desk – everyone bar Seb. He had his headset on, so his inertia wasn't immediately obvious, but it was impossible to focus on anything other than his opening words to Fletcher.

William, sorry to ask but would you mind explaining the background to Richard Barnard's unusual request?

William, can we think about how we can accommodate Richard's needs?

William, what the actual fuck was that all about on

Thursday? And by the way, he's stalking me!

'Seb. Seb. Sebastian Faber!'

'Sorry, Vicky, yes.'

'Where were you there Seb?'

'Err... don't know. What is it?' Seb replied curtly.

'William's after you.'

Shit

'Did he say why?' asked Seb.

'No. Christ, you look like you've seen a ghost. Everything alright?'

'Err... yes, thanks.'

He started to dial his number.

'No. In his office.'

Then Vicky's line rang, she put her game face on and picked up.

'Rupert, morning. Yes thanks. Well remembered. We were in Vienna for the weekend. You *have* to go. Now, did you get my email on ARM?' And she was off.

Seb got up and walked off the trading floor to the office. As he approached, he saw a woman standing with Fletcher in the doorway and was struck by her physical proximity to him. They could only have been a few inches apart, almost intimate in their postures. And this a man for whom maintaining distance, emotional and physical, was a defining characteristic. Fletcher saw Seb approaching and said something hurriedly to his attractive companion. She walked away swiftly without looking back, a visitor's pass in her hand and a coat and handbag under her arm. Not a Blounts employee then. She cut an impressive figure in an expensive looking trouser suit as she walked down the corridor to the lifts.

'Come in Seb,' said Fletcher.

'Door open or shut?'

Chapter 20

'Open, nothing terribly important. I just wanted to say that I felt that Thursday went well, and that bloody cheat Barnard seems to like the cut of your jib. He flew back on Sunday and hopes to have his clinical trial data ready for us to market in about six months, all being well. And don't get your knickers in a twist about his cloak and dagger facade. Just his nature.'

Seb was at a loss as to what to do. He had been partially disarmed, but not completely. It wasn't his imagination. Barnard had been very specific indeed about the opportunity, and the consequences of refusing it.

'He seemed to want a response from me,' said Seb.

'He did, but I covered that off.'

'What did you say?' asked Seb, aware that he was flirting with impertinence.

'Enough to send him home with us retained as his advisor for the IPO. That'll be all, Seb.' Fletcher's brusque tone emphasised the finality of his message.

Seb was being treated like a moron. He was being groomed and it was a deeply uncomfortable sensation, one that he couldn't tolerate for much longer.

'William, just so you know, my response would have been no. I hope you would agree with that decision.'

Fletcher's disposition pivoted from convivial to furious in an instant.

'Shut the door.'

Seb's pulse quickened as he did as instructed.

'Listen carefully to me. I know how this business works and you evidently don't. If I choose to massage an ego or give a client the impression of control, I will, and I don't need your advice and I most certainly don't need your blessing. You're a decent salesman and you've quickly carved yourself a nice little niche here, but if you think for one second that you are indispensable let me swiftly disabuse you of that fantasy. That will be all.'

Seb's fight or flight instinct was leaning towards combat. He stood looking at Fletcher who had delivered his speech from the comfort of his chair with his legs crossed and back reclined. Seb didn't move an inch. Fletcher stood up.

'I said...'

'And I heard you.'

Seb took out his phone and handed it to Fletcher.

'He sent me that message on Friday night when I was at home with my family. I think he was watching me from my mother's garden.'

Fletcher scanned the message and handed the phone back.

'Total fantasy. What could possibly have led you to that conclusion?'

'It is an observational comment. He had no prior knowledge of my whereabouts on Friday night. We found fresh footmarks at the rear access point to the property. We heard what we both considered to be laughter, immediately followed by a car starting in the lane at the boundary of the field and driving away.'

'We?'

'Me and my brother.'

'I see. That message was sent at 10.47pm. I guess you and your brother may have taken a few drinks by that point?'

'Yes, we had. But we know what we heard. And saw.'

'You sound perfectly ridiculous, Seb. You had a weekend bag at your desk on Friday. You told Vicky that you were going home for the weekend, and she told me. In passing you understand. Richard called me on Friday suggesting dinner

Chapter 20

that evening to continue the discussions regarding his IPO, but I told him you were unavailable, as you were going home for a family gathering. Mystery solved. But listen carefully. I couldn't care less what you do in your own time, but I do care about what you do here. I know you've been asked to keep an eye on Richard but until we have any concrete evidence of malfeasance, he remains a highly valued client of the firm. Now go back to your desk and get on with your work.'

Seb held his gaze for a few seconds, the depth of the desk separating the two former warriors, before calmly opening the door and, taking care not to be rushed, walking back to his desk. He couldn't however erase the rage that was etched in his face.

'What the hell just happened?' enquired Vicky.

Seb didn't answer. Instead, he sat down heavily at his desk and stared through his screens.

'He hasn't just fired you, has he?'

'No Vicky. He hasn't just fired me,' he spat back.

He didn't need to look at Vicky to know that his tone had caused offence.

'Sorry for snapping. We just had an exchange of views. It's fine, really.'

'Ok. If you say so.'

'One thing though. William said that you told him I was going home for the weekend. Absolutely no problem, but how did that come up?'

'He wandered over when you were off the desk and asked me what the bag was for. Pretty directly. He's taking a keen interest in his new protégé. Sorry, perhaps should have mentioned it.'

'Don't worry. It's nothing, really.'

It was very definitely something.

CHAPTER 21

Penny had seen Seb return to his desk and overheard the exchange with Vicky. She marched up to him with her handbag tucked under her arm.

'Coffee, Mr Faber!'

'I'm alright Penny, but thanks.'

'That wasn't a question. Let's go.'

Penny's maternal instincts were so all-encompassing that resistance was futile. She whisked him to the coffee shop next to the office and told him to find a seat while she bought the drinks.

'Ok, Seb. I have never seen you like this. What's going on?'

'Maybe nothing. I just don't know.'

'Well, it doesn't look like nothing. Come on!'

Seb decided that Penny was someone he could confide in. The pressure in his head was explosive.

'I could be being very naïve, but some things were said on the golf course that I can't ignore.'

'That South African biotech company? Can you be more specific?'

'I probably shouldn't.'

Chapter 21

Penny sipped her coffee before probing any further. She was good at this.

'Ok, but whatever it was that worried you, you put to William?'

'Yes, just after it happened. And he just brushed it off. I came in today to address it with him, but he called me into his office and dismissed the whole thing as normal business practise. I couldn't believe it. I still can't believe it.'

'And you shared your disbelief with William, and he reacted?'

'He reacted alright. Dismissed it, and me, and lost his cool. I've never seen him like that.'

'Me neither. So, what the hell did you say to him?'

'Not much, but I think I may have been a *little* confrontational. It probably didn't help.'

'Oh Lord, Seb, what did you do?'

'I just stood my ground, but I probably shouldn't have. I wanted to crawl across the desk and rip his head off, if you really want to know.'

'Well thank God you didn't do that, at least. Apart from anything else he was in the Army as well, wasn't he? You might have got your ass kicked.'

'Royal Marines. And maybe. Maybe not.'

'Listen Seb, I know William as well as anyone round here. He's a very private guy and sometimes, like a lot of you fucked up public school boys, more than a little odd.'

He knew his army officer background and general bearing led to Penny making assumptions about his education, but this didn't seem the moment to put her right.

'The main thing is that I trust him. He's been a big supporter of you since you walked through the door, before you walked through the door come to think of it, and if you did question his decision making in some way, he probably took it personally. Whatever it is, I'm sure it'll work out.'

Seb's brow furrowed.

'Really?' said Seb.

'Really what?'

'He talked about me before I got here?'

'Yeah. Must be a solider thing or something. He announced to the team at the end of the morning meeting that we had a new salesman joining, a 'good man' who would do 'great things'. It was quite arresting. The last thing I thought we needed was another damned army boy, but how wrong was I!'

Her face turned crimson as she finished the sentence. Maternal or not, Penny was fond of Seb. Very fond.

CHAPTER 22

Seb needed intelligence on his target, and his new target was Fletcher. He left the office the second the market closed and sped home with new purpose. With his helmet barely off his head, he fished his notebook out of his backpack, flung himself onto the sofa and started to sketch out a matrix of people he knew, or could readily access, who had potential links to Fletcher.

The British military is a small world, and the officer class a microcosm within it. It took only a few minutes to jot down a dozen names who probably had some story to tell about Fletcher. Bathurst was clearly the easiest one to access. His service in the forces overlapped with Fletcher's by a few years and his appointment was always seen by the civilian majority at Blounts as yet another job for the boys. Bathurst was, however, ineradicably bound by rank, and his loyalty was unambiguously directed upwards. Definitely not a safe person to probe.

The next closest to Fletcher on the spidergram was Callum 'Cal' Stewart, a wild Scottish aristocrat who Seb had crossed paths with in Northern Ireland. Cal was the same age as Seb and had gone straight into the Royal Marines after a brief and calamitous three weeks at Edinburgh University. Having spent a good deal of time and money fending off affray and indecent exposure charges, Cal's father decided that the military was the only thing left for his son and heir, and that some distance between father and son would help Cal learn to stand on his own two feet. At six hundred and twenty-seven miles, The Commando Training Centre in Lympstone was the furthest possible officer training academy from Bliffie Castle, so that was where Cal went. Or that was how the story was told at least. If Seb had got his maths right, he would have served as a young officer for the last two years of Fletcher's service.

There were a few other Royal Marine officers he knew of, and half a dozen army officers who would have been direct peers of Fletcher's in their respective regiments. They may not have served with Fletcher, but whether it be at regimental dinners, shooting parties or jollies at the Cresta, Seb felt it likely that most of them would have come into contact with him at some point or other.

Then there was the financial community. As far as Seb was aware, Fletcher had gone from the Marines to Blounts in the mid-nineties. The only person on whose discretion he could really rely, and who had been at the bank for the entirety of Fletcher's employment was O C-B. But Seb could walk down to lunch with him on any given day and pick his brains, so he decided to start with Cal. He hadn't spoken to him for years, but he knew it wouldn't matter. As he scrolled for his number in his phone, Seb chuckled to himself as he remembered their shared service. Bloody awful, but bloody fantastic too. A bond forged quickly, and permanently.

'Is that Major Stewart?' enquired Seb.

Chapter 22

'At your service, Faber. Bugger me sideways. Lovely to hear from you, Seb.'

'Hope you're well and all that. Listen, are you in London any time soon?'

'As it happens, I'm in London tomorrow for a funeral service.'

'Oh. I'm sorry.'

'Don't be. Old git I never liked, and he fucking hated me. Wakes are good dos though, so should be a riot.'

Same old Cal.

'A relief to hear that you haven't let the burden of rank change you. Can I meet you before your event kicks off? You'll be a bloody shambles afterwards.'

'Very wise. The service is at three. Shall we say lunch at the Army & Navy at one?'

'Perfect. Look forward to it.'

'Oh, Seb, for what do I deserve the pleasure?'

'I just want to pick your brains about something. Nothing major.'

'Sounds intriguing. By the way, it's so funny that you should call. Your name came up over dinner with Sam's godfather, my old CO.'

Seb's mouth suddenly went dry.

'Oh really. Who's that?'

He knew.

'Fletch of course.'

Seb remained silent.

'You must know him. William Fletcher. Said he recruited you into his bank. Wouldn't shut up about you actually.'

His bank. Seb stiffened at the possessive adjective.

With that, the avenue for information was slammed shut. Seb had been close to Cal but since he hadn't been asked to be godfather to any of his three children, evidently not as close as Fletcher.

'Ha, 'Fletch'. He's very firmly William Fletcher at work. I thought you might have crossed paths with him.'

'Oh, we did. Some interesting stuff together actually. Anyway, see you tomorrow. One o'clock sharp.'

CHAPTER 23

Seb felt obliged to meet Cal even though it was patently going to be a wasted exercise now. He had his cover story prepared by the time he walked into the Army & Navy Club, having spent the rest of his evening thinking up a plausible reason for calling Cal out of the blue, after five years of no contact whatsoever.

He found Cal in the bar talking to the teenage girl behind it whose bubbles of laughter indicated that she was being well entertained. Cal was never hard to spot. He had a distinguished looking face dominated by his thrusting angular jaw which, combined with his almost comically feudal height, meant that he dominated any room. Dressed in a bespoke blue double-breasted bird's eye suit, he looked every inch the man Seb had so admired.

'Sebastian Faber, City stockbroker, no less! You haven't changed one bit.'

'Neither have you Cal. Can't believe it's been so long.'

'I heard about Selection. Fucking bad luck. I hope you got my letter.'

'I did, sorry I didn't acknowledge….'

Cal cut in.

'Don't be an arse. Tough blow. You would've made an excellent operator. Anyway, what can I get you? We can squeeze a few in before lunch. If I'm honest I like to be in a pleasant haze when I go to a memorial. All that structured grief is a bit of a ball ache, isn't it.'

They drank two swift pints, talking about this person and that, and who'd got married, divorced or died, then sat down to eat. Almost as soon as their napkins were unfurled, the question came.

'So, what was so important that you needed to see me in such a hurry after half a decade?'

Seb was careful to not look overly rehearsed. But he was.

'Can I speak in total confidence?'

Cal's chin jutted even further across the table, obviously displeased with the question.

'Of course you bloody can. Come on Seb. After what you did for me? God knows I owe you.'

'You don't owe me a thing. But this is very sensitive for reasons that will become clear.'

'Well get on with making them clear then, why don't you?'

'Ok, so, I want to leave my job and re-join the military. The Royal Marines to be specific. And I need your help to make it happen.'

Cal tilted back in his chair, folded his arms and considered Seb with assessing eyes.

'You can't be serious!'

'I'm very serious.'

Cal leant in, elbows plonked heavily on the table.

'You were invalided out of the Army. Forced out. I'm sorry to tell you but The Royal Marines don't accept retired soldiers whose arm falls off if the wind changes direction.'

Chapter 23

'There's a new operation. I've discussed my situation with the leading shoulder reconstruction surgeon in the UK. He does all the international rugby players. It would make me pretty well indestructible.'

'Mate, I'd have you by my side in any situation tomorrow, but we both know you have no chance of passing the physical, miracle doctor or not. Apart from anything else, you're ten years older than when you joined the Army. The return-on-investment argument has swung sharply against you. Sorry to say it but there are other younger blokes out there who are simply a better bet.'

Even though Seb was just playing a part, he was beginning to be irritated by the bluntness of the message he was being given. It was his turn to lean back and cross his arms defensively, no longer sure where his performance ended and his actual indignation began.

'Don't be daft, Seb. We're all trying to find a way out and you've landed a cushy number that presumably pays you silly money for making a few telephone calls before getting pissed for the rest of the day. Be grateful for what you've got.'

Seb took a deep breath, unwound himself physically and mentally, and reminded himself why he was there.

'I don't know. Perhaps you're right. Grass is always greener, I suppose. So, you mentioned some interesting stuff you did with Fletcher?'

A natural enough deviation from the conversation and a plausible extension of a previous one.

'He was my first Squadron Leader in Poole.'

RM Poole. SBS. Seb had heard that Cal had served with the SBS, but the first-hand confirmation triggered a sharp stab of intrigue. Or was it envy.

'We only served together for a brief period but, as you and I know Seb, that's all it takes to get the measure of a man.'

And that was the end of the discussion. They ate lunch and shared a bottle of the club claret, and Cal asked for the bill.

'Everything to your satisfaction, Your Grace?'

'Certainly was, John. Compliments to the chef.'

Seb stared at Cal with his mouth hanging open.

'Your Grace? The funeral…'

'…is my father's. Yes. And as much as I despised the man, I had better not miss it.'

CHAPTER 24

In the days and weeks that followed the episode in his office, Fletcher reverted to his dogmatic, emotionally unavailable self, and nothing more was said. Seb looked out for it, but couldn't detect even the slightest change in his manner towards him. It was as if nothing had ever happened. While he was certain that this was a mere hiatus, Seb was in no hurry to see him blow again, so he just went about his business. And so did Fletcher. He saw him every working day, several times a day, but it was always in group meetings so there was no requirement to deviate from the matter in hand and just shoot the breeze, and he doubted if Fletcher was capable of trivial social interaction in any event. There were no personal exchanges with Fletcher at all until an invitation appeared in his inbox.

Fletcher: Date for your diary. Client shooting party, Fri 5th October, dinner the night before, you can stay in the house. Annabel will send you the details.

Faber: Great. Thanks William.

Fletcher: You do shoot, don't you?

Faber: I'm decent with an SA80. I shouldn't embarrass you.

Fletcher: Good.

CHAPTER 25

Seb had done some digging to prepare himself for what to expect, O C-B being his most bountiful source of information. Apparently, this shoot was one of half a dozen days Fletcher hosted at Ickling Hall, a Jacobean manor he'd inherited via a circuitous path from a distant cousin he'd never met. The shoots were commercial and helped pay for the relentless upkeep of the house and estate. Unfortunately, the house was not quite grand enough to open to the paying public, but much too grand to enjoy as a family home. However, set in the heart of rural north Norfolk, with nine hundred acres of arable land and woodland, it had a shoot that was nationally recognized.

He drove up to Norfolk after work on Thursday. As instructed, he drove slowly though the pretty little village of Ickling, straining hard to spot the small, offset signpost to the Hall sunk into a grass verge at the edge of the village. He turned right off the main road down a narrow, unmarked lane. It was dark, but the moon cast just enough light to see a looming mass set on an elevated position on the other side of the quarter-mile estate wall. After following the lane for a few minutes, the boundary wall recessed to reveal

Chapter 25

an imposing splayed entrance, flanked by two triangular lawns and defended by a dozen staddle stones. He turned into the gravel drive and proceeded under the elaborate ironmongery of the entrance arch, its vast wrought iron gates latched open in anticipation of the guests' arrival. The drive meandered past a small lake and up a short incline to the house. There were already several cars parked in a neat line with their noses up against a topiary hedge to the right of an ornamental turning circle. His low-key Golf looked distinctly out of place next to the fleet of Range Rovers and Land Rover Discoverys. The chat around the trading floor was that Fletcher had a small armada of vintage cars, but if that were true, all bar one were garaged elsewhere on the estate. A red E-Type was in place for all to see.

He stepped out of his car and heard roars of laughter from deep within the house. The party had clearly started. He grabbed his bags from the boot and stood for a moment to take in the grandeur of the four hundred year old building. As he approached the house, the door swung open and a striking woman in her early forties strode out and offered an outstretched hand.

'You must be Sebastian. I'm Phoebe Fletcher, welcome to Ickling Hall.'

'Seb. Good to meet you. And thanks for putting me up.'

'Not at all. Delighted to have someone young in the place. The rest of the guests look as if they could well be dead by the morning.'

She showed him into the galleried entrance hall, the oak panelled walls hung with ancestral portraits, assorted fighting blades and a vast dusty tapestry depicting a mediaeval battle scene.

'Agincourt. Don't ask me why. Now let's get you settled,

then do come down and join us for a drink before dinner. Up a few steps I'm afraid.'

She led him up the grand staircase which clung to two of the four walls in the double height hall, rising to a gallery that emerged twenty feet above the stone floor below.

'Halfway. Hope you've got plenty of stamina.'

He grinned at the back of her head as he followed her along the landing, not entirely sure she wasn't flirting with him.

'Up we go again.'

The stairs to the second floor were narrow and steep. It was impossible not to notice, and then be slightly hypnotised by, her bottom neatly presented in tight black Capri pants swaying from left to right with each stride. The second-floor landing was L-shaped and served four bedrooms. Seb's was at the end of the landing and was easily four times the size of his perfectly decent bedroom in London.

'The door with the white handle around the corner is the bathroom. Inexcusably barbaric to have to share, but just the one up here I'm afraid. En-suite wasn't terribly popular in the early 1600s.'

Seb walked over to the window and looked out into the moonlit night.

'This is quite a place,' said Seb.

'Well, the kids are constantly terrified, and it's the gloomiest, coldest house on earth for four months of the year, but we like the summer hols here and it is a great place for a party. I'll leave you to it then. See you in the library when you're ready.'

He sat on the vast, iron-framed bed and sank into its exhausted springs. Ornate wooden cornicing, complete with cobwebs, contributed to the musty fug of the room.

Chapter 25

A distinct smell, but not unpleasant. He'd been assured by Fletcher's PA that the dress code would be casual, so he tidied his jeans up with a fresh shirt and grey flannel jacket and went downstairs. He stood in the entrance hall and listened for the source of the laughter, following the escalating rumpus along a lengthy dimly lit corridor, past an inactive kitchen and several closed doors to the last open one on the left.

'Ah, here he is. Well done, Seb, found us easily enough?' said Fletcher. Even factoring in him being in his own home, that was an unnervingly effusive greeting.

'I did. What a stunning house'

'It is a bit of fun, until you get the first bill for the fuel oil that is!'

The assembled group of older, senior men wobbled about in a chorus of guffaws. All bar one, a tall blond heavy-set man with thick dark spectacles, who was unmoved by Seb's arrival. At that moment three black Labradors chased each other into the room, skidding on the flagstone hall floor and collectively misjudging the ninety-degree corner, as they probably always did and always would. While the dogs charged around, sniffing everything at nose height, Fletcher took control.

'Right, introductions. Of course, you know Roger, Jim and Fraser.'

He did. They were CEOs of companies Blounts advised. A mixed bag but, on balance, pretty good company.

'And I think you'll remember Sven and Kjetl from AB Venden.'

He shook hands with all the men. Judging from their hearty enthusiasm and rosy glows, they had a significant head start on him.

'Last, but not least, let me introduce you to Felix Oberlauffen. Felix is the CIO of Orpheus Capital.'

'A great pleasure to meet you, Sebastian.'

Seb had absolutely no idea why it was a great pleasure, or what Orpheus Capital was. Fletcher handed him a gin and tonic in a heavy crystal tumbler, and the evening began. After enough drinks to know they'd had them, a gong sounded. The men spun round like a troop of meerkats to see Phoebe Fletcher standing in the doorway with all her gymkhana-mum sex appeal, looking cock-a-hoop.

'Dinner is served!' she beamed, and gave the handheld gong another thump for good measure. 'Sorry everyone, just bought this thing and simply had to give it a go.'

The dining room was situated at the physical heart of the house. Dimly lit, with half a dozen wall mounted lamps, it was dominated by a deep inglenook fireplace with a five-foot mantle and a grate the size of a child's bed. It was needed; the room had no other source of heating, but the fire had clearly been blazing for some time and for now the room was pleasantly warm as they found their seats. There were hand-written place cards at each setting and the guests shuffled around to find their names. As Seb started to circle around the table, he felt a delicate hand on his arm. He turned to see Phoebe leaning into him and felt a heavy bosom pressing against his side.

'I hope you don't mind but I've put you next to me. This lot will send me straight to sleep, or worse, spend the whole night trying to get into my knickers.'

'With William at the other end of the table? I'm sure they're not that bad.'

'Oh, they are, and I seem to give off the impression that I just might be too.'

Chapter 25

Phoebe had a glint in her eye as she delivered the line. Seb's pulse quickened. She saw the impact she had made and filled the void that Seb's stunned silence had created.

'Don't be silly. I'm just pulling your plonker. Anyway, I'm not risking it, and I have a job for you I'm afraid. The moment that fire looks like anything other than a raging inferno, leap up and throw another log on. You'll know if you haven't because I won't be in here anymore. You've never felt cold like it.'

'No problem. Can I pour you some wine?'

'Go on then. The white please.'

As he poured, Felix Oberlauffen took the seat to his left and three serving staff appeared with multiple plates in their hands.

'Where have they been hiding? I'm sure I walked past an empty kitchen down the corridor.' said Seb.

'Below stairs, naturally,' replied Phoebe, with comedy affectation. 'Actually, we have a little family kitchen on the ground floor, but the big kitchen is in the basement. Sadly, just contract caterers for these events. Our roster of staff consists of an octogenarian gardener who comes for four hours a week and a cantankerous woman from the village who comes in on Mondays to clean up the mess from the weekend.'

The eight diners were served very efficiently and, as the last plate was positioned, William stood up with a knife and crystal goblet and tapped on it with unnecessary pomposity to get everyone's attention.

'A few points of order while there's still a chance of you remembering them,' and he outlined the plan for the evening, which was basically eat, get drunk and get to bed while you can still do it under your own steam. The plans for the following day's shoot were also needlessly lengthy, and amounted to 'meet at eight for breakfast and follow me'.

Phoebe was the perfect hostess, dividing her time equally between Roger Wittingborne to her right and Seb to her left. Roger was the CEO of one of the largest car retailers in the country, a highly amusing Lancastrian, and a very rich one. He might have done very well on the working men's club circuit telling bawdy jokes if he hadn't used his wit to sell motor cars. The same could not be said of Felix Oberlauffen, who had apparently had a charisma bypass. He was earnest and humourless, and a dozen other words that make for a dreadful dinner companion. Seb tried to get off the subject of investment management, but Felix clung to it for dear life. To compound the agony, he kept putting his hand over his glass when the waiters tried to top it up; God forbid he loosened up a bit or lost a modicum of control. Thankfully, the guest to Felix's left took some of his attention and, where he could, Seb picked up the thread of Roger and Phoebe's conversation and held on tight. But then, surprisingly, Felix said something rather interesting.

'Ya, so we were looking at a small UK deal, a small telecoms business, Fibrefill. You know it?'

He did. A once feted market darling with a billion-pound value, now trading at seven percent of that.

'Some gung-ho college kids from the valley outbid us yesterday. Six months work for my team. We were bidding a hundred million and we hear they were way ahead of us. Worth picking up a few shares, no? Might push the share price up a bit and get those asshole kids to pay even more for it.'

To which he chuckled away at his own hilarity. Seb smiled, remained silent and took another tug on his glass of

Chapter 25

claret. Felix filled the void.

'Might struggle to buy a unit. Perhaps William could sell you a few of his.'

More jowl wobbling chuckles. Seb had just been given information he couldn't un-know.

The fact that a crashingly dull Austrian private equity principal had fed him with inside information of the most sensitive nature and encouraged him to use it for his own gain, was interesting, but hardly shocking. Fletcher to be insider dealing was hard to believe, and he didn't want to. He cast his eyes up to the end of the table to see his host delivering some tale that held his half of the table's rapt attention. He delivered the punch line to much noisy appreciation and slowly turned to look down the barrel of Seb's gaze, aware of being watched. With a little nod of his head and tip of his glass he toasted him across the table.

The rest of the dinner passed in an ever-accelerating blur. The room was getting communally drunk, Oberlauffen being the only island of sobriety, submerged by the rising waters around him. All their voices were now competing for airtime which made for a cacophony that carried all the way to the below stairs loo. Phoebe had had enough. She leant forward and whispered in Seb's ear.

'Go with me on this.'

'Err...ok,' said Seb, uncertainly.

Phoebe leapt up.

'For Christ's sake Seb, I gave you one job. The bloody fire's out!'

It wasn't out, but it was the perfect excuse for a change of scene.

'Right, everyone. Back to the library. I'm sure the boys will have been feeding the fire there for me.'

Phoebe swept her glass and a bottle of red off the table and marched out of the door and down the hall to the library, closely followed by the now rather shambolic collection of drunk, middle-aged men. She made straight for a very large, near-black wooden sideboard and opened a cupboard door to reveal a CD player, with a small pile of CDs next to it and quickly rifled through them.

'This should wake everyone up.'

She pushed the disc into the player and pressed play.

'Is this the real life? Is this just fantasy?'

Phoebe could sing more than passably well, and she knew it. She also knew every word of *Bohemian Rhapsody* and all the other tracks on the Queen Greatest Hits CD. Buoyed by her confidence and a couple of bottles of wine, half the men, the British half, burst into song, Seb included. The two Swedes and the Austrian looked at them with frank confusion.

'*Any way the wind blows*. Right, who wants to play snooker?' said Phoebe.

'Sure, I'll play,' responded Seb, a fraction too quickly.

'Come on then,' said Roger, 'Fraser, thee and me, let's be having you.'

Fraser ran a Cambridge spin-out company in advanced imaging technologies. They had aspirations to transform the medical and industrial imaging marketplaces. Thus far it was a shed on a science park, with lots of maths PhDs drinking supermarket own brand instant coffee out of chipped mugs. But Seb had sold the hope and the market had bought it. Prof Fraser Pope was the smartest of them all.

'You any good at this, Sebastian?' said Phoebe.

'Very.'

Chapter 25

'Oh brill!' she replied, reciprocating his comic bravado with equally over the top joy. 'Plenty of time to waste in your wicked youth?' and she bumped her hip against his provocatively as she walked past him to break. He was, in fact, the 1991 Feltham Young Offender Institution dual pool and table tennis champion. So she was right, his time there hadn't been entirely wasted.

Fletcher and Felix sat on the sofa by the fire and started making a dent in a bottle of vintage port while the earnest Swedes, having spotted a chess board set up for play on a table by the window, embarked upon a game in total silence. Phoebe and Seb won the snooker without much difficulty, crowned the one-eyed kings in a land of blind drunks. As well as scoring all but one of his team's points, Seb also successfully debated the near infinite outcomes of a single shot with the Emeritus professor, his coup de grace being an observation about the impact of air temperature on the rigidity of the cushions.

Sven and Kjetl had already sloped off to their beds, a half full bottle of vodka left on the table, and Fletcher and Felix had wandered off half an hour earlier, ostensibly hunting for cigars in the study, not to return The fire had been left untended and was a now just a small pile of embers and the central heating, such as it was, had long since clicked off. The red wine was chilling in their glasses and even their foreheads were cold to the touch.

'Bedtime I think,' said Seb.

'Yes, I'm done.' confirmed Roger.

'Me too,' said Fraser.

Roger and Fraser walked out of the room without saying another word, narrowly missing several pieces of furniture in their wake. Phoebe started to busy herself collecting up glasses; Seb volunteered his assistance.

'That's very good of you, Seb. There isn't much, but if you could grab the bottles and follow me to the kitchen that would be kind.'

She turned off the lights deftly with her elbow and they set off along the hall and down the stairs to the basement kitchen, the only room in the house that retained any heat. She put the glasses down by the sink and pointed Seb to the bottle bin where he put the three empty claret bottles and the dead bottle of port.

'Freezer for that vodka please. In the scullery.'

'Scullery?'

'Little kitchen off the main one where troops of kitchen staff did the washing up when this house has such luxuries. Now just the home for our big freezer. Through there.'

Seb did as asked, and when he came out Phoebe was pouring two fresh glasses of red out of a half-finished bottle.

'Come on then. Might as well finish this off.'

She was leaning back against the Aga holding both glasses, inviting him to take his from her. She was a bit drunk and so was he, and she held his gaze for a little too long. He walked over to her and took it from her hand, held close against her chest. They both sipped the wine and, realising that the situation was getting more compromising by the second, Seb took a step back. She immediately took a step forward.

'Do you find me attractive, Sebastian?'

He stood stock still with his mouth open, trying to process the question.

'You're very attractive, but you're also my boss's wife. I'd really better go to bed now.'

'Oh him, he hasn't fucked me for years, not properly

Chapter 25

anyway. Too busy with all his little schemes.'

Seb was rooted to the spot.

'But I bet you would Sebastian. Will you take me to bed?'

As she spoke, she took his free hand in hers and pulled it to her left breast. He resisted but not before he had felt the weight of it in the palm of his hand. His body was preparing for an event that his brain knew couldn't happen. She looked down at the bulge in his jeans and cooed with excitement.

'I can see you want me, Sebastian.'

He stepped back from her and put his glass down on the countertop.

'I think that's bedtime. Good night, Mrs Fletcher.'

'Oh, how boring! I suppose I'll just have to sleep in one of the empty bedrooms and think about you while I play with myself instead then. And don't you feel bad while you're playing with your lovely cock thinking of me. You know you will, but your sweet little girlfriend never has to know.'

Seb span around and walked briskly out of the kitchen and up the three flights of stairs to bed.

He lay awake half the night in fear of a knock on the door, every creak of the landing floorboards sending him into palpitations. She didn't appear.

CHAPTER 26

He woke to voices outside his bedroom window, clambered out of the cavernous bed, walked across the ice-cold floorboards and looked out. It was just after seven and a morning fog was draped over the lake below a cloudless sky. Directly below, he saw a woman with a small overnight case talking to Fletcher. They had a brief, intense exchange, a quick embrace and she climbed into the back of a black Mercedes being driven by a heavy-set man in a suit and tie. No taxi markings. It was her, again. The woman he'd seen outside Fletcher's office.

He had a one-minute shower, shaved and dressed himself in the traditional tweed ensemble required of all the guns, his borrowed from an old army buddy. He wanted to be anywhere in the world but Ickling Hall as he walked down to breakfast, which was being served in the basement kitchen he'd so recently beaten a swift retreat from.

'Morning Seb. Sleep alright?' said Phoebe, with no trace of embarrassment.

She was busy at her Aga producing a vast array of fried food using all four ovens and both hobs, and didn't miss a beat. Nothing, absolutely nothing, in her tone or demeanour

Chapter 26

to suggest that she had tried to sleep with him in her family house with her husband, his boss, within earshot.

'Sit down and pour yourself some coffee, or is it tea in the Faber household?'

The way she asked the question made it clear there was definitely a wrong answer. He served himself from a vast serving dish laden with every hot breakfast fare imaginable and poured himself a large mug of coffee.

All the other guests were mid breakfast and seemed to have shrugged off the effects of the booze like the old pros they were. The Swedes had evidently paid a recent visit to Farlows of Pall Mall and, to the amusement of the rest of the party, some of the price tags were still visible on their matching outfits. They were both fabulously rewarded fund managers so neither would have noticed the ten thousand pounds leaving their bank accounts, nor understood the social suicide of turning up in brand new kit for a day of driven pheasant shooting.

Fletcher walked in accompanied by a world-weary looking man in his sixties with large grey mutton chop sideburns and thick bushy outcrops sprouting from his ears.

'Morning all. I trust you slept well, and you have a good breakfast in you. Let me introduce you to Vic. Vic here has been retained at Ickling as Head Gamekeeper for forty-three years so listen clearly to everything he has to say, and we will all have an enjoyable, safe day. All yours Vic.'

'Right, first things first, we have some novices I am told. Would that be you two gentlemen?'

Vic glanced towards the two Swedes, but Fletcher chimed in.

'And our friend Sebastian. He tells me he's good with a rifle, but everyone knows Paratroopers can't shoot straight.

He can join me on my peg and I'll keep an eye on him.'

Fletcher enjoyed his moment and Seb went with it, straining to look entirely unruffled.

Those that had them collected their own guns. The Swedes were each issued with a 20-bore; 12-bores had been deemed a bit too much for them to handle, a point that wasn't made any too subtly. Fletcher took a pair of elaborately engraved guns from the rack and handed them to Vic.

'Put these in the car would you please Vic?'

He then took a much less ornate gun from the rack.

'This will do for you Seb. My first 12-bore. You should be able to handle it.'

They all climbed into the back of an old, long wheelbase Land Rover Defender with bench seating down the sides, joined by the three dogs who came charging out of the house at warp speed, leaping into the boot of the car with all the excitement of working dogs about to go to work. Fletcher sat up front and Vic drove them down a track that ran from the back of the house, past the stables and into the undulating woodland beyond.

None of what Seb had had to cope with the previous night could be addressed immediately, so he focused all his energies on just getting through the day. He shot more than his fair share of birds, much to Fletcher's irritation, and contributed willingly to the general conversation, but when Phoebe appeared with the soup and game pie lunch, he was careful to avoid her. Hard to do in a small, one-room shooting lodge without causing offence, but he could tell that Phoebe was playing the same game; perhaps in her sobriety she had some shame after all. Once the formalities of the day were over, and as soon as he could politely do so, he made a rapid escape.

CHAPTER 27

Seb decided not to share the tale of Phoebe's advances with Sophia, unable to see any way of describing it without implying some element of complicity. He kept the other bizarre aspects of the shooting party to himself too. Sophia would only repeat what she'd already said and make him feel weak for not taking more affirmative action after the whole Sunningdale episode again. And he *was* being weak. He was quietly hoping the whole thing would go away if he ignored it for long enough. Patently, it wasn't going to.

Back in the office, he slumped at his desk looking straight though his screens mindlessly. The only distraction came from O C-B who was in mid and expansive flow.

'Clinical data? Well, suffice to say they have an embarrassment of riches in that department. Two Phase 2 proof of concept trials completed on the back of the successful Phase 1 trial last year. Failed?? Of course, I accept they didn't achieve their primary end point. On the other hand, they demonstrated beyond doubt that the dosage levels they chose were insufficient to achieve efficacy. A critically important outcome, I'm sure you'll agree. The new trial your money will pay for will use the higher dose range they have already demonstrated to be safe and well tolerated in the Phase 1 trial two years ago. Remembering, of course, that this indication has expedited FDA review and no alternative approved treatment exists anywhere in the world. They can pretty much name their price when they come to sell it. We are one trial away from lift-off for this company so we must all get behind it and see this journey through. The book? We are in very good shape. A number of Tier 1 names already joining the register, so you'll be in very good company. Nicely covered with a dozen big accounts to come back to us. Seven million pounds at strike? Thank you, Jeremy. I'll make sure we look after you when we do the allocations. Bye for now.'

He put the phone down and walked over to Charles Bathurst who was looking as gruff as ever.

'Put Viper Capital down for £7m. That covers the book nicely I think.'

'Him again. Bloody hope this goes well, or we've blown up one of the bank's most important accounts!'

Despite being the Head of Sales, Bathurst found it almost impossible to praise his team members, and most particularly O C-B, whose prandial excesses he could barely tolerate. He was ever hopeful that he would trip up and give just cause for dismissal, but he never did. Ollie ignored the remark and strode purposely over to Seb.

'Glass Bertie? I think we've earned it, don't you?'

'Great order, Ollie. You almost convinced *me* that the thirty million they've expended to prove the drug doesn't work was money well spent. And 'well covered?''

'I was being prophetic. With Jeremy's order, it now is. You'll join me.'

'Why not. Actually, I could do with a drink.'

Chapter 27

'Goodo. Let's go to Balls. We can have a good natter over a sandwich.'

Seb lowered his voice.

'Fine. But do you mind if we go to the Carter Lane one. A bit of a schlep but I don't want to bump into anyone from here. I'll explain when we get there.'

They set off to lunch with the temporary impunity afforded them by their success. Ollie's order had closed the deal and Seb's clients had provided the bulk of the balance of the thirty-five million placing, so there was precious little Bathurst could do about it. They ordered their sandwiches and a bottle of the white burgundy and took a corner table in the subterranean City bolthole.

'One can't help but notice that you have looked a bit vexed lately. What's up, mate?'

Seb took a large sip of his wine and considered his response.

'A lot of strange shit. This can't go any further or I'll be fired. Or worse.'

Ollie squeezed Seb's forearm fraternally across the table.

'I am the very soul of discretion, Bertie, you should know that by now.' Seb did.

'OK. So, this is it. I think Fletcher's a crook. I think he's insider dealing and taking personal bribes from clients, and I don't think he's working alone.'

'Crikey. What's brought this on?'

'Conversations I've overheard or been involved in with various clients over the past three months, brought to a head at a surreal evening at the shooting party on Friday.'

'Am I to know which clients?'

'Probably best not just yet. It sounds silly saying it out loud, but the less you know the better.'

'Golly. How very Le Carré!'

'Or Jilly Cooper. You want to know the weirdest part of the night at Ickling Hall? Fletcher's wife tried to seduce me.'

Ollie sat back in his seat with a look of awe on his face.

'You lucky bastard! I sat next to her at an otherwise appallingly leaden client dinner last Christmas. She was particularly taken by the Lotus, and it was all I could do not to invite her back to Chelsea then and there to rev her up, so to speak. Suffice to say she didn't try and seduce *me*. What on earth did you do?'

'Nothing, of course.'

'Of course?' pressed O C-B.

'Of course!' insisted Seb.

'Quite right, the boss's wife. And you have the stunning Sophia so why would you? But by heaven, after a good evening on the Fletcher claret, it took some turning down I bet.'

Seb let the comment drop, implicitly answering the question to Ollie's satisfaction.

'The point is that she's aware of his behaviour too, and she didn't seem to mind telling me about it. She was a bit drunk but she's nobody's fool.'

'And where was her husband when all this was happening?'

'In deep conversation with a private equity principal. They separated from the rest of the party to smoke cigars, or so he said.'

'How did she take being turned down?'

'She was pretty frustrated. I get the feeling she's used to getting what she wants.

'I bet she is. Must have been mortifying in the morning?'

'It was for me. She acted like nothing had happened, then

Chapter 27

did her best to avoid me. I couldn't get away fast enough.'

Their conversation was interrupted by the waiter arriving with their club sandwiches.

'Well as thrilling as all this sounds... dear God, the breasts on that woman.'

'Ollie!'

'Sorry, back in the room. OK, you have to decide how you respond to what you've seen and heard. I'm fairly sure you have a duty to report any suspicions of this nature to compliance.'

'I know, but if I'm wrong about it, it'll be the end of my very brief career in finance, no question. And right now I can't prove any of it,' said Seb, exasperated.

'It isn't your responsibility to prove it. It *is* your responsibility to report the suspicion. The subsequent investigation will unearth the wrongdoing, if there is any.'

'It should but given who's involved, there's a good chance it wouldn't and Fletcher would find a way to get rid of me.'

'To be honest, it all sounds a bit unlikely to me Bertie, but I suppose it's possible.'

'And if I am right, the only way I can protect myself is to get hard evidence of his illegal dealings. And that means playing along with it all for a bit longer.'

Ollie put his drink down and set his gaze on Seb.

'I hadn't realised that you'd started playing along at all. What have you got yourself into?'

'I haven't done anything illegal, but I haven't done anything to stop it either, which is almost as bad.'

At that moment the door of the disabled loo opened, and a young woman stepped out looking flushed and ruffled. They both knew her.

'Oh look, it's Vicky. I wonder what she's doing here,' said Ollie.

She walked briskly up the stairs and out into the street without looking up.

'Bit odd,' said Ollie.

'Keep an eye on that door,' said Seb.

'What on earth for?'

'Just keep looking.'

They sat in silence staring at the door. A minute later the door swung open again and Paul Flynn bounced out looking like the cat that got the cream. He was careless enough to glance around the room, and clapped eyes squarely on Seb and Ollie. His face fell as he slunk out, knowing they probably wouldn't say anything but would know exactly what was going on. Which was enough.

'Oh dear. That's back on again. I guess the last place they expected to get rumbled was here,' said Ollie. 'She is an awful minx. I have an invitation to her wedding on my mantelpiece. Perhaps one last taste of the forbidden fruit.'

Seb drained his glass and poured himself another.

'I very much doubt it, but it's not my problem. This one is.'

CHAPTER 28

Seb needed evidence, and he needed help to get it. Luckily for him, his former profession had plenty of talent in the area of reconnaissance, and he knew someone who was amongst the best of them. Seb had heard that Charlie was now working freelance in London, so he let Ollie go ahead of him back to the office and made the call. It was a number he hadn't used for many years, and he wondered if it would still work. It did.

'Charlie, it's Seb.'

After a discernible pause, Charlie responded.

'Sebastian Faber. Jesus H Christ!'

'I know. There's a lot of stuff to catch up on and we will, but just now I need your help on something important. In your line of work. And I need to discuss this face to face. Are you free any night this week? I'll happily come to you. Where do you live?'

'Wow. Shit. OK. I can't do tonight but I could get away for an hour tomorrow after work. I live in Battersea. The shite bit mind.'

'Tomorrow night's perfect,' said Seb.

'But why don't I come to your place? Would be nice to

see how you're living these days.'

Seb considered this for a microsecond. Charlie and Sophia in his flat together felt like a very bad idea indeed.

'...Nothing to see but a messy bachelor pad. Battersea is pretty much on my way home from work. Let's meet at The Latchmere? Say seven o'clock? Won't keep you long.'

'Yeah, that's fine. Nice to hear your voice Seb. I've missed it.'

CHAPTER 29

Charlie was already entrenched in a corner booth, with two pints of Guinness, when Seb walked in at two minutes to seven.

'Look at you in your posh suit. Sure, do I have to call you sir again?'

She spoke with a Belfast accent, but with none of the harshness that English 'News at Ten' viewers were accustomed to hearing.

'As I recall, you never did,' said Seb.

Charlotte 'Charlie' Walsh was a former member of 14 Intelligence Company, the British Army's plain clothes reconnaissance unit deployed in Northern Ireland, and the only Special Duties entity that permitted women amongst their ranks. '14 Int' were amongst the best people in the world to deploy into a situation where you needed to gather intelligence on the enemy covertly, before neutralising them. Charlie, as most of the men called her, was granted her nickname on account of the fact that she was as physically robust as most of the men she served with, and more mentally tough than any. That, of course, plus the useful coincidence that 'Charlie' shared a syllable with her actual name, military nicknames rarely being complex constructs.

The truth was that Charlotte became Charlie the day her father and youngest brother, still no more than a child, were blown up by a car bomb. Her father, a fast-promoted member of the Royal Ulster Constabulary, was the target. The little boy sleeping on the back seat was 'collateral damage', as the local commander of the IRA described it. She walked into the recruitment office for the Royal Irish Regiment the very next day.

They embraced warmly, more like siblings than lovers. Theirs was a very unlikely friendship. Their paths had crossed twice during their army careers, the first time in the Balkans by chance and then, by design, in Northern Ireland. Had Charlie been seen socialising with a uniformed British officer, she would have been executed by the IRA as a traitor and a spy. As a result, the few times they did meet were meticulously planned, and utterly thrilling. However, by the third and final time, for reasons neither party could explain, the sex part was all done.

'Go on then, I've to get home and feed the family so tell me, what problem can't the great Captain Faber sort out himself?'

'I need some information from a sensitive source, and I need to not get caught getting hold of it.'

Seb explained the background and the nuances of his situation, while Charlie made detailed notes in shorthand, before firing a series of questions about Fletcher's circumstances, patterns of behaviour and character traits. The Q&A took them halfway into their second pints before Charlie put her pen and notebook down.

'Well, the good news is that I have a solution that'll work for you. The bad news is that it's feckin' dangerous. Also

Chapter 29

highly illegal and, for a couple of reasons, you'll have to do it yourself.'

Seb plonked his pint glass loudly on the table.

'Shit, Charlie. I thought this was what you did these days?'

'It is, and I know what I'm doing. And I know for a fact that the only person who can get this done is you.'

'What the...' Charlie stopped Seb in mid flow.

'Will you shut up and listen. The sort of evidence you need can either be recovered or generated. Given enough time and resources, we can recover any physical or digital evidence. That is something I could do, if I thought that there was anything there to find. And I don't. I would bet your arse that he hasn't left a trail behind him. I've wasted a lot of my time and my clients' money doing forensic analysis of the contents of dustbins and computer servers. He's ex-SBS for Christ's sake. He'll have thought about the chances of being investigated and dusted the ground behind him after every step.'

'Makes sense. He's about the most measured bloke I've ever met.'

'Right. So, if we can't recover any evidence, we need to generate it. We need to record his private conversations. You say his work line is already recorded by compliance, so he won't use that. That leaves his home's fixed line and his mobile. If he has a wife and kids in the house I doubt he'll make his dodgy calls there, so he'll use his mobile for the calls we need to record.'

Charlie paused to take a sip of her pint, enjoying the whole business of giving an intelligence briefing once again.

'I can give you an interceptor device that can pick up his calls from a radius of about 500m. It's a unit about the size of a 1980's ghetto blaster so would need to be hidden in a van. All we need is his mobile number and his location.'

Seb slid forward in his seat and picked up the thread.

'I have his number in my phone, although City Police do practically nothing but look out for suspicious people in vans, so that won't work.'

'Even if you could locate a device near the office, you'd still be wasting your time,' said Charlie.

Seb threw her an exasperated look.

'Now you're confusing me.'

'If you'd just shut up and let me speak, I'll explain.'

'Sorry. Go on,' said Seb.

'You have *a* number for Fletcher, but unless he's trying to get caught, he won't make these calls on that number. He'll have a separate pay-as-you go SIM card, acquired under a false name. It's what I would do. We don't know that number, so the remote interception solution is out. That creates a new challenge. We, or rather you, have to physically access his mobile phone.'

Seb's brow furrowed into a tight knot.

'For fuck's sake! He never puts it down.'

'Oh, calm down will you. I'll come to that in a minute. We have two different approaches available to us. We can put an RF device in the handset which will transmit voice data to a lightweight receiver. It's small, and it can listen in up to 1km from the source. The microphone is tiny, and it'll easily fit in the Nokia he uses, but it's powered off the phone's battery so that'll run down at about twice the normal rate. If he notices it, he might be prompted to change his battery and he'd find the RF bug wired to it straightaway.'

Seb opened his mouth to interrupt but Charlie silenced him by placing her index finger on his lips.

Chapter 29

'Which leaves the last option, a simple voice recording chip. Uses far less power than the RF bug and it's powered by its own tiny battery cell. Unless he's weirdly au fait with the chipset of a mobile phone, you can deploy it where it wouldn't be noticed even if he were staring straight at it. You get up to seven days' voice recording from the latest devices. Unfortunately, there is one obvious drawback.'

'I have to retrieve the device when it's full.'

'Clever boy.'

'Doubling the risk of being caught!'

'Doubling a very small risk, if you listen to me and do exactly what I say.'

'Jesus, Charlie! How do you expect me to get his mobile away from him once, let alone fucking twice?'

He was beginning to lose heart, but Charlie continued quickly.

'Ok. You said he takes the phone everywhere with him. That won't be true.'

She spoke with such authority that Seb instantly remembered why he trusted her.

'What about when he takes a dump? He probably tucks a broadsheet under his arm like half you weirdos.'

'Jesus, I don't know. He must take himself off to the Corporate Finance traps. Never seen him in the ones on our floor.'

'What about meetings?'

Seb considered the question for a moment before replying.

'I've never seen him take a call in a company meeting, and it's a serious offence if anyone else's phone rings. But he always wears a jacket, so I'd bet he has it with him on silent if I had to guess.'

'And he never takes off his jacket in the office?'

'He takes it off in his office, and he's generally without it when he leaves it to prowl around the floor.'

'Like the morning meeting?'

'Yes. He throws caution to the wind with shirt sleeve order for the morning meeting,' said Seb, drily.

'And he doesn't carry his phone in his hand or trouser pocket?'

'Never. One of my colleague's phone rang in the morning meeting not long after I joined. Fletcher made him present on a different stock every morning for the remaining three days of the week. Won't even allow them visible on our desks.'

'Helpful. Where does he hang his jacket? On the back of his chair?'

'Shit no. He has a coat stand in his office. He hangs it on his tailor's wooden coat hanger along with his tightly furled black umbrella and his suede-collared fawn overcoat. You get the picture.'

Charlie ignored the caricature and stuck to the task in hand.

'How long does the meeting last?'

'About fifteen minutes. But it varies. A little as five minutes on quiet news days.'

'And he's in there every day?'

'Without fail. Stands in the same spot scanning the floor for any absentees or obvious inattention. He likes us to be frantically scribbling away writing notes when the analysts are talking.'

Charlie turned to a clean page in her notepad and handed it and the pen to Seb.

'Draw me a sketch of the trading floor and Fletcher's

Chapter 29

office. Mark with an 'X' where he stands in the morning meeting.'

Seb did as instructed and handed it back to Charlie who used the edge of the bar menu to draw a straight line between the 'X' and Fletcher's office door. A line that clearly passed through two other offices and the lift shaft.

'No clean line of sight. So, unless he locks his office behind him every morning, that's your window.'

'But I have to be at the bloody morning meeting,' Seb countered impatiently.

Charlie didn't skip a beat.

'OK, so under what circumstances can you legitimately not be there?'

'Holiday, grave illness or death.'

She thought for a moment.

'What about a client meeting?

'At seven fifteen? Never happens.'

Charlie shrugged, irritated, her patience wearing thin.

'You could try working with me on this you know. The drama queen shite is pretty boring and I've a family to get back to.'

Seb, chastened, took a deep breath, sat up straight and put his mind to work. After thirty seconds the silence was broken with an idea.

'I know, I'll pull rank,' said Seb, his chest puffed out with pride.

Charlie's eyebrows shot up.

'Go on.'

'Call my direct line at 07.16. You pretend to be someone with some information on Barnard. Ask me to meet you in Fino's Café in five minutes. I'll grab my jacket and jump off desk and head for the lifts. I won't get in them, instead I'll wheel round to Fletcher's office, fish his phone out of his jacket and do what I have to do. Then I'll head out of the building for my fake rendezvous. When he asks who called, I'll say it was a lead on Barnard. He knows I've been tasked to get information by Mark Simpson. He's a higher-ranking director, so basically Fletcher can't do anything about it.'

Charlie continued to make notes as he spoke. Then put her pen down and looked up with an expression that Seb decided to interpret as admiration, even affection.

'Not bad. I think that could even work. But he could ask who you met, and what the information is. To make the story failsafe, use a real person with no possible crossover with Fletcher, and have a document with you that does actually contain something about Barnard's past. Don't volunteer it, it'd look far too rehearsed. Only produce it if he pushes.'

'OK, sure. As for the name, you're a real person with no connection with Fletcher. Let's just keep it simple.'

Charlie started to fidget in her chair, her eyes looking everywhere but into Seb's.

'Yeah, well, that brings me to the second reason why I can't do this myself. I've met William Fletcher. A couple of times actually.'

She looked uncharacteristically coy.

'We served together on a few operations in the mid-nineties.'

'And he would remember you after all these years?'

'I would fucking hope so,' said Charlie, tartly.

Seb chuckled.

'You bad woman. He must have been married by then.'

'Engaged.'

'Oh well, that's alright then,' said Seb, mockingly. 'And

Chapter 29

there I was thinking I was special.'

'Ah, bless,' said Charlie, patting his hand.

With no warning, Seb suddenly lurched for his mobile phone and started feverishly scrolling through the 'options' menu.

'I've just remembered, this mobile has a recording function. I could try and goad him into saying something compromising and record him for posterity. I may not need you after all.'

Charlie snatched the phone out of Seb's hand and examined it carefully.

'Why'd they give *you* the latest Nokia?'

'I'm very important you know.'

'Important, my hole. You're right though, it does, but it only lasts for thirty seconds and the recording ends with a very loud ping. You'd need to be a lot more skilled than you'll ever be to record anything useful without being caught. You just do exactly what I tell you with the equipment I provide, and you'll be just fine.'

'Yes staff!'

'That's more like it, Faber.'

She finished her pint and grabbed her things.

'Give me a couple of days. I'll come to yours to show you how to deploy it. It'll only take a few minutes but it's not something I want to do in a pub. Maybe I'll meet the new girl?'

Seb was momentarily taken off guard.

'How did you know I'm seeing someone?'

'I didn't 'til just now. And I'm happy for you, so I am.'

One look into her eyes confirmed her sincerity.

'I should know better than to try to keep a secret from a spy,' grinned Seb.

They hugged warmly, holding the embrace as old lovers do.

'Thanks again, Charlie. I'd be stuffed without you.'

With her head still resting on his shoulder, she whispered in his ear.

'No you wouldn't.'

CHAPTER 30

Sophia wasn't there when Charlie came to the flat the following week. Seb told himself that her absence that evening was unplanned, but he knew it was consciously unplanned. There was no upside to the two women meeting and swapping notes.

It only took five minutes for Charlie to show Seb how to deploy the recording unit. Then it was his turn. The tiny black device had an even tinier ball of sticky gum on one side to hold it in place, and the Nokia 6820 had a perfectly shaped recess above the SIM card where the bug sat unobtrusively.

Charlie was nothing if not meticulous. She hung Seb's jacket on a wooden coat hanger on a peg in the entrance corridor of his flat, told him to walk five paces away and, while his back was turned, slid the phone into a pocket. A different pocket on each of the trial runs. It took him no more than thirty seconds to find and extract the phone, deploy the device, and return it to the jacket. She waited till he'd completed three attempts before passing comment. He looked at her complacently, ready for his gold star.

'I can give you five reasons why you would've just got

caught, fired, prosecuted and convicted.'

'What? That's ridiculous! How?'

'Come here under the light. See that, fingerprints, all over the screen and the casing.'

'I can't wear gloves! It's too bloody fiddly.'

'No, but you can hold the phone with your fingertips. And you can give it a wipe when you finish. Particularly the screen.'

'OK, I suppose. And the others?'

'On the first go you put the phone back in the right chest pocket, and it came from the left. On the first and second goes you put the phone back upside down. On the third you put it back upside down, and facing out not facing in. On all three goes you left the jacket at ten degrees to the perpendicular on the hanger. He's the sort of man who would never do that. So, as I said, five different mistakes, any of which could fuck all this up. And assuming Fletcher's office has a desk, why are you trying to make life hard for yourself? Put the phone down and *then* get the bug out of your pocket. Use the hall table. Now let's do it again shall we?'

Seb did it another dozen times and his performance was marked, as before, after each series of three goes. He scored a zero-error count on his final three efforts.

'OK Seb. I think we're ready. You have your document on Barnard?'

'Not yet,' replied Seb, strung out and irritable.

'Well make it believable, or even better, make it true.'

Seb gazed at her, wide-eyed.

'You really don't think much of me, do you?'

Her eyes didn't leave Seb's for one moment.

'You know I do.' She paused to draw breath. 'At this very

second I may even love you in a funny kind of way, so just do what I tell you and get the job done.'

Seb's cheeks flushed as his exasperation gave way to affection.

'I will, Charlie. I will.'

CHAPTER 31

He wanted to get it done as soon as possible, and that meant the very next day. As the analysts gathered by the sales desk for the morning meeting, Fletcher strode onto the floor and took up his usual position behind the squawk box. He was, as ever, jacketless.

Steve Hoddler, the Head of Sales Trading, started proceedings with the usual round up of global equity index activity and economic data, and Seb, like the rest of the team, worked hard at looking like he gave a shit. As Hoddler ceded the microphone to the retail analyst, who had something of nothing to say about the M&S results, Seb's phone rang. He quickly put his headset on and hit the flashing button on his dealer board.

'Hi. OK. Where are you now? Can it wait twenty minutes? Shit. OK, I'm coming down.'

He spoke clearly and loudly enough to be sure both O C-B and Vicky could bear witness to his end of the call, if he ever needed them to.

His heart thumping, he pulled his headset off, swept his jacket off the back of his chair and strode to the right-hand bank of lifts where he couldn't be seen by Fletcher, or

Chapter 31

anyone else engaged in the morning meeting.

He walked straight past the lifts, turned left onto the wide corridor that accessed the four senior executive offices, and stepped past the open door into Fletcher's office, the last one on the right.

The light was on. So much for Charlie's insistence on doing the training in a half light from a distant source. He pulled the door, leaving it an inch ajar and went straight to Fletcher's jacket on its hanger. As she'd predicted, the shoulders and hem were exactly parallel to the floor.

Seb patted down the jacket to locate the phone. It was in the right-hand hip pocket. Careful not to touch the screen, he took the phone out with his left hand, noting that the phone was upright and facing inwards, slid the battery cover off and put both phone and cover on Fletcher's desk. He then reached into his own hip pocket with his left hand and pulled out the tiny, clear plastic zip-lock bag containing the bug. He teased open the bag and extracted the device with the thumb and index finger of his right hand.

As he'd practised endlessly, he put the bag back in his left hip pocket and picked up the phone. Unlike the practise runs, though, his fingers were now clammy and as he closed in on the target location with the tiny device, it slipped from his grasp and fell to the carpet-tiled floor.

He swore sharply under his breath and quickly scooped it up, placing the device in the target space, pushed it down firmly with his thumb, compressing the gum ball, slid the cover back onto the phone and, taking care to duplicate the way he'd found it, returned it to Fletcher's jacket pocket. As the phone hit the silk lining of the pocket, he heard a sound. A rattle. The bug had come loose. It had never happened before. He fished the phone out and took the cover off yet again. The unit was loose in the battery compartment. He held the bug up to the light; the gum was covered in fibres from the carpet tiles.

A panicked glance at his watch. 07.21. It was a quiet news day. The meeting would be shorter than normal. Fletcher would be back in no time. He slowed his breathing and tried to tease the gum ball back to a more adhesive surface, but it was the size of a squashed petit pois. Impossible. He tried again and it stayed in place. He put the cover back on and raised it to the vertical. No noise, but he knew that wasn't enough. He gave it a vigorous shake and there it was. Abort.

A thunder of feet. Out of the corner window, he could see the analysts making their way back to their room. The meeting was over. He retrieved the bug and returned Fletcher's phone to his jacket, this time not giving any thought to the orientation. The corridor was already a busy thoroughfare. Seb reached into his jacket and pulled out an A3 envelope and went straight to Fletcher's desk. The door opened before he got there.

'What the hell are you doing in my office?'

Seb span round with the envelope still in his hand.

'I needed to leave this with you.' He handed it to Fletcher.

'What's this?'

'Information on Barnard. An old friend just met me downstairs. Sorry to leave the meeting, but she couldn't wait.'

He'd said too much.

'She?'

'Ex-Army. Does some security stuff now.'

Fletcher took the envelope from Seb and stared intently at him, saying nothing. Asking everything.

Seb broke the impasse.

Chapter 31

'I'll leave it with you. Need to get on with my calls.'

He didn't wait to be discharged, walked around the motionless Fletcher and was halfway out of the door when he was frozen to the spot.

'Wait!'

He turned around to see Fletcher staring at his jacket, the shoulders an inch off square. and the left lapel slightly, but noticeably, ajar.

'You've interfered with...

'Your jacket. Busted.'

'What the hell...'

'Welsh and Jeffries. I thought Gieves and Hawkes, but my curiosity got the better of me. I'm sorry, but I've always admired the cut of your suits.'

Fletcher's mask of displeasure was transformed by a flicker of vanity.

'Yes, well. If you keep your nose clean you might be able to afford my tailor one day.'

Seb smiled obligingly, span on a sixpence, and escaped.

CHAPTER 32

A brown A3 envelope marked 'Do Not Bend' was in amongst the marketing detritus and takeaway menus on the mat in the communal entrance hall. He walked into the flat with it in his hand, to find Sophia had let herself in and was busy in the kitchen preparing their supper. Halfway through dicing two chicken breasts, she gave him a kiss, careful to keep her sticky hands away from him. Seb slumped down on the sofa and studied the envelope.

'What's that?' said Sophia.

'No idea.'

He opened it and slowly slid out a photograph. A dark image. A man and a woman. Bodies almost pressed against each other. A hand on her breast. His hand.

'You've gone pale, what is it?'

He couldn't say anything.

'What is it Seb?'

He was cornered. He wanted to run out the door.

'I'm being blackmailed.'

She stepped forward, plucked the photo from his grasp, no longer any thought of the state of her chicken covered hands, and examined it. She brought the photo close to her eyes and took her time, taking in every awful detail. Her eyes glistened but she spoke calmly.

'Who is she?'

'Fletcher's wife. She came on to me after the dinner at that shooting party, and I knocked her back.'

Seb responded as if he was in the witness box, but not the dock.

'If it's not an unfair question, why is your hand on her tit?'

'She grabbed my hand and put it there.'

She looked at the photo again. Phoebe's hand was either obscured by the profile of her breasts or had been digitally removed. Either way, there was no evidence to back up Seb's version of the event.

'And you, with all your might, couldn't stop her. Is that it?'

He could have resisted her. And he hadn't pulled away instantly. He'd been aroused, and actually he'd thought he'd been pretty saintly walking away as he had.

'This must be a still taken from video. She took me by surprise. My hand was there for a split second then I told her that she'd had too much to drink and took myself straight off to bed. I promise you that's all that happened...'

She looked at him closely.

'Why were you alone with her anyway?'

Her eyes were welling up.

'I was helping her clear up at the end of the night. We were taking everything down to the kitchen.'

'And everyone else had gone to bed?'

'Only just. I was being polite. She was my hostess and she's my boss's wife. I didn't think for one second that she'd make a pass at me, let alone grab me like that.'

Sophia paced around the room, stopping on two occasions to look at the photo.

'Did you kiss her? Take a moment before you answer that question.'

'I don't need a moment. No, I didn't.'

She looked down at the image again.

'Why didn't you tell me this happened?'

'Honestly, I couldn't think of any way of explaining it without looking like I was in some way to blame.' He took a breath. 'And the truth is that I *was* letting her flirt with me. But I was doing it to get information on Fletcher, which I got, but I guess I could have given her signals that she felt she could act on.'

'What, like a fucking boner pointing straight at her!'

She shoved the photo into his face with her finger pointing at the offending bulge.

There was nothing he could say, so he didn't. Sophia dropped the photo onto the coffee table, folded her arms and stared at the floor while she considered the evidence. At last, she lifted her head to deliver her judgment.

'I believe you.'

Seb started to speak but was cut off.

'I believe that this was all that happened because I imagine I'd be looking at something much more horrifying than that if you had taken it further. But you should have told me.'

'I'm sorry. It was a mad situation. I didn't want to drag you into it.'

'Well I'm in it now, boyo. Why are they doing this to you? First Barnard, now Fletcher. This is getting scary. Do you know what you're doing?'

'I've got to get more information before I take it to

Chapter 32

Simpson, and then to the police. And I know I'm finished if I get this wrong.'

'Well hurry up and get whatever it is you need, so we can get the fuck on with our lives. Please!'

'I will. I have a plan.'

'I hope it's a bloody good one.'

She returned to the kitchen to finish preparing their supper, the clacking sound of her chopping vegetables, much more vigorously than before, bouncing off the walls.

Seb picked up the photo and tried to work out where the camera was hidden, whether other cameras could have been positioned around the house, and where.

In the kitchen there was silence as Sophia stopped chopping the vegetables before she called out, 'But did you *have* to have such a massive hard on?!'

CHAPTER 33

Seb sat in his flat trying to take stock of the three months that had elapsed since he'd met Sophia. So much had happened, all of it on fast forward. They wanted each other, and they were consenting adults, but the usual practice was three dates - or was it three months - before sex. They'd broken that rule twice within days of meeting each other. In the three months that followed they'd met almost daily and spoken multiple times a day when apart. They sent each other kooky little texts. Got drunk together. Dragged themselves through hangovers together. They'd lied to friends to get out of events. Even kept toothbrushes in each other's flats. They zipped around London on Seb's Vespa having coffees and lunches in eclectic little places that Seb would never otherwise have visited, and where Sophia was invariably greeted with a jubilant embrace.

They shared confusion over the displays in the Tate Modern. Shared sadness at the demented pacing of the tigers at London Zoo. They stole a thousand kisses in quiet residential streets. Crisp, dry, bitterly cold. As romantic as anywhere in the world. The feeling of Sophia's body pressed against his, wrapped tightly in his arms, was an addiction.

Chapter 33

Theirs was a connection that was conceived of raw physical attraction but had gestated, born and nurtured by their shared philosophies on the world. They were bound by the things they shared, and the bonds were only strengthened by the things they did not, independent in their thoughts but united in the principles they lived by. Be curious. Ask questions that you don't know the answers to. Say yes to things that take you out of your comfort zone. Listen to others. Read. Learn. Be kind. Be decisive. Stand up for those who can't. Take risks. Be prepared to fail. *Be prepared to fail.* They were throwing all of themselves into each other, more exposed than either'd ever been before. Aware of the risk of failure. Of loss. But the thrill of it, the exhilarating rush. It made the hazards seem irrelevant, carrying them to a higher plain.

The doorbell rang, and he buzzed Sophia up, opening his door to greet her as she climbed the stairs. Before she even had her coat and scarf off, he blurted it out. He had a lot he had to say.

'We've been going out for nearly four months. That's pretty much my record. I think we should step things up. Go away together for a few days. I thought maybe a long weekend skiing.'

Sophia draped her scarf on the coat hook and stood stock still, facing Seb.

'Are you sure you can cope with the commitment of a *whole* long weekend away with me?'

She was joking, maybe.

'Shut up and listen for a sec. If it's great, and I know it will be, will you move in with me?'

She looked into his eyes, a million calculations behind her perfectly still face. There was something about the way she was looking at him, searching for answers, that made him continue. When he did, his whole manner had changed.

'But listen. Before you answer, there's something you need to know,' he said.

'If it's about girls I don't want to hear it. God knows I'm not telling you my war stories. Everyone's allowed a past you know.'

'This isn't about girls. You'd better sit down.'

Seb's seriousness wiped the light from Sophia's face. She hung her coat up and sat down; he carried on standing.

'When I was seventeen, I put a drug dealer in hospital and ended up going to a young offenders' prison for six months.

He waited for a reaction. Sophia didn't move, focused on his eyes. There was more to tell.

'Go on.'

'He tried to sell drugs to Emily after school one day, and he threatened her. Sexually. I had to stop him. It was just one punch, but he fell and smashed his head on the kerb.'

Sophia leant forward, her face a picture of confusion.

'That's bloody awful, but you were just protecting your sister, why…'

'Why was I charged, and convicted?'

'Yes. That's crazy.'

He got up from the sofa and started pacing.

'Because I knew the dealer. He was my dealer. He was also my boss.'

Seb watched her shrink away from him.

'I did a few small jobs for him just to pay for my drugs. Deliveries of weed and hash mostly. But other stuff too.'

'You don't need to tell me all this. Not now.' His distress

was unmistakeable, and instinctively she held out a hand towards him. He ignored it.

'Yes, I do. You have to know who I am. All of it.'

He sat down on the opposite end of the sofa to Sophia, staring straight out of the window at nothing at all.

'My Dad. I told you that he died in an accident. He did, but it was my fault. He was trying to rescue me from a cliff face. The tide was coming in. I couldn't move. He tried to climb up to me, but he slipped.' Seb had to stop. He took a deep breath to gather himself. 'What I'll never forget is his face. He looked up at me as he fell. Didn't look down once. And he didn't make a sound.'

He broke off again, forcing back the tears. Sophia moved along the sofa to sit next to him, her hand on his thigh.

'Everyone said it was an accident, but it only happened because I climbed where they told me not to.' He bowed his head, defeated, overwhelmed by the intolerable memory.

'You were a thirteen-year-old boy. That's what thirteen-year-old boys do!'

Seb just shook his head, still locked in the past, and rushed on.

'Mum tried to keep us at our schools, but she couldn't manage it. I was bullied at the local school. I just took it for a while, but in the end I fought back. And I got a taste for it. I started bunking off lessons. Went for anyone who looked at me the wrong way. I was drinking in the afternoons, smoking weed. Even did pills and coke when I had the money for it. That's when he offered me the jobs. Just a few local drop offs, nothing big. But when I tried to stop, he said he would get Emily involved. I thought it was just a bullshit threat, so when I saw him outside the school gates with her, I went straight at him. I couldn't drag my family into my shit. He never expected it from me. Christ, Sophia! The noise when his head hit the kerb. And then he didn't move.'

Seb stopped and turned to face her as he said, 'It was a long time ago. I'm not that guy anymore. And I know I never will be again. But it happened, and I can't let myself go any further with you without your knowing what I was.'

He sat motionless and waited for Sophia to digest what she'd heard. It was her turn to pace around the room, arms crossed. After a while she paused, moving slowly towards the open fireplace and picked up the framed family photo from the mantelpiece, looking at the five happy faces thoughtfully.

'You must have loved your father very much,' she said, eyes still glued to the image as she put the photo back on the mantel carefully and turned to face Seb.

'You have a lot of people that love you and believe in you. I want to be one of them. But I need you to know that if I walk in through that door with my bags in my hand, I may never, ever want to leave.'

Then, at last, he wept as he stood up and folded her in his arms.

'If you decide to walk through that door, I'll never let you go.'

CHAPTER 34

'You're doing what?' said Seb's mother, after Seb tried to casually introduce the skiing trip into an otherwise un-newsworthy telephone conversation.

'We're going away for the weekend,' said Seb.

'But you've only just met the girl.'

'Mum, we've been together for four months.'

Seb heard his mother take a long drag on her cigarette before she continued.

'For a normal person this would be entirely unremarkable. But this is serious, isn't it, my love?'

'What do you mean a normal person?'

'Oh, you know what I mean. Don't you think it's about time we met her?'

'You'll meet her soon enough.'

Another drag on the cigarette.

'No. It won't do. You can't go gallivanting off with a girl that none of us have even met!'

'I'm not gallivanting, it's a weekend break,' Seb protested, but immediately wished he hadn't.

'If you don't bring her home to meet us, I'll just have to camp in your flat 'til she turns up.'

'That's a bit extreme isn't it, Mum?'
'Not in the slightest. So, what's it to be?'

* * *

Resistance was futile. Seb decided to host dinner for his whole family in his flat. There was safety in numbers, and importantly he could turf them all out at the end of the evening. His siblings, normally so hard to nail down, were unusually eager to meet his new girlfriend and a date was set.

The night came, and Seb and Sophia were busying themselves with preparations.

'So, what's your mum like?'

'Protective, extremely hard to please. You'll like her,' said Seb, with a smirk.

'Oh piss off. I'm sure she's lovely.'

'She really is, and she'll love you,' he said, smiling. 'It's my sister you really need to worry about.'

The doorbell rang before Sophia could come up with an answer, and Seb pressed the intercom.

'It's me.'

'Great. Come on up.'

He pressed the entry button and there was a thunderous galumphing up the stairs.

'Harry was at a loose end, so I suggested he come over now and get his inquisition over with before the others get here. Hope that's OK,' said Seb.

A firm wrap on the door announced Harry's arrival and Sophia took a deep breath as Seb opened the door. The bear-framed Harry wrapped his arms around his brother with a bottle of wine clasped in each hand.

Chapter 34

'Sophia, this is my little brother Harry. You spoke briefly on the phone.'

'Nice to meet you in person, Harry,' and she held out her hand.

'And lovely to finally meet you, Sophia.'

Harry bypassed her hand and kissed her enthusiastically three times on the cheeks.

'You've done your homework,' said Sophia.

'Indeed I have.'

His words were heavy with the implication that his homework had been extensive.

'Oh God,' she replied, throwing an accusing look at Seb.

'I haven't said a damn thing. Don't let him wind you up.'

'Sadly true. He's been boringly discreet. Let's get stuck into these and see if we can't make up for lost time.'

'Only if I get to hear all about your adventures as an international playboy, Harry.'

'Well, all the good stuff he's told you is true.'

'Shame. I was hoping it was the bad stuff,' said Sophia.

While Seb worked away in the kitchen the two of them sat in the sitting room and exchanged edited highlights of their lives. Judging by the howls of laughter, they seemed to be hitting it off.

After a while, Harry appeared in the kitchen.

'You lucky, lucky bastard. She's bloody fantastic. Only fair to warn you that you better watch your back. I think she's quite taken by me.'

'Thanks for the heads up,' said Seb, grinning.

'My pleasure. Got any crisps?'

'They're in the top cupboard but you can eat them in here. I need you both to help plate the starter, while I get on with the vegetables.'

It was like an episode of The Generation Game; Seb demonstrated how he wanted the plate to look, and Harry and Sophia followed obediently. Their hands were still covered in avocado and melon juice when the doorbell rang again. Seb pressed the intercom button with his elbow.

'Hi darling,' his mother's voice, needing no introduction.

'Hi Mum. Come on up,' said Seb, and he let her into the building.

Sophia rushed to the sink to wash her hands.

'Tea towel! Where is your feckin' tea towel?'

'Relax,' said Seb, handing her the one that was right under her nose.

She dried her hands hastily as Seb opened the door to his mother who stepped in with bags full of pudding, cheese and wine. She put the bags by her feet and focused her attention on Sophia.

'Mum, this is Sophia.'

They took a moment to take each other in. Mary stepped forward and hugged her as she would her own daughter.

'Sophia, how lovely to *finally* meet you.'

'Let me help you with these,' said Sophia, reaching for the bags by her feet.

'That's lovely but Harry will take care of them, won't you, Harry.'

Harry leapt forward to sweep up the bags.

'Pudding in the fridge, cheese left out please.'

Harry did as instructed, Seb poured the drinks and they all milled around in the kitchen while Seb busied himself with the food preparation. Once all the vegetables were simmering away, he dried his hands on the back of his jeans and picked up his glass.

'Right, let's go through while we wait for Emily'

Chapter 34

They transferred to the sitting room and sat on the sofas at the near end, the dining table in the bay window overlooking the street.

'So, Sophia, Sebastian tells me you're doing a masters in fashion. What's the plan when you finish?'

The genesis of the question wasn't about her career. It was about her life choices. Most particularly whether they involved her son.

'Well, I've been sponsored through the masters by Yves Saint Laurent in exchange for promising them two years of my time after I graduate.'

'How lovely, will that be here in London?'

'London or Paris. I just have to take whatever I get.'

'Well, Paris isn't that far away, is it?'

'No, Mum, it isn't,' said Seb, giving his mother a cease-and-desist glare.

'It's all very exciting, Sophia. Could I ask you to help me in the kitchen? I have a dozen cheeses I need to unwrap, so they'll be alright in a couple of hours. All French and Irish you'll be glad to know.'

Mary set about unpacking the Tupperware box as Sophia fetched the cheese board.

'I have so looked forward to meeting you. He won't thank me for saying this, but Seb's been a bit lost since he left the Army. It was the saving of him you see, and it was just so cruel, the way it ended. But I can see the spark back in him again now, and I thank you for that, truly.'

At that moment, Seb walked in to fetch another bottle from the fridge.

'What are you two talking about?'

'Absolutely none of your business, so top up our glasses and leave us alone like a good boy,' said Mary.

The doorbell rang.

'That'll be Emily,' said Seb. He buzzed his sister up and Sophia moved to greet her, visibly tensing as Emily approached the door.

'Hello, hello, hello. Fucking dreadful day topping off a fucking dreadful week. Give me wine right now please brother,' announced Emily.

She looked over Seb's shoulder at Sophia, and whispered.

'Shit Seb, she's gorgeous. Please, God let her be dull or, better still, stupid.'

Sophia stepped past Seb to greet Emily with a respectful handshake.

'Emily, I'm Sophia, we spoke briefly on the phone.'

'We did indeed, and as feared, you're impossibly gorgeous, and I hate you very much indeed for it. I'm sure we can find a nicer man for you than my brother.'

'Sounds like a plan. Why don't we enjoy this evening, and we can start our search in earnest in the morning.'

'And funny too! I am completely redundant!' said Emily.

'Don't sound so bloody miserable,' piped up Harry. 'You're the one happily married with two kids! Speaking of which, where is Geoff tonight?'

'Performing some bloody awful German dirge at the Wigmore Hall. He'll try and pop in afterwards if we're still going.'

'We will be,' confirmed Harry, with absolute conviction.

They stood at the kitchen table and watched Seb proudly do the final assembly of his starter and take the pork belly out to rest.

Seb's family took turns to ask about every aspect of Sophia's life, and the one she aspired to. Sophia tentatively launched into the well-rehearsed pitch that she had given to

Chapter 34

St Martins and Yves St Laurent as part of the sponsorship process. 'Skirts by Sophia Deschamps' was to be the name of the brand, unique to her and doing exactly what it said on the tin. The .com web domain of her name was secured, as were multiple variants of it and, with the help of her tutor at college, she had a four-year business plan written, complete with a twenty-tab financial model.

When she was given a moment's pause, she asked each of them insightful open questions that allowed them to talk about their own lives. Mary told great stories of life as a theatre sister at St George's Hospital in the swinging sixties where she'd met Anthony, the swashbuckling Irish surgeon who stole her heart.

'You'd have enjoyed meeting him,' said Mary, more matter of fact than melancholic.

'Having met you all now, I'm absolutely sure that I would,' said Sophia.

And that was all that was said about Seb's father.

Mary had been sitting quietly for while with a look of intense concentration on her face.

'It's quite amazing,' she exclaimed.

The room jumped to attention.

'Sophia, as I sit here listening to you, I can't hear any trace of a French accent. It's quite uncanny how completely Irish you sound given your entire life has been spent in France.'

'That's easy to explain. My entire life has also been spent with my mother. She didn't speak a word of French to me for the first ten years of my life. She had a morbid dread of my speaking English with the sort of American accent she saw other bilingual kids pick up from MTV, so she made it her mission to get this Cork accent hard wired.'

'What a sensible woman,' said Mary.

'Sensible would not be the first word I would choose to describe Mum. I'd say fiery would be closer to the mark.'

'Lucky Monsieur Deschamps,' said Harry.

'Harry, really!' pleaded Mary.

'I'm not in the least bit offended, Mary. I'd say that Papa does consider himself very lucky indeed.'

They finished the starter and Seb served the pork belly to coos of admiration, some of which were genuine, the noise intensified as each voice competed for ever more scarce airtime.

They'd finished and cleared the main course, and Mary was serving the chocolate roulade, when the doorbell rang.

'Who the hell can that be? Everyone I care about in the world is here,' said Seb, and pressed the intercom button.

'Hello?'

'Seb, its William. Can I have a word?'

Fletcher had never been to Seb's flat. Why on earth would he?

'William, err, OK. Sure. I have guests but come on up. Up the stairs, first door on the left.'

He turned to the open-mouthed audience around the table.

'It's my bloody boss, for God's sake.'

Seconds later, there was a knock on the door.

'William, come in.'

Fletcher stepped into the flat and scanned the room.

'You're busy, I can see. I won't keep you long. Could we speak somewhere quiet?'

His only acknowledgement of the fact that he'd burst into a family dinner party uninvited was a half grin directed to the table as he strode into the kitchen. Seb followed behind him.

Chapter 34

'The information you gave me on Barnard. Who else knows about it?'

'Me, my source, and you.'

'Ah yes, your source. Who is this woman?'

Seb didn't hesitate.

'I'm afraid I can't say. She works in intelligence. An old colleague. I'm sure you understand.'

Fletcher most certainly didn't understand and was about to erupt.

'And Mark Simpson OK'd it,' said Seb.

He'd played the trump card. Rank. Fletcher became a degree less belligerent.

'Well, until this information is verified, don't pass it on to anyone. Do you understand?'

At that moment Mary Faber walked into the kitchen. Incensed.

'As you didn't introduce yourself, I will. Mary Faber, Sebastian's mother.'

'William Fletcher, Seb's boss.'

An entirely unnecessary hierarchical classification. Mary Faber and William Fletcher faced each other in an uneasy standoff. Mary elected to end it.

'We'll since he's not actually at work it would be fair to say that I'm his boss just now, don't you think?'

Before Fletcher could muster a response, she continued.

'Mr Fletcher, as you can see, we are enjoying a family dinner but if we hunt around I'm sure we could find another chair.'

If she had had another thousand goes at it, she couldn't have been more disingenuous.

'No, no. I'll be off. Sorry to disturb. I'll see you first thing on Monday then Seb.'

Fletcher popped his head back into the sitting room.

'Do carry on. Enjoy your evening.'

Both his tone and delivery suggested their enjoyment was somehow in his gift. As Seb closed the door behind him, Fletcher span round to Seb with a parting shot.

'Lovely family. Pretty girlfriend, too. Sophia, is it?'

He hadn't ever mentioned her name to him.

'You'll remember what I said.'

And he left, not waiting for any response. Seb was chilled to the core and wore it on his face as he sat back down at the table.

'What the hell was that about?' bellowed Harry.

'He's just a prick who feels the need to remind everyone who's the boss. Constantly,' said Seb, doing his best to maintain levity.

'Be careful there my love,' said Mary, lighting a cigarette to settle herself.

'I will. I've got it under control.'

Seb caught Sophia's eye as he said it, and his mother spotted it, but said nothing.

'*Ding dong, the witch is dead*, let's get this party back on the road shall we,' said Emily, and so they did. But Seb's head was never fully back in the room.

CHAPTER 35

The departure day arrived. Their bags were packed and waiting for them in Sophia's flat, a walk away from Victoria where they could catch the train to Gatwick. Seb went to work, and Sophia to college, both brimming with excitement about the three days ahead. He had a series of meetings in the morning, and by the time he got back to his desk at noon he realised his mobile phone was dead. He plugged in the charger, and it sprang to life with a crescendo of pings and illumination. Two missed calls and a text message from Sophia. The text message, sent hours earlier, was terrifying.

I'm in the C&W Hospital. Probly nonthing serious.
Come if youcan. A&E. x

He'd never seen so much as a single typo in any of her previous texts or emails. He rang her straight back but was immediately diverted to voicemail. He left his desk without a word to any of his colleagues and was at the Chelsea & Westminster A&E department twenty minutes later giving Sophia's full name to the absurdly perky receptionist, who needed three repetitions of her surname before she looked up again.

'Found her,' she beamed. 'Sophia Deschamps?' pronounced phonetically.

'Yes.'

'She was brought into A&E by ambulance at eight-thirty this morning and was transferred to ICU at eleven fifteen.'

ICU. Oh Christ…

'Down the corridor, lift to the third floor. Left out the lift', and she gave him a bright toothy smile as if she were directing him to the lingerie department in Peter Jones.

He ran to the lift, paced back and forth in it like a caged animal, and crabbed sideways out of it as the doors were still opening. He rang the bell at the intensive care unit and was met by a matronly nurse who calmly asked for his name and relationship to Sophia. 'Boyfriend' sounded pathetically adolescent as it left his lips.

'Ah yes. She asked us to look out for you when she first came in. Please, let's step into the family room. The doctor will be with you in a moment.'

Ushered into the empty room, he cast his eyes down the corridor to the half-dozen visible beds but couldn't see her. The nurse shut the door firmly behind him.

Family rooms in hospitals are wretched places. Family rooms in intensive care units are the most wretched of all, places where the very worst news is delivered in featureless, halogen lit spaces. The car-boot-sale artwork hanging on the pockmarked walls is studied in more depth than the artist could ever have imagined it might merit, hours of desperation needing any diversion available. Plastic coffee. Plastic food. The percussion of beeps and pings from the orchestra of monitors in the room beyond, amplified every time the door swung open. And when it does, the occupants of the room freeze in terrified suspension.

Chapter 35

After a while, a doctor of middle age and Indian ethnicity stepped into the room.

'Mr Faber.'

'Yes.'

'I am Dr Mistry, and I am the physician in charge of Sophia's case.' His diction was measured, and precise.

'I have spoken to Sophia's parents, and they are getting on a plane to London shortly. I wouldn't normally share this information with someone outside the immediate family, but the last thing Sophia did was tell her parents to expect you to be here when they arrived.'

'The *last* thing she said?!'

'Yes, Mr Faber. Let me explain. Sophia fell down a concrete flight of steps and has taken a severe bang to her head. She has brain swelling and her raised intercranial pressure is likely caused by a cerebral oedema, further exacerbated by a bleed caused by the trauma.'

Fletcher. Seb had dismissed his thinly veiled threat as being empty and had kept it to himself. He hadn't warned her.

'What do you mean fell? Why would she fall? Were there any witnesses?'

Seb was shouting, attracting attention from all the staff on the unit.

'Actually, there is a reason why she could have fallen. I'll come to it in a moment, but my priority is to manage the bleed and reduce the brain swelling. In these cases, we use barbiturates to induce a coma which has the effect of reducing the metabolic rate of brain tissue, as well as the cerebral blood flow. With these reductions, the blood vessels in the brain narrow, decreasing the amount of space occupied by the brain, and hence the intracranial pressure.

The hope is that, with the swelling relieved, the pressure decreases and some or all brain damage may be averted.'

Brain damage. Separately, two inert words. When combined, the most terrifying prospect imaginable. He'd seen the consequences of brain damage. A living death. The person you knew gone forever, replaced by a stranger with a mere physical resemblance of their whole self. Seb listened, appalled, but before he could gather himself to respond, Dr Mistry continued.

'Her brain injury is our immediate focus, but I'm afraid there is a secondary condition. Sophia has acute liver failure. For reasons yet to be established, her liver is functioning at less than twenty percent of full capacity. Observers at the scene said that she fainted. That was likely to be caused by the cerebral oedema that is consistent with the condition. We have stabilised her for now and are running more tests to establish the extent of the disease and the precise cause, but I need to caution you that at this stage it is our expectation that full functionality may not return. For that reason, we have placed Sophia on the national transplant list for a cadaverous liver.'

Seb couldn't keep up with the galloping pace of this horror. He had never known fear like it. Never felt this helpless.

'Can I see her?'

'Yes, but be aware that she has had quite an insult to her forehead. Her appearance may look alarming to you at first.'

Seb shook his head, dismissing Dr Mistry's concerns out of hand.

'But before I take you to her, I need to ask you some questions about Sophia. Personal questions. She was somewhat incoherent when she came in and we sedated

Chapter 35

her soon after she was admitted to the unit.'

'OK. Fine.'

He was desperate to see her, exasperated by the delay.

'How much alcohol does Sophia drink?'

'A few glasses of wine a night, sometimes more. Not every day. A lot less than me.'

'Understood. And is she a recreational drug user? Particularly those that involve needle use?'

'Jesus no. She doesn't take any drugs, not with me. Not since I've known her. And certainly not heroin!'

'Thank you. And her sexual history. Are you aware of many partners?'

Dr Mistry asked the question without any hint of embarrassment or discomfort.

'Jesus! What is this?'

'I'm sorry Mr Faber. I know this is difficult, but we need to establish the cause of the liver failure as quickly as we can.'

'I don't know her sexual history. She's a normal twenty-five-year-old girl who drinks wine and has the occasional cigarette when she's out. What else can I say?!'

'That's fine Mr Faber. And was she in good health would you say?'

This gave him pause.

'Thinking about it, she has had one or two headaches recently and she was complaining about being tired all the time. She's looked pretty washed out in recent weeks, but we put it down to too many late nights and not enough sun.'

Dr Mistry hurriedly scratched the notes into her file with his heavily chewed Bic biro.

'That is very helpful, Mr Faber. Let me take you to her now.'

He saw her but could barely recognise her. Her head was heavily bandaged, both her eyes enflamed. She had a drain in her skull, oxygen apparatus in her nose and had been catheterised. In her right arm a saline drip, a blood oxygen monitor on her index finger. A large cardiac monitor was attached to her chest via tentacles that disappeared under her blue hospital blankets. When he'd left her flat shortly after six that morning, she had never looked more perfect. Tousled hair and eyes half open, buried in the thick winter duvet. He held her free hand between both of his. It was warm, which was a surprise. Her hands were almost never warm.

'What happens now?'

'All being well, the brain inflammation will abate over the next twenty-four hours, and we'll be able to perform the brain function analysis.'

Seb glared at the doctor with an ashen face.

'You shouldn't worry too much about that. The swelling was managed quickly post trauma. The test is largely precautionary.'

Largely?

'What does she know?' asked Seb.

'Very little. Her liver function test results came back after she was placed into the coma, and she was pretty confused by the time she got to us in ICU.'

Seb held Sophia's hand, listening to the sounds of life support all around him. Another noise, a buzzing in his pocket. An overseas number.

'This could be her family,' he said.

'Please take the call outside. I'll find you if there's any change.'

Seb walked as briskly as he could without causing a

Chapter 35

disturbance and stepped out into the corridor.

'Seb?' An urgent female voice with an Irish accent.

'Yes.'

'This is Sophia's mother. Are you with her?'

'Yes I am.'

'Thank God. How is she?'

He didn't know what she'd been told.

'She's stable and in no immediate danger. Not much change from what you will have been told, I think. When will you get here?'

'We land at Heathrow at one fifty. We'll get a taxi straight to the hospital.'

'OK, Mrs Deschamps. I'll be here. Don't worry.'

The second the words left his lips he cursed himself. How preposterous that platitude was, and how impertinent it must have sounded. He was neither a doctor nor the next of kin, merely a boyfriend of a few months. She'd worry herself sick, of course she would, and so she should. Her girl was as near to death as she had been since the day she first came into the world. Seb shook his head to try to rid himself of intolerable thoughts. He was buzzed back into the unit, only to be told that Sophia was resting and not to be disturbed.

'We'll call you when we have more information, but I suggest you go and get a coffee and something to eat.'

He couldn't eat, but he did get his third coffee of the morning at one of the hospital cafés. He used the time to tell work and his family what had happened and where he was. Every one of them offered sympathy, but he wore it uncomfortably. His phone rang while he was emailing Bathurst to update him on his whereabouts. Dr Mistry was summoning him back to ICU with some urgency. This time he was met at the door and the doctor showed him to his tiny office off the main corridor.

'We have stopped the bleed and the measures we have taken to reduce the brain swelling and associated intracranial pressure are working. We will start to bring her round in a few hours if she continues to make the progress she has demonstrated since this morning. Her liver disease is, however, very advanced and I'm afraid very probably irreversible. She has some form of hepatitis. We will know soon which variant we're dealing with, but it won't change the outcome. A transplant seems to be the only course of action.'

Seb took a moment to process this. He paced around the room, arms folded for a moment.

'How long will she have to wait?'

'Well...'

The briefest of pauses, but it was deafening.

'...that is something the liver specialist will discuss with Sophia's parents when they get here.'

He knew more than he was letting on. As he was thinking about what they could be hiding from him, a penny dropped.

'Hepatitis. Sexually transmitted. Oh my God. I could have given her this.'

'And she could have passed it to you. For now, that is not important. But we do need to get you tested as soon as possible. There are a number of treatment options with very good outcomes, particularly as you are currently fit and well. And there is no certainty that you will have contracted the disease.'

The focus being diverted to his wellbeing felt impossibly perverse.

Chapter 35

'There's nothing wrong with me! She's the one lying unconscious in there.'

Seb's raised voice caused Dr Mistry to take half a step back. He gathered himself.

'I'm sorry, doctor. I know you're all doing your best.'

Before he could respond, Seb's phone rang. The same overseas number.

'It's Sophia's mum. Can I take it in here?' Seb asked.

'Please do, I'll be outside.'

'Sebastian, we're about five minutes away. Where is Sophia?'

Her mother was speaking with urgency, but not panic.

'She's in intensive care on the third floor. I'll meet you in the main reception area and show you the way.'

CHAPTER 36

He hurtled down the stairs to reception with little idea of what to expect, even less of what to say. He should not be meeting Sophia's parents this way. A black cab pulled up and they stepped out as he reached the front entrance. They hurried into the building, her mother with just a handbag and her father with a small overnight case, with no idea as yet where they would be going with it.

'Seb?'

'Mrs Deschamps.'

'Jude, please.'

She hugged him fiercely and Serge Deschamps' handshake was no less robust. They'd never met, but they weren't strangers.

'How is she?' Jude asked resolutely, as they made their way in together.

'She's doing OK. I'll show you up.'

Seb led them up to ICU and waited in the family room while they spent time with Dr Mistry, and then at Sophia's bedside.

They came back forty minutes later, their faces taut as they tried to digest what they'd been told.

Chapter 36

'They say she has hepatitis. They asked us how she could have contracted it, Sebastian. They want to speak to you and get you tested. I don't really know what to say. She had some piercings in Thailand. She said they were safe and clean, but you can't know. She's had boyfriends. I don't know. I don't suppose it matters now. We just need to save her.'

It was Jude Deschamps who spoke, Serge standing beside her in silent support. She walked up to Seb and reached forward to hold his hands in hers.

'I hope to God you're not sick too.'

At that moment, the door opened, and Dr Mistry came in with a tall grey-haired man in a threadbare white coat and half-moon spectacles. The ranking doctor spoke.

'I am Professor Harrison. I'm the senior consultant hepatologist here at the Chelsea and Westminster. Dr Mistry and his team will manage her head trauma, and I will treat her liver disease. Sebastian, we have shared with Sophia's parents that she has acute liver failure caused by an underlying hepatitis infection. As you will doubtless know, most forms of common viral hepatitis are transmissible through sexual intercourse. So, we need to establish your own health, and while you show no obvious signs of liver disease, it would appear that Miss Deschamps didn't either. We rarely see end stage liver failure without some prior warning, but it does happen, generally masked by the usual complaints of modern life. I need to caution you all to the fact that her condition is acute. Her disease is very advanced and that's left us with just one single treatment option, a liver transplant. We'll treat the underlying disease, of course, and do everything we can to preserve what is left of the diseased organ, but we cannot predict with any degree of accuracy how long it will continue to perform a useful role. Furthermore, it transpires that Miss Deschamps has an unusually rare phenotype which makes a compatible match harder to find. In practical terms, that means that despite being at the front of the queue she may not survive long enough to receive an organ from the national register.'

They were stunned into silence and looked aghast at Harrison as he produced three trifold pamphlets from his white coat.

'We will continue with the viral and immunological tests but as I fear time is not on our side, we had better get going. Live liver donation. It's all in here. All Miss Deschamps' blood relatives should be made aware of it. Common procedure these days.'

'Sophia's an only child.'

'So I understand. That is indeed a shame. Siblings are much the best candidates in these circumstances.'

Jude glared at Harrison, appalled by the absolute pointlessness of that observation.

'I understand however that there are cousins, and I would also suggest that you are both tested without delay. Dr Mistry will help you with that. Let's reconvene in my office at nine o'clock tomorrow to make some plans.'

With that he turned on a sixpence and left the room abruptly before he had to deal with any time-consuming emotional response from his traumatised audience. Aware of the tension caused by his professor's less than tactful lecture, Dr Mistry was the first to break the silence.

'Let me assure you that Professor Harrison is one of the finest liver specialists in the country, and only has Sophia's well-being in mind.'

'Let's hope so,' replied Jude, the expression on her face saying all that needed to be said.

CHAPTER 37

They all three went straight to the phlebotomy unit and had their blood drawn. The surge of adrenalin that had carried them through the last few hours was draining away, and Seb took an unobserved moment to look closely at Sophia's parents. He could see elements of her in both of them. He'd seen photos of them, but he needn't have; her descriptions had been so rich in detail. Her father's face was heavily lined and dignified. Her mother looked a good deal younger than her husband and retained a beauty that she'd passed undiluted to her daughter.

They were exhausted. Jude was the first to acknowledge it.

'Darling, you look dreadful. You must eat a proper meal otherwise you'll end up in here yourself. Seb, do you know somewhere nearby you could feed my flagging husband?''

Before he could answer, Serge protested gruffly.

'Absolument non. Je dois rester ici.'

He continued in English, not to exclude Seb.

'Sophia could wake. I must be here when she does.'

'And you will be. They said it will be a few hours yet, and I'll call Seb if there's any change.'

'And what about you?' asked Serge.

'Her flatmate, Tilly, is due here any moment. I told her that Sophia was still sleeping but she insisted on coming, bless her. I'll pop to the hospital canteen and pick up something if I need it. Now off you go.'

As she kissed her husband, she produced a small blister pack of tablets from her bag and slid them into his jacket pocket.

'I'll count them when you get back, so I will.'

He huffed with mock indignation but took them with him as he was told.

* * *

Seb and Serge walked three minutes down the Fulham Road to the little family run Italian restaurant he'd often been to with Sophia. The owner greeted him enthusiastically.

'No Sophia tonight?'

Seb hesitated. Serge stepped in.

'Today Sophia is sick, but she will be back quite soon we hope.'

The tilt of his head. The tone of his voice. The lack of any detail. It was clear that it was serious, and to be left there.

'Of course. Please send her love from me and Victoria,' he replied, ushering them to a quiet corner table.

They ordered two lasagnes and two glasses of the house red. Under normal circumstances, a proud man wouldn't talk at length about his daughter when meeting her boyfriend for the first time, and Serge Deschamps was undeniably a proud man. But these weren't normal circumstances. So, they ate their pasta and talked about Sophia. Serge was tender and pensive, as he reminisced

Chapter 37

over moments from her childhood, all of them adding colour and depth to the stories she'd already shared with Seb in their brief time together, before he looked across the table and spoke more briskly.

'And what about you Sebastian? Sophia calls her mother every Sunday and we have heard your name a lot in her stories. A soldier. A banker. A man of honour, no?'

He held Seb in a penetrating gaze. There was no aggression in his voice but there was an intensity that tilted the question into an enquiry.

'I'm just a man, M Deschamps, but you should know that I love and honour your daughter. I really don't think anything will ever change that.'

He spoke simply, and from the heart. The truth needed no gilding.

'Bon,' her father said, raising his glass. 'And please! Call me Serge.'

'Serge. And Seb will do for me.'

'Then Seb, I make a toast. May God bless our darling Sophia.' They drank together, as one in their desperation and hope.

Serge put his hand into his pocket and pulled out the tablets, and a tatty envelope. He popped two tablets out of the foil and washed them down with his tumbler of water, one after the other, saying with a shrug,

'My heart sometimes gets a little too boom di di boom.'

He picked up the envelope and pulled out photos of varying sizes and shapes, sun bleached and warped.

'Sophia's mother thought you would like to look at these.'

He carefully and delicately passed each photograph to Seb, one after another, a brief explanation accompanying each one, each precious captured moment described with a tender smile. Sophia as a baby on a picnic blanket. The two-year-old Sophia on her father's shoulders walking through the vines in the height of summer. Her first day at school. Her First Holy Communion. In dungarees as a very tomboyish nine-year-old. The chic teenage skier. A proud family portrait on graduation day. Seb pored over each photo and felt his eyes begin to sting. He gripped himself quickly, but Serge saw clearly enough.

'Non, Seb. We have no time for sadness. There is work to do.'

Serge's sky-blue eyes were glassy, but he would not yield.

CHAPTER 38

Sophia's parents were waiting outside Professor Harrison's office when Seb arrived shortly before nine the next morning. Her intracranial pressure and temperature had spiked in the early hours and the decision was made to halt the tapering of her sedation while they stabilised her. When it became clear that she wasn't going to wake any time soon, Jude had accepted Seb's offer of his spare bedroom on her husband's behalf, and ordered Serge to go and get some sleep, asking Seb to go with him. She'd stayed put at the hospital all night.

Seb woke at six and found a note by the kettle saying simply, 'See you at 09.00. Serge,' written in a spidery hand.

At exactly 09.00, Harrison opened his door and ushered Sophia's parents in.

'Mr Faber, if you would be so kind as to wait outside for a few minutes. What I have to say concerns only Sophia's parents.'

With the flash of a forced smile, Harrison shut the door in his face.

'Do take a seat M and Mme Deschamps. OK, first things first. The trauma team conducted an MRI on Sophia's head, and the preliminary indications are good. The bleeding has stopped, and the swelling is significantly reduced. That, combined with her relative lucidity on arrival and the fact that she had no obvious peripheral neurological problems, continues to bode well. Now, to the underlying condition. Sophia has Hepatitis B. How she contracted it is of no matter at this moment, but I'd venture the roadside piercings in Thailand may be the culprit. What does matter is that the virus has caused a vast amount of damage in a relatively short period of time. The extent of her liver disease is profound and irreversible. Without a transplant, she remains in grave danger. Which brings me to my next point. It is highly unusual, actually something of an anomaly, but neither of you is a suitable donor for Sophia.'

He seemed almost to expect them to join him in his enthusiasm for the rarity of the outcome, something to write up in a peer reviewed journal perhaps, and then gathered himself again.

'We were always very unlikely to recommend that M Deschamps be the donor. The age gap and general health concerns would all but rule out his candidature. But Mme Deschamps, you are still just on the outer envelope of clinical relevance. However, your tissue match result is positive, that is to say, in lay terms, negative. Anyway, there it is.'

They both stared at him with absolute incredulity, trying to take in what they were being told, and understand the consequences. All while attempting to rationalise the gallingly insensitive picture of complacency perched on the desk in front of them.

'What in God's name do we do for her now?'

'Well, Mme Deschamps, we continue to hope for an

Chapter 38

organ to become available from the national register. Which remains a possibility, albeit not one we can rely on. And we, by which I mean you, appeal to everyone who loves your daughter to come forward and get tested.'

Professor Harrison's mobile phone rang.

'You'll forgive me...Harrison, yes, understood.' He hung up. 'Sophia is regaining consciousness. You should go to her. We can continue this discussion later.'

Raging against both the message and the messenger, they hurried straight up to ICU, barely acknowledging Seb as they passed him in the corridor. He held back instinctively to give them some time alone with her, and while he stood there not knowing quite what to do, the eminent Professor popped his head around the corner.

'Mr Faber, a word please.'

Harrison sat down in his button back 'Chairman's' chair and reclined to the precise angle that would allow him to look down his nose through his stage prop spectacles at Seb.

'I'll be brief. Sophia has Hepatitis B, and you didn't give it to her as I am pleased to say that you have tested negative. That means that you are no longer my concern. The best you can do is be supportive of Sophia and help her parents where you can. She's waking up, so give it a minute or two then I would go up and see her.'

He rotated forty-five degrees to his left dismissively, apparently contemplating the multiple framed certificates that covered most of one wall of his office.

'In light of what you've just said, that isn't really the best use of my time, is it Professor?'

Harrison span back to the perpendicular.

'I'm not sure I follow Mr Faber.'

'Well pay attention, and I'll explain.'

CHAPTER 39

The encephalopathy that had caused Sophia's fall came and went in waves. It gave her windows of clarity against a backdrop of semi-consciousness, and she was fully conscious when her parents walked into ICU. Sophia could see the fear in her parents' eyes as they came towards her bed, before they realised that they were being watched. As soon as they saw she was awake, they changed their expressions. Sophia smiled, determined to be equally in control.

'Hi Mum, hi Papa. I'm sorry to put you through all this. Bloody hell, you look worse than I do!'

'I should say so my love. Quite the cry for attention,' said Jude.

'I know I look a sight, but they say my head will be OK, no 'permanent impairment' was I think how they put it,' said Sophia.

'Well done, ma cherie.' Serge was overcome with emotion. He held his daughter's hand and leant forward to kiss her cheek. As he did, he whispered in her ear, 'We will help you my beautiful girl. It will all be good in the end.'

The intensity of her father's feelings alarmed her.

Chapter 39

'What's wrong with me Dad?'

Her father stroked her face and looked up to Dr Mistry. 'Doctor?'

Doctor Mistry spoke with both sensitivity and clarity. It was a blessing that the pompous Professor Harrison had abdicated this responsibility. Sophia wept quietly, which made her parents all the more determined not to. When live donation was explained, she looked into her mother's eyes.

'You've tried, haven't you?'

'We both have my love, but they say we can't help. You wouldn't want any part of our geriatric old livers anyway.'

They all managed a smile as the lie hung in the air, then drifted away harmlessly. Sophia was suddenly and totally overwhelmed. In the few minutes she had been awake she had been swamped with information that changed everything about her life. Trying to absorb it had drained her of all her energy. She took a long deep breath.

'I'm tired, Mum. Could we talk more a bit later?'

Her mother leant forward and held Sophia's freckled cheeks in her hands, as she had done all her life.

'Sleep, my love. We'll be here when you wake up. We like Seb by the way.'

A broad grin broke through the fatigue and fleetingly lit up Sophia's face, before her eyes closed and she was away.

CHAPTER 40

From: HR Department
Sent: 22 December, 09:07
To: Sebastian Faber
Subject: Unauthorised Absence

Seb

It has been brought to our attention that you have been absent from work for large periods without a formal request for compassionate leave or registering annual leave. Any further such absence will be reported to your divisional head and may result in formal disciplinary proceedings.

Please acknowledge receipt of this email and consider this a formal warning.

Regards

Samantha Old
Head of Disciplinary Affairs, Human Resources

Chapter 40

The email sat heavy in his inbox. He read it over again. *Don't react. Breathe. Send a polite reply. No, don't send any reply. Don't give them that, don't give him the joy. Divisional Head? Annual Leave? I've come in every day since Sophia was admitted. Every single fucking day.*

He put his headset on and started dialling Fletcher's extension. Before he pressed the last digit, he stood up and threw his headset against his screens, causing the rest of the sales team to jump like startled rabbits.

He was halfway to Fletcher's office before Bathurst caught up with him.

'No Seb. Not like this.'

He gripped Seb's arm and steered him towards the lifts.

'Time I bought you lunch.'

He had Seb's jacket in his other hand.

'You'll be needing this.'

Of all people, Bathurst would have been the very last one he would have expected to intervene. Nothing was said until the lift doors closed.

'I was blind copied on the email. Total bloody nonsense. Leave it to me.'

The lift doors opened before Seb had the chance to respond.

'City Club I think,' said Bathurst, and marched at a military clip to the Old Broad Street sanctuary.

It was only noon, but the bar was already half full.

'Two pints of bitter please.' Bathurst didn't ask Seb what he wanted.

'We'll have a table in the bar and please decant a half decent bottle of claret. Nothing special.'

Seb had never seen this side of Bathurst. He'd never really seen any humanity in him at all.

'First things first, that email has been sent to get a reaction. So don't give them one.'

Seb was still dumbfounded at his boss's transformation and had the sense to keep quiet. The beers were poured, and he drank a third of his pint in one long draught.

'We can both guess who instigated this. Some sort of test I should fancy. He's effective, but fundamentally, he's a bloody odd bloke. Between you and me, you understand. But he's loyal, and God knows he likes you. Got me my job too, as it happens. Leave the email to me and do your best to let me know about your hospital visits in advance. As long as I know where you are, that'll do for now.'

Before long, they moved to the dining room and shared an uneasy forty minutes eating their stodgy club fare. Seb felt as if he'd bumped into a teacher in the school holidays, who felt obliged to be unnaturally friendly to him.

'Bad business with your young lady. Lots of clever chaps taking care of her no doubt. On her feet before you know it, I'd venture.'

And that was it. Relatively speaking, this was an empathetic eruption, but it was short lived. The moment the last drops of wine were drained from their glasses, Bathurst brought the lunch to an abrupt close.

'Right, let's get back. You go ahead and I'll sort the bill.'

He waved away Seb's offer to pay or even contribute to the bill and was back to being the socially inept man that Seb felt rather more comfortable with.

CHAPTER 41

The days that followed were all-consuming, and testing. Somewhere in the middle of it all, Christmas happened for the rest of the world. Seb made daily visits to the hospital on his way home from work; soon a familiar face at the Chelsea & Westminster, he quickly became fluent in the medical vernacular relating to Sophia's conditions. Her medical team performed an endless series of tests to monitor her brain and liver functions. Her brain function, mercifully, had been saved but her liver was dying and taking her with it.

As each neurological test gave her a future, a liver test swiftly took it away again. Professor Harrison was doing what he could to prolong the remaining functionality, buying as much time as possible while her parents prayed and, more practically, searched for a miracle. By week two all that remained of the head injury was a patch of short hair where her head had been shaved to give the long-since-removed intracranial catheter access. The rescue therapies had taken her out of immediate danger, and she was comfortable. Comfortable, bar the fact that she was entirely aware she was dying, her renewed mental acuity allowing her to comprehend it in all its horror.

At their daughter's insistence, Sophia's parents left her bedside and the hospital for a few hours for the first time since she was admitted. They'd resisted it ferociously, but in the end Sophia told them to 'bugger off and let me sleep'.

Jude's phone rang while she was holding up a strappy top against an obliging sales assistant in a boutique on The Kings Road, buying Sophia a special something to give her a lift even for a moment. She'd left her husband, not much of a one for shopping, drinking coffee and reading Le Monde in a café a few doors down.

'Mme Deschamps, Professor Harrison, come in as soon as you can. Sophia has taken a turn for the worse.'

'What? Oh Christ, what's happened?' said Jude.

'I'll explain when you get here. Are you far?'

She dropped the blouse on the counter and ran out of the shop to the café, where Serge was sitting at an outside table in the winter sunshine.

'The hospital called...'

Nothing more needed to be said. Serge had seen his wife running towards him and was on his feet dropping a handful of coins onto the table before she spoke. He hailed a taxi with a savagery that made nearby pedestrians jump out of their way. They were only a ten-minute walk from the hospital, but it would be a one-minute taxi ride.

Professor Harrison was waiting in the reception area when they arrived, which only added to their terror. A man with his level of self-regard wouldn't do that unless in extremis. He didn't make eye contact with either of them. Arrogance or nerves?

'Come with me. We'll talk on the way up. Sophia's liver function has collapsed to almost nothing in the last hour.

Chapter 41

That has put an enormous strain on the rest of her organs which means her heart and lungs are now compromised as well. We're managing each as best we can and have halted her decline, but I need to be clear with you that we've entered a new phase.'

Sophia was back in ICU, the curtain drawn around her bed. She was partly sedated and back on all the life support infrastructure she'd started on weeks before. They tried not to show their shock at her appearance. Their poorly masked alarm was difficult to hide, but thankfully her drug-induced torpor saved Sophia from seeing the truth in her parents' eyes. Her jaundiced, gaunt face had lost all its lustre. Her eyes were sunken, her lips dry and flaky.

'We're here my darling. We are right here,' said Jude, holding Sophia's lifeless hands in both of hers.

There was nothing more she could say. Their daughter was ebbing away in front of them. Serge had seen enough. He turned to Professor Harrison, standing behind them.

'You come with me,' he said, jabbing his index finger viciously at Harrison's white coated chest. He strode into the corridor and Harrison followed.

'What will it take to save my daughter?'

'We will do everything we can to recover the function of the other failing organs but if she doesn't receive a transplant very soon, she will be even more highly compromised.'

'You mean she could die?!'

'Yes, I do, M Deschamps.'

Serge Deschamps walked around the corridor in circles, kneading his forehead with his weathered hands. He stopped abruptly.

'You can buy a liver, no?'

'Actually no, you can't. That's an illegal practice in Britain and most progressive western societies, M Deschamps. Some Asian countries have an underground trade in human tissue, but the incidence of infection and rejection compared to NHS performed transplants is unacceptably high to justify the risk. Quite apart from that, Sophia is far too ill to travel, so it's completely out of the question.'

'But she won't get one here, will she? If this was your daughter, what would you do? Tell me! What should I do?'

His roar of despair echoed down the barren hospital corridor. He was shaking with frustration. 'We can't help her. We can't save my daughter!'

'M Deschamps, try to stay calm. My advice is that you continue to ask as many friends and family to come forward as you can. She's already at the highest level of priority for a cadaverous organ, and we'll do everything we can to stabilise her and maintain all her other functions in the meantime. Beyond that, I'm afraid there is nothing more we can do, unless of course you are given to prayer. In which case I can gladly direct you to the hospital chapel.'

On any other day Serge would have punched him, but he was already halfway down the corridor, in the opposite direction to the chapel.

CHAPTER 42

Seb was oblivious to this terrifying escalation because he was stuck at work, sitting in a meeting room without his phone, unaware that it had been peppered with missed calls and messages. He was sitting across the table from the very last person in the whole wide world he wanted to see; Richard Barnard, waiting for Seb to deliver a pitch to his board of directors. As far as Seb was concerned, Blounts had already won the IPO mandate, and the meeting was merely a chance to bring the non-Exec directors up to speed. He'd spent the previous evening preparing the slide deck. It was rushed, and largely generic. In part because he hadn't had a decent night's sleep since Sophia was taken ill, but mainly because he couldn't have cared less. He'd done the best he could to adapt previous pitch documents to fit the new mandate, and Saki had sent him some slides on the target markets for an appetite suppressant. Seb had produced two slides on the investor marketing process himself, including a list of institutions they would expect to approach.

He sat down on the opposite side of the table to the client with Simpson, Fletcher and Saki on either side. After some trivial small talk led by Fletcher, centring on England's rugby supremacy over the Springboks, they handed round the slide decks and started to turn the pages. Simpson set the scene by reeling off stats on how much money Blounts had raised for client companies in the past three years and had found several ways to manipulate the data to demonstrate that they ranked first in several league tables, all of them entirely of his own making. Fletcher had a slide on equity capital markets that he rattled through, managing to deploy the phrase 'my team' seven times. Saki then demonstrated his specialist knowledge of the subject matter, which included a valuation slide. Seb's blood suddenly ran cold. The valuation range that the unbiddable analyst had come up with was between seventy and ninety million. The same price as the previous venture capital round, and a hundred and thirty million pounds lower than the value Barnard had suggested to Seb on the golf course.

Seb hadn't read Saki's slides. He'd just copied and pasted them into the deck as the final action before he'd saved it and sent it off for printing. Fletcher and Simpson were seeing it for the first time too. Before Saki could deliver his company valuation, the final bullet on the slide, Barnard erupted.

'What is this?'

He jabbed at the presentation with such force that the coffee cups all rattled in their saucers. Saki continued manfully.

'This is my price range based on a discounted cash flow model, with the assumptions all set out on the bottom of the slide. We can obviously play around with the assumptions.'

'Play around? Yes, you play around with them Mr Patel, because you clearly have no understanding of the size of the markets we're addressing.'

Chapter 42

'Well, I do Mr Barnard, but as your drug candidate has very little clinical data, I have to apply a low probability to your revenue projections, and a heavy discount rate to the cash flow arising from them.'

Simpson and Fletcher were throwing daggers at Saki, who was now under a full-blown attack from all sides. All bar one. Just before the two senior men could speak, Seb stepped in.

'He's right, Richard.'

Barnard, and the rest of the suits in the room, were temporarily stunned into silence. Seb continued.

'Saki is one of the most respected biotech analysts in London. He knows exactly what he's doing. His challenge is that H57 currently only has anecdotal evidence of efficacy, strong though that may be. If I were to be candid, his valuation is arguably generous for what you have today.'

Barnard's board were all watching their CEO as they would a lit firework before it launches. Seb was heading straight towards it.

'However,' he went on, 'your ongoing Phase 2 trial will report before we come to market and that will allow Saki to change his discount rate and risk adjustment factors, which will generate the net present value you, and we, think fair.'

He managed to keep his breathing slow and heart rate down as he faced off with Barnard. But it wasn't over.

'Would it not have been a good idea to model that scenario Mr Patel? Your people are well known for your diligence are they not?' probed Barnard.

Racial profiling, discrimination scarcely dressed up as a compliment. Saki was well capable of handling this moment, but it was Fletcher's turn to sound presidential.

'And he is, Richard. We'll model the upside scenarios

and get them to you later this evening. Let's move on to the more interesting bit of who we will target as cornerstones in the listing. Seb?'

Seb managed to stretch two slides over ten minutes, miraculously without repeating himself or running dry. He knew just enough about the European biotech market to make a respectable show of it; he did, however, have to make a concerted effort to look as if he cared one way or the other.

Johan Smith, Barnard's Finance Director, didn't say a single word. Both of the crusty old non-Exec Directors asked a few process-related questions to which they already knew the answers, purely to justify their fifty thousand pound directors' fees and first-class travel from their country homes, at which point Fletcher abruptly concluded the meeting.

'If all that's settled then, let's take this discussion to No 1 Lombard Street. I have a table booked for one o'clock. Seb, Saki, we won't drag you out. I know you both have plenty to be getting on with.'

Seb looked at Fletcher and then Simpson, whose very slight shake of the head acknowledged the hierarchical slight that had just been handed out to the two most junior people in the room.

As they filed out of the room Seb felt a sharp tug on his upper arm. He spun round to find Barnard's face almost pressed against his.

'You'll remember our chat at Sunningdale. It will help with any questions of valuation, I hope.'

'I remember. Don't worry,' said Seb, as neutrally as he could.

They all squeezed into the lift, Saki and Seb stepping out

at the first floor.

Just as the lift was closing, Barnard fired his parting shot.

'Sebastian. You never said that your brother was a cricketer.'

CHAPTER 43

Naturally, Sophia's parents ignored Professor Harrison's superfluous offer of the hospital chapel and focused all their energy on finding a donor. They appealed desperately to both sides of the family, calling their siblings directly to explain the heart-breaking situation they faced. Three aunts, four uncles, eleven first cousins. Included in that list was Jude's brother-in-law, the last person on earth she would ever want them to have to ask for help. Pascal Deschamps had never attempted to hide his dislike of her. In his eyes she was a flighty Irish woman living in the house he grew up in; a house in which he could no longer feel at home.

She didn't have to suffer the awkwardness for long. Pascal flatly refused to submit himself or any of his family to the tests. He answered unequivocally that he and his wife were too old to be of use, and his children too young to have their own lives endangered in such a way.

'You cannot say there is no risk. There is always risk. And don't approach my children. They would make their decision from the heart, and they have their own lives to lead.'

Serge had started the conversation calmly enough,

Chapter 43

but erupted when his brother dismissed their request so absolutely and with so little thought. Jude was standing close by her husband and could tell how the exchange had ended without any explanation.

The conversations with Sophia's Irish aunts and her uncle went quite differently. They all volunteered themselves without hesitation and said they would discuss the situation with their children, who would have to make their own decisions. As they talked, it turned out that both of Sophia's aunts knew their blood type, and neither were compatible donors. Her uncle, an accountant who was the introverted polar opposite of his flibbertigibbet younger sisters, didn't know his blood type. He'd barely been sick a day in his life and had had no reason to. The net result was that Sophia's uncle and all seven of her Irish cousins stepped forward to be screened. As soon as one cousin volunteered, the others followed. Christian duty was as much the force behind their decisions as familial bond; it was the right thing to do. Simple as that. They didn't really know what they were putting themselves forward for. They were anxious about what they knew, but more so of what they didn't, and descended on Cork University Hospital the very next day en-masse.

Five of her seven cousins had the wrong blood type and fell at the first hurdle. Siobhan and Sinead were a blood type match however both, highly unusually, failed the tissue match. It was always a possibility that the family couldn't provide a suitable donor, but given the number of potential candidates, not one that the medical team had thought likely. The whole week was a special torture for Sophia's parents, for Seb and, of course, for Sophia. She was weakening. Her clinical team were using all their collective experience and expertise to keep her organs functioning, to keep her alive, but the trend line was inexorably downwards. Then she was saved.

CHAPTER 44

Serge and Jude found Professor Harrison in his office settled on the edge of his leather topped desk, his Senior House Officer standing awkwardly next to him. Dr Andrews was an earnest looking man of slight build and pallid complexion. He looked as if he'd spent most of his life reading books in dark corners, avoiding natural light and social interaction with equal commitment. Jude gave him a smile to put him at ease.

'We have a compatible organ for Sophia, and we have taken her straight to theatre to prep her for surgery.'

Jude stood stock still save for the slow extension of a hand to grasp her husband's. For a moment, she was silent, staring into Harrison's eyes, searching for anything that might suggest she had misheard or misunderstood. She had not. She and Serge pulled each other close, but there was no sense of celebration. As good as this news was, it was a fresh shock, and the start of a new and dangerous journey. And Sophia's salvation was some other family's tragedy, for the organ to have become available. Jude broke away from her husband and drew breath as she took a moment to contemplate the horror that was unfolding to an unknown family in an unknown place.

'I thank God for this news. I do. But are we to know how this happened? Who our daughter's guardian angel is?'

'In fact, yes. A thirty-two-year-old male of otherwise perfect health. But you can thank him yourself when he comes out of recovery.'

Sophia's parents looked at each other with disbelief, then back to Harrison who was enjoying the moment.

'Seb?' said Jude.

'Indeed,' said Harrison.

He capitalised on the open-mouthed silence of his audience and continued.

'Mr Wallace will perform the surgery. He is our most experienced transplant surgeon so Miss Deschamps and Mr Faber couldn't be in better hands. He will come and see you shortly and give you a quick briefing.'

They were so full of questions they didn't know where to start.

'When did he get tested...Does Sophia know...Why didn't he say?'

'He volunteered. In fact, he insisted on the screening process the moment we knew he was Hep B negative. It took a week of tests to establish his physiological compatibility, but he was warned that the psychological assessment would be more protracted. Living organ donation in the UK has to be approved by the Human Tissue Authority. In essence, it needs to be proved that the donor is of sound mind and understands the near and long-term risks, both physical and mental. Mr Faber and Sophia have both been interviewed by the HTA's independent adjudicator and considering the urgency, they have accelerated their usual ten-day process to just twenty-four hours. Their report has just been emailed

Chapter 44

through and suffice to say, they have approved Mr Faber as a living donor. He and Sophia insisted that it remain private, lest his candidature was ruled out at any point.'

'Oh, God bless him. God bless that boy. It hasn't yet been six months since they met,' said Jude.

'Well, indeed. The brevity of the relationship was the biggest hurdle to overcome. We have a duty of care to the healthy on which the HTA gives no ground. It appears that Mr Faber made a statement that left the panel in no doubt of his commitment. I have read the transcript of the interview contained in the report. He is a man of singular purpose, I must say. We have managed to prolong the useful life of her liver long enough to prevent widespread organ failure. So, she is well enough to undergo the operation, and we can be quietly confident of a positive prognosis.'

For all his social ineptitude, Professor Harrison wasn't the enemy.

'Thank you for all you have done for my daughter and for my family,' said Serge, with a depth of sincerity that was impossible to ignore, even for as cold a fish as Harrison. Completely out of character, the consultant reached out and gave him a reassuring squeeze of the arm.

His haughty facade cracked a little, 'You are so very welcome. I think everything will be OK now.'

So astonishing was this unguarded sentiment from Harrison's lips, it was as if the Lord God Almighty himself had spoken.

'Does Seb's mother know?' asked Jude.

'She does. Sebastian called her half an hour ago when the panel's decision came through.'

Jude made straight for the door and found Mary hovering in the corridor. She went to her with her arms open and engulfed her in a tight embrace. There was no need for words. Serge put his arms around both women and they shared a silent moment of thanks and praise. Professor Harrison, who wasn't quite done with the spotlight after all, reappeared and herded them back into his office.

'Let's have you all back inside. I must go to theatre and brief the surgical teams, but Dr Andrews here has lots of information to share with you that will answer the many questions I know you will have.'

With that, he swept out of his office, leaving Dr Andrews alone with Serge, Jude and Mary. He took a deep breath and summoned all the social and professional confidence he could muster.

'If I may, I will explain what is going to happen now.' And so he did.

After they were fully briefed on the surgical details and the respective post-operative pathways, Dr Andrews walked them up to a waiting room outside the operating theatre, a space smaller and even less appealing than the ICU family room. Four white walls and eight plastic 'easy' chairs. No coffee table. No magazines. A small, miserly framed print of an English rural scene hanging slightly askew.

The barrelling presence of Mr Wallace suddenly erupted into the quiet of the room, as he rattled off what they should expect of Sophia and Seb in the hours and days after their operations. His rumbustious confidence filled them all with hope.

They were all encouraged to go off site and have lunch, even 'do a bit of shopping', as Sophia and Seb would be with the team for three to four hours and the canteen food was 'bloody awful'. He was right about the food, but they weren't going anywhere anyway.

Chapter 44

They sat, and paced, and made shuttle runs to the coffee machine. Jude produced a bag of knitting, the clicking of her needles a comforting, homely soundtrack to their vigil. Mary did The Times crossword, then went to the shop to buy a copy of The Daily Telegraph and rattled through that one too. Serge was encouraged to rest by his anxious wife, and he did try. His eyes closed. His brain stayed wide open.

After an hour a nurse came in, startling them all. Aware of the alarm she was causing just by standing there, she was quick to say that Seb's operation was over, that it was all very straightforward and that he was in now in recovery. He was due to go to the general ward in an hour or so. Some of the tension in the room ebbed for a moment, and Serge and Jude thanked Mary all over again for the phenomenal sacrifice their son was making. And she, once again, deflected it.

* * *

A little under three hours later, Mr Wallace strode boldly into the room.

'All done. No complications. I've done my bit, so it's over to our clever chums in the medical team now.'

A whimsical nod to the age-old tussle between physicians and surgeons. Piano players and piano shifters as the physicians would have you believe. With the enormous weight of anxiety now greatly relieved, they were all three suddenly struck by a tsunami of fatigue. They took a moment to breathe, to take stock, to gather themselves for what lay ahead. But the thing that lay ahead was now a future. It was something they could all find the energy to embrace.

CHAPTER 45

Seb was up and about with no obvious impairment twenty-four hours after his surgery and was discharged three days later. Sophia's was bound to be a more convoluted recovery, but Professor Harrison and his team were there to nudge her back on track whenever intervention was required. Her body had accepted Seb's transplanted liver tissue, and it was functioning as hoped.

Her recuperation was all the speedier for her impatience. After a few days, she started to feel like her old self, and her old self was bored out of her mind. After more than a month lying in a hospital bed, she wanted to re-join society and be part of it again at the very earliest opportunity. Professor Harrison's moment of empathy was not repeated. New patients with their own crises came under his care and demanded his attention. He'd concluded his contractual and moral responsibilities and wished Sophia and her parents a formal farewell. She walked out of hospital with her parents at either shoulder eight weeks to the day from her fall. Seb dashed ahead to take the triumphant photo that would forever document her survival.

The next vital step was to get her parents home. They'd

Chapter 45

been sleeping in her room in the Pimlico flat while she was in hospital, and she needed it back. They'd moved to a two-star hotel round the corner, which was both profoundly unpleasant and unsustainably expensive. They needed to get back home and pick up the life they'd dropped so abruptly eight weeks earlier, and the malodorous nature of the Park Place Hotel helpfully spurred on their departure.

Life as a liver transplant patient was a bit different from her previous life, but as Seb was quick to point out, a lot different from being dead. Sophia, being Sophia, wanted to live life without limits. The fact that she couldn't drink a bottle of wine every evening initially depressed her until she accepted Seb's pointed observation that she'd never drunk a bottle of wine every night of the week. The word 'moderation' was the problem. Sophia wasn't programmed to be moderate. But her situation wasn't the joyless vacuum she'd projected for herself in the early hours and days post diagnosis. They were both thrown out of orbit psychologically, however. The point had been made to them in the consultation phase pre-surgery, with what felt like unnecessary emphasis at the time, that for Sophia having her life saved by Seb, having part of him living inside her, was going to be confusing. It was. She owed him her life and she didn't want to. For Seb, it was like a surprise pregnancy too early in a relationship. It can serve as a bond, but generally doesn't. They were biologically bound together. Obligated to be together, and to stay together. And it was choking them.

At first, they tried talking about it. Then they stopped talking about it. Then they broke up.

As break ups go, it was a poor effort. It began on a Saturday night in a pub in Chelsea. An emotional scene in a neutral location, neither really knowing what they were doing but both with a primal sense that it needed to happen. They left each other alone for seventeen hours and six minutes. Then Seb sent Sophia a three-word text.

I hate this x

Her reply was even briefer.

Me too x

That was all that was said until Seb cracked once again on Monday evening, but this time he picked up the phone and called her. They searched each other's voices for signals while desperately trying to avoid giving them. He suggested they could go to the cinema, and they rationalised the plan for each other.

'No reason why we can't meet as friends… Perfectly normal… We're grown adults, we can make sensible decisions.'

Patent nonsense.

They met outside the Odeon on the Kings Road and hugged nervously. Seb bought the tickets to *The Guru*, an infectiously upbeat tale centred on an Indian Bhangra dance teacher who unwittingly has a brief but high-profile career as a professional sex coach. It was mercifully light-hearted. Seb still couldn't help reaching for her hand which she grasped without hesitation and held throughout. At the end of the film, they shuffled out into the night and hugged again, which became a gentle kiss on the lips, then more lingering. Sophia pulled away.

'What are we doing? This is playing with my head. Please don't mess with my head.'

'I'm sorry.'

They were adrift, at sea and listing. This wasn't working and they both knew it. They hugged one last time and went

Chapter 45

their separate ways. Bewildered and dismayed, they were completely at odds with the cheerful crowd milling around them.

Tuesday, Wednesday and Thursday all came and went. On Friday evening they both had drinks with their own friends, all of whom were at a loss as to why they'd broken up. Both typed multiple text messages and sent none of them. Both concluded that they were no longer wanted, that the other had started to move on, or worse.

After a miserable night, Seb showered, put on his running kit and shut the door behind him. He ran to try to clear his mind. It was 7am on a perfect spring morning, the night crowd not long to bed, the bustle of the day still hours off. As he crossed Albert Bridge, 'her Bridge', a layer of complication fell away. With each stride around Battersea Park his fears lessened, and as they did his strides grew longer and life got simpler. By the time he completed his second lap, he was in no doubt. He ran back to his flat faster than he knew possible. Everything was so blindingly obvious. She was beautiful, smart, creative, and magnificently ungovernable. And she loved him. God, he hoped she still did. Pouring with sweat, he grabbed his phone the second he got back to his flat. It went to voicemail. He had a few seconds to decide whether leaving a message, this message, was a good idea. The beep came while he was still hesitating.

'Soph, it's me. I…um…I need to talk…err give me a call when you get this. Bye.'

Had she screened him? Was it really all over? Fuck! Was she with someone? As he was working himself up into a lather, his phone rang.

'Sorry, missed your call. I'm somewhere in the West Sussex countryside and the reception's shite.'

'Oh. Who with?'

He wished he sounded less anxious. She could hear the panic in his voice.

'At Tilly's parents' house. She decided I needed a decent meal and a change of scene. They've been lovely actually. Long walks and messy dogs.'

Despite her urban chic, Sophia was a country girl at heart. They had projected their future together in countless fantasies, and they all involved long walks and messy dogs.

'I really need to see you. I've been doing a lot of thinking.'

'So have I, Seb.'

The interruption, and pointed use of his name, filled him with dread.

'I've been just so sad all this week, and the only person I want to talk about it with is you,' said Sophia.

'I know, I'm exactly the same. I feel exactly the same.'

They spoke for a little while longer, but Sophia was conscious of being a guest in her friend's home and didn't want to be rude. They made a plan to meet at the café in Battersea Park at five o'clock the next day, which was the earliest possible time she could get back to London given the particularly sumptuous Sunday lunch Tilly's mother had promised them.

Seb got to the café twenty minutes early just in case she had the same idea, but the predictable gridlock in southwest London put paid to that. A few minutes after five she arrived, red in the face and flustered, and found Seb sitting at an outside table overlooking the rowing lake. He leapt up to greet her.

'Let's get a coffee and go for a wander,' said Seb.

It was as perfect an evening as could be imagined. After an unseasonably hot April day, families and groups of young

Chapter 45

Londoners were packing up their picnics and winding up their first jumpers-for-goalposts football games of the year. Lovers, young and old, were drifting in and out of this oasis of calm in the heart of London. And among them, unnoticed, were Sophia and Seb, walking their own path, the direction immaterial. They linked arms and walked down the central boulevard towards the bandstand. At the bandstand, they cut towards the river, crunching over the gravel paths of the ornamental garden.

'I was here yesterday running, and all the stuff we agonised over, the weirdness of this whole thing, just fell away. Whatever it was about, I don't feel it anymore. I just see this beautiful, kooky, freckledfaced girl that I chased off the tube and damn near killed myself to follow.'

She smiled but carried on walking, looking up into the middle distance.

'OK, Sebastian. This is how I feel. I'm young, and you're a man, so neither of us feel quite ready to know our destiny, much less have it forced on us. At the same time, I am completely and hopelessly in love with you, and the idea of anyone else with you...'

She just shook her head.

Without knowing how they got there, they were now on the promenade on the south bank of the river, as the early evening sun start to descend behind Chelsea Bridge. They turned to face each other.

'There is no one else for me,' said Seb.

He pulled her towards him and kissed her slowly and deeply. She kissed him back just as intensely. It was as electrifying as their first kiss, but so much more powerful. They drew away momentarily, just long enough to look into each other's souls, confirming what they already knew, before dissolving into each other again.

Sophia opened her eyes to see a family with four young children approaching them over Seb's right shoulder. She grabbed Seb's hand and marched him on.

'Come on you.'

They walked a little further towards Albert Bridge and found an unoccupied park bench, sitting for several minutes in total silence, watching the world go by.

'Soph.'

'Yes Seb'

'Just so I get this right, have we just got back together?'

'I think we probably have,' she said with a glint in her eye. 'And you owe me a skiing holiday, mister!'

She squeezed his hand and rested her head on his shoulder. Seb could smell the soft fragrance from her hair as she nuzzled into him, and nothing in the world had ever felt more right.

CHAPTER 46

They flew to the mountains four days later. Sophia had listened respectfully to, and equally respectfully disregarded, the notes of caution from her parents. Her wounds had healed, her liver was working perfectly. 'If not now, when?' was her counter, and it was hard to argue against.

Seb's family had been regular visitors to the Alps until his father died. But they initially lost the will, then the wherewithal, to take skiing holidays in the dark years of Seb's decent into delinquency. A decade later he talked his way into the regimental team with the promise of providing maximum entertainment on and off the snow, even if it killed him. He delivered on his promise, and it very nearly had on more than one outing.

Their fellow Gatwick to Geneva passengers were the usual collection of middle class, middle earning, middle England. A homogenous bunch, thought Seb as he looked around, but not all bad. Once checked in and through security they found seats in the departure lounge and Seb was dispatched to get the coffees. He joined the short queue behind a young family. He was just beginning to suspect that there was something familiar in his frame of vision, when he locked eyes with their mum.

'Seb, shit. Wow.'

'Lou?'

Seb looked at Lou, at her husband, and her two little girls.

'Wow. Look what you made.'

They did the double cheek kiss thing, and while Lou remained frozen to the spot, Seb introduced himself to her husband.

'Hi, I'm Seb.'

'Yes, heavens, sorry. Seb this is my husband Dominic, and these two are Flo and Ella.'

The infant kids were peering through their mother's legs at the interesting new man putting their mum and dad on edge. Lou, who had flushed pink and was all of a dither, pulled herself together.

'Seb is an old friend from yonks ago. What's it been, twelve years?'

It had been much less.

'You've been a lot more productive that I have.' Gallant to the last.

If ever a Starbucks server was a hero, it was when theirs placed the coffees and juices on the counter and provided a diversion. Dominic swept them up hurriedly.

'I'll grab a table. Nice to meet you, Seb. Girls, come along.'

Lou held her ground for a moment.

'Where are you off to?'

'Chamonix, just for a few days.'

'Lovely. Are you…'

'With my girlfriend, Sophia, just over there.'

They both turned to look over to Sophia who had her

Chapter 46

face buried in a book. The Starbucks star interrupted again.

'Sir, what will you have.'

Lou took her cue.

'I'll leave you to it. Really nice to see you Seb.'

She re-joined her family and Seb ordered his coffees, avoiding the temptation to check back at Sophia or look at the table where Lou was sitting. He carried their drinks back to Sophia, who looked up from her book with amusement.

'She's pretty.'

Seb thought about responding with some form of explanation but decided against it.

'Isn't she,' he replied with strained nonchalance.

Sophia gave Seb an affectionate little kick and dived back into her dog-eared novel, completely unthreatened by what she had seen. Such was her faith in Seb, and her confidence in herself.

The rest of the journey passed without event, and their coach pulled up in the darkness outside their hotel in Chamonix a few minutes after eight o'clock. They'd booked a room in a small, centrally located hotel which turned out to be occupied by an incongruous mix of a dozen twenty-something Aberdonians, a young family with three pre-school children, and them. The Aberdonians split roughly into two groups. Half were fishermen, for whom the trip represented a once-in-a-lifetime holiday, and half were offshore oil workers who could, if they so chose, go each and every year. All of them completely unintelligible to Sophia, Seb, or anyone not actually born and bred in Aberdeen; their accents were so broad Seb only got one word in three, and Sophia none at all. They endured the backslapping and forced integration of the welcome drinks and, as soon as they could without giving offence to the husband and wife hotel owners, broke away and headed out into town.

They walked on past the Casino and into the pedestrian streets dotted with bars and boutiques, passed by groups of ski boot-clad revellers returning to their accommodation from their après ski venues. Their skis and poles came clattering from their shoulders to the road as they slipped and tripped, miraculously managing to stay more or less upright. Definitely British. They shared the town with highly polished couples in fur lined jackets and blow-dried hair, women and men, sipping double espressos in the cafés. The French. Sophia and Seb were not out to party; they wanted solitude. They turned their backs on the town centre, heading up a narrow lane leading up towards the Brevant mountain on the northern side of the valley.

It had been snowing very lightly when they arrived in the resort, but now the snow was falling in large fluffy flakes foreshortening their horizon and, illuminated by the phosphorous domes lining the lane, cocooning them in a silent pocket of peppered light. The lane rose up and out of the village where it joined the footpath that followed the east-west line of the valley, lying just below the steep forested slopes of the mountain. They turned left towards the cable car station and a few minutes later found themselves at the bottom of the piste. High above them, a group of piste bashers were going about their nightly routine, lighting up small sections of the mountain as they carried out their work with practised efficiency. It was irresistible, Seb and Sophia ran straight up the slope until they were out of puff, and collapsed on the snow, looking down over the town below.

Out of sight, 3842m up in the darkness, loomed the Aigille de Midi, the cable car station that was the departure

Chapter 46

point for the Vallée Blanche, the world famous 20km off-piste trail which ran over a deeply crevassed glacier looping round to the Chamonix valley. Seb had skied it once before and hadn't much liked the experience. He and two fellow members of the Regimental Team, all profoundly hungover, had had to concentrate very hard indeed not to be blown off the mountain before the skiing even began. The eighty metre walk down a knife edge arête was hard enough to negotiate without fifty mile an hour gusts trying to carry them off into the abyss. He'd been scared witless, and the memory of it was still vivid. For a paratrooper, Seb didn't much like heights.

'Shall we ski the Vallée Blanche tomorrow? The snow will be perfect,' said Sophia.

'Yeah, why not,' Seb replied.

His chest had tightened as he agreed to the plan, and silence resumed. They drew each other close and gazed over the hazy vista below; their footprints in the snow were already obscured.

CHAPTER 47

They woke up to a Wedgwood blue sky. The snow had continued to fall until the early hours of the morning, and they were woken by the scraping sounds of shopkeepers and hoteliers clearing pathways and pavements. They'd fallen into deep sleep quickly, the result of fatigue, a little wine and blissful post-coital collapse. That sleep had, however, been rudely interrupted by the noisy return of the Aberdonians at three in the morning. They'd set up camp in a room next to theirs, but Seb's strong suggestion that they call a halt, delivered in his boxer shorts but with unmistakeable resolve, had driven them down to the dining room and ultimately the kitchen, where they had helped themselves to the wine and generally been something of a nuisance. The broken furniture could be passed off as accidental, defecation in the Nutella jar could not. The Gendarmes removed them all at gunpoint before breakfast.

Seb and Sophia were tired, but the crispness of the air and the magnificence of the freshly covered mountain-scape soon refilled them with energy. They had breakfast, hired skis and presented themselves at the ESF office at 08.30 to hire a guide. Despite their remarkable efficiency, however,

Chapter 47

keener and better organised observers of weather forecasts had anticipated the perfect conditions and had booked all of them days in advance. Seb and Sophia conferred. There were many ways to navigate the Vallée Blanche, and though a guide was advisable, and an absolute necessity for all but one route, they both had some knowledge of the mountain, and the conditions were as perfect as could be hoped for. Partly driven by a mutual wish to impress, they decided to press on and ski the 'Route Classique', the relatively benign and most travelled route from peak to valley.

The journey from the valley floor to the Aiguille de Midi station was breath-taking. The highest cable car in the world ascends to within nine hundred and thirty metres of Europe's highest peak.

The cabin was full to capacity, with lots of nervous chatter in several languages. A nuggety ESF guide with long grey hair contained by a white towelling sweatband was briefing his group of half a dozen young Englishmen. The deep crevasses in his bronzed leathery face told their own stories.

'Follow exactly my path. No overtake. Wide base like zees. Enjoy yourselves, huh. You're on 'oleeday!'

Sophia and Seb leant into each other and enjoyed listening in. The cabin docked on arrival at the top station and everyone disembarked, following the signs that led them through a granite tunnel to the departure point which was on foot, down the arête.

The gradient of the slopes on either side of this knife edge meant that anyone unfortunate enough to lose their footing died, their bodies eventually recovered on the lower slopes some thousand metres below. Every few years someone did. Those with guides, the overwhelming majority, stopped in the tunnel where their poles were collected and bound into one manageable bundle to be strapped to the guide's back, more Sherpa then ski guide. This was to give their clients a free hand to hold onto the safety rope, while the other held their skis. The guides then roped their clients together and in turn to themselves; a safety measure that generally heightened their terror rather than lowering it.

'Let's get out ahead of these guys, Soph.'

She nodded in agreement. Once out of the tunnel, the arête lay before them, and beyond it in every direction, endless alpine peaks were set against a cerulean sky. Just as Sophia and Seb were about to comment on the extraordinary panorama, a gust of wind along with a complementary barrage of snow jabbed at them without warning, very nearly knocking them off their feet.

'Fuck! Let's get this done. Give me your poles and stay close,' said Seb.

Sophia handed over her poles to Seb who tied them together with his, and onto his backpack with the length of cord he'd always kept in the bag, but until that point had never actually used. They set off down the path, Seb in front on the basis that if he fell, his fourteen and a half stone bulk would probably take her with him, but he could probably cope with her eight stone frame if she tumbled into him. They made their way down the steep path at a sensible pace until it branched off in two directions. The wind continued to lash at them. They needed to get off this ledge. The path to the left was longer and more serpentine, but a lesser gradient. To the right, there was a steep descent down frozen snow steps, but a more direct line to the plateau where they could put on their skis. His first experience of the arête had been on the right-hand path and, after a cursory look, he decided

Chapter 47

on the left. They snaked their way back on themselves as it carved a channel in the two-metre-deep snow, a welcome but temporary respite from the wind. As the path hairpinned once again, the full extent of the precipice opened up before them. They both instinctively tightened their grip on the guide rope, taking even greater care as they placed each bootstep on the icy path. After eighty metres of acute concentration, the path fanned out to a hard, windswept plateau on which they swiftly unbound the poles, clipped themselves into their skis and started the descent.

Now off the plateau and out of the wind, the fun really started. They saw the peak of Mont Blanc to their right and dozens of junior peaks jostling for attention in front of them. Seb set off first, but before long Sophia had overtaken him effortlessly. The elegance of her movement, the strength, balance and courage that it implied, was mesmerising. Seb was centred, balanced and strong. Nothing flamboyant, but perfectly functional. Sophia continued to make great sweeping turns down the centre of the Glace du Mer, leaving uniform parallel tracks in the virgin snow. Seb, giving his competitive instincts free rein, let his skis run and drew level with Sophia halfway down the upper section of the glacier. For a kilometre they skied side by side, intermittently crossing in front of each other, creating a double helix pattern in their wake. And as with each strand of DNA, separate but inexorably bound together on the same journey. As they reached the vast left-hand turn to the lower section of the plateau, Seb drew ahead by a few metres and stopped, giving time and space for Sophia to react and join him. They were euphoric, experiencing a shared joy that neither had ever known before. They locked hips and kissed.

'That was amazing. You are amazing,' said Seb.

She felt the full force of him. His love. And she yearned for it. She loved him. She drew her lips away from his, looked up, and paused.

'I love you, Seb.'

He held her gaze and drank in every glorious detail of her smiling face.

'And I love you, Sophia Deschamps. I will always love you. Will you marry me?'

He hadn't planned it, and she hadn't expected it, but he didn't have time to worry.

'Yes. Oh, God, yes!'

And they stood alone in the brilliant sunshine, cradled by the peaks, swept up in a moment that would change them forever. Sophia wasn't thinking entirely clearly, but she knew she needed this miraculous moment to be recorded. The first of the guided ski groups was approaching, and she waved frantically at the guide to attract his attention, digging around in Seb's backpack for her tiny new digital camera.

'Monsieur, désolé pour vous arrêter...'

'Pas de problème, comment puis-je aider?'

'S'il vous plait, pouvez-vous prendre une photo. Nous venons sommes engagé'

The camel train of six Englishmen had now all arrived at the scene.

'Engaged! Shit man. No way. Congratulations!' And a spontaneous round of muffled, gloved applause erupted. The enthusiastic whooping that followed attracted the attention of the next two groups descending the glacier and within a couple of minutes their solitary, intimate moment was being shared by twenty-five happy, smiling faces, as

Chapter 47

joyfully spontaneous as the engagement itself. The photos were taken and soon there was something that resembled a reception line, with every member of the impromptu gathering filing past Seb and Sophia on their skis, delivering their hearty congratulations. Then they were alone again. Forever changed.

They wanted to let their families know, to share their delight, and hurriedly checked their phones. Seb had no reception, but Sophia had one bar. She called her mother. The phone rang but after a few seconds the line went dead as the solitary bar withered away. It would have to wait.

'Let's get off this mountain and celebrate!' And with one final lingering kiss, they set off down the mountain.

The mid-section of the Vallée Blanche was steeper and more crevassed than the top. With self-preservation firmly in mind, they followed the precise line that the first guide had chosen for his group and picked their way down to the third section, a gentle six kilometre cruise down the terminal moraine field at the snout of the glacier. There followed the central, partially tracked-out trail which snaked around the car-sized granite boulders defining the structure of the lower glacier. The skiing was undemanding and gave them plenty of time to take in everything around them.

Seb's phone buzzed in his pocket and, without stopping, he fished it out to see who it was. It was a text from Fletcher. An abrupt message just saying, 'Call me'.

'I've got a text, so my phone's got reception. We can call our parents.'

'Great. Let's call when we get to the end. The steps up to the train are just down there,' said Sophia, pointing it out with her pole. 'Who is it anyway?'

'Work. Nothing important' said Seb, starting to stuff the

phone back in his pocket.

Sophia skidded to a halt in front of Seb, forcing him to take quick action not to collide with her.

'It's your bloody boss, isn't it? What does he want now?' Sophia asked impatiently. 'Nothing. Usual crap, but who cares.'

She snatched the phone out of his hand and read the message.

'Enough now!'

She pushed off down the mountain, picking up speed and putting some distance between them. Still moving, she took off her mittens, tucked them in her jacket, and tapped out a message with her thumbs, half an eye on what was in front of her. Then she span round one hundred and eighty degrees and continued down the track skiing backwards. Seb, who'd hared off after her, was just a few feet away.

'Sorry. Had to be said. We don't need him now,' said Sophia, eyes full of laughter, and she tossed the phone back to him. Seb caught it and looked down, his eyes fixed on the screen.

So, he didn't see it coming.

CHAPTER 48

Sophia was declared dead on arrival at the hospital, but she was gone long before that. She had been killed instantaneously, they said. The contact with the boulder was catastrophic. The rock that had thrown her off balance was half-buried under the fresh snow. Had she been facing forwards she would have seen it. Even if she hadn't, her arms would have taken some of the impact, and she would have lived. She would be alive now. Loving him. Not dead. Not fucking dead.

Seb had watched it all unfold. Utterly helpless. She was bleeding from the impact site and from both ears. Not breathing. Lifeless, dilated eyes. He performed CPR exactly as he had been trained to do, but his training also told him there was no hope. She was gone. He screamed for help, knowing there could be none. A final appeal to a God he had long abandoned and who had now abandoned her. The first guided group of skiers were out of earshot. He had to wait ten minutes for the next group to arrive. More panic. More redundant first aid. A helicopter summoned, but the paramedics took their time with Sophia. No call for haste. Her delicate face was still happy. Still, and forever, to be loved.

CHAPTER 49

The petrified silence of the emergency room cubicle was disturbed by buzzing. Sophia's phone was ringing in her jacket pocket. Seb unzipped it and retrieved the phone. *Mum M* illuminated on the screen. The phone smelt of Sophia.

'Jude, it's Seb. Sophia called you to say that we got engaged. But then she fell. She hit her head on a rock. She's dead, Jude. Sophia's dead.'

Three people died that day.

CHAPTER 50

It wasn't until he lay in bed, their bed, in the first of the unbearable, endless, sleepless hours to come, that he looked at the sent messages on his phone.

Not today…today he's all mine!

Sophia (Faber!)

CHAPTER 51

Jude was not made for this. Her heart was too open. Total incredulity, followed by horror, followed by incalculable despair. All light was extinguished. Cut off from life forever, a glass wall between her and the rest of the world. The first weeks saw her fly into spontaneous fits of violent fury; against property, her husband, herself. She had attended Mass every Sunday of her life. She had prayed to Jesus, Mary and all the saints to give thanks for the gift of parenthood. The gift of Sophia. Jude's life had overflowed with a happiness that filled her every day. She had a purpose, and that was to cherish her little girl, and keep her safe, so that Sophia too would one day enjoy the divine joy that motherhood, and only motherhood, offered. But now that treasure had been ripped away. For no reason. There could be no conceivable greater meaning; there was nothing but the purest form of agony. The daily torture of the few seconds of peace on waking, followed by the devastation, relived hour after hour, day after day. There was no escape in the conscious world. Jude's free-thinking, unburdened spirit laid her emotions bare. No curtains to draw or shutters to fasten to keep some part of her functioning. She was demented. She denounced her God, in foul language that would previously have been unimaginable.

Serge withdrew into himself, binding to the horror so tightly that it had no space for expression. His rigid lack of emotion only aggravated his wife's hysterical episodes. He walked his fields, seeing ghosts of Sophia behind every vine. He'd taken to sleeping in the afternoons, any means of avoiding the naked truth. His darling girl was dead. His only beloved child. His hope and his future. And he feared the pain so much that he locked it all away in the depths of his being and used all his energies to keep it there.

CHAPTER 52

Seb was with Sophia's parents the night before the funeral. They sat around the kitchen table while he tentatively showed them the photos on the mountain, and shared the story of their trip and their engagement. Serge took the pictures from Seb apprehensively, taking a moment to gather himself before looking down at each precious image. Jude, her head on her husband's shoulder, looked on. They seemed to take some comfort from knowing that Sophia had been as happy as she had ever been on that day. The unrestrained joy shining out from the photos even made them smile a little; it was a look they knew well in their life-loving daughter.

It didn't last, and Seb didn't stay to eat. Jude was engulfed by the agony of grief again, distraught, shrinking back into the rocking chair in the corner of the kitchen, weeping and staring around sightlessly. Serge took Seb by the shoulder and walked him towards the front door.

'This is not my darling wife. You must not see her like this. But when she can find life again, I know she will want to have you in our lives.'

As Serge opened the door, Seb stopped and turned to Jude.

Chapter 52

'I'd give anything for us to have her back. I can't do anything at all to change what's happened, but you need to know that in the last minutes, hours and days of her life she was as happy as it's possible to be. And that she talked about you both every day. Every single day.'

He was sobbing now.

'She loved you with every bone in her body, and she loved me. I was so blessed to have her love. I'll carry her with me every day for the rest of my life.'

Jude looked up and stopped rocking, moving over to Seb and holding him close. She couldn't speak, but her loving maternal impulse was strong. She was simply following her natural instinct to give comfort to someone in distress, a first step on the journey towards her survival. It would never be the life she longed for, but it would be a life.

CHAPTER 53

The funeral was held in the medieval village church where her parents were married and Sophia was baptised, had taken her first Holy Communion and been confirmed. Jude was guided by her husband's and sister's steady supporting arms as she took her place at the front of the church.

Seb was tortured by thoughts of what would never be. They would have been married in this church. They would have drawn crowds of tourists as their gaily dressed friends walked up the ancient, cobbled street. The bells would have rung for them. The whole village would have turned out. Her father would have wept with pride and joy and suffered the natural feeling of loss in sharing his daughter with another man, another family. Seb could only imagine how Serge must long now for that benign loss.

He was there with his family but no friends. Many of them had offered to travel to France to support him, but he'd politely and firmly declined. The church was full of people who had known Sophia all her life. Her aunts and cousins. Her school friends and university mates. The community of farm labourers. Local shopkeepers. The dentist. Doctor. Mayor. This was not the celebration of a

Chapter 53

life that could be appreciated. Not yet. Despite the heartfelt and well-meaning eulogy from the priest, it was impossible for anyone there to find any meaning in this appalling waste.

There were two more eulogies; one from her French Godfather and another from her Irish Aunt Margaret. They both spoke of the essence of Sophia. She was so interesting and so very kind. She captured attention with her creativity, her beauty, but she listened as much as she spoke, not just waiting for a moment to get her next point across, but really listening, wanting to understand what she was hearing, and what lay behind the thought. She filled a room with her infectious presence but wanted others to flourish around her. Her death removed colour from life. It changed verse to prose, and prose to bullet points.

Seb listened intently. He had known death, but nothing could be like this. He was at the funeral of the girl he loved, the girl he was going to marry, and yet he felt like an outsider in a sea of unfamiliar faces. Perhaps they blamed him. Perhaps they should.

The wake was originally planned for the Deschamps' house but moved to the tasting barn to cope with the number who wanted to be there. Some declined the offer of wine out of respect; it wouldn't feel right. Some drank quickly and silently. A group of half a dozen of her London friends formed a circle and drank at pace, sharing their stories about Sophia, their own form of catharsis and remembrance. Jude contained her grief long enough to support her husband as they circulated amongst the mourners, accepting their condolences and thanking them for their kindness. When she saw Mary, they embraced as would sisters. Neither woman spoke; there was no need. When they let go, they looked into each other's eyes and

Mary simply said, 'I know.'

Seb stayed close to his family nursing a glass of wine, avoiding getting pulled into any of the huddles, until he felt a tap on the shoulder. He turned round to be met with the moist eyes of Sophia's flatmate, Tilly.

'I know you saved her life. She swore me to secrecy and nobody else knows. But I know. And I think you're a bloody hero.'

'I'm not, you know.'

She didn't respond but kissed him on the cheek.

'Come and meet the rest of the gang. They'd love to meet you.'

'You're kind, Tilly, but I won't.'

'OK, but we're not going anywhere, so if you change your mind.'

'Sure. Thanks, Tilly. Really, thank you.'

As Tilly walked back to her group, Seb grabbed a bottle and took himself away from the crowd. He walked up to a solitary tree on the hill behind the house, sat down and poured himself a glass. His family had all seen him take his leave and let him be for a while, but after twenty minutes or so, his mother looked up at the forlorn figure in the distance, then to Emily and Harry.

'Go to your brother,' she said, and they set off together in the dying light. When they reached the tree they sat down on either side of Seb, shoulder to shoulder and offered up their empty glasses which he filled. They shared a few minutes of mutual reflection until, with an empty bottle in hand, Seb broke the silence.

'Time to go. isn't it.'

'Yes, it is,' Emily replied, kindly but without hesitation.

And with his sister's words and a knowing smile from

Chapter 53

his brother they headed back to the wake, said goodbye to Sophia's parents and set off for home.

CHAPTER 54

Seb was offered a week of informal compassionate leave after Sophia's funeral. He rejected it, which was a mistake. The staggering banality of stockbroking came into even sharper focus. He went to work in a haze and conducted his tasks mechanically, courteous enough to avoid drawing attention, exuding enough passive hostility to repel the pity that was magnetically drawn to him. Then it would hit him like a runaway bus. Abject despair. Which became rage, and then apathy, a cycle that repeated itself a dozen times a day.

He got through the Monday by making a series of pointless calls to clients who had never known of Sophia's existence and were equally unaware of her death. He collected the endless feedback comments from results meetings for the companies he represented. It was 'results season', so fund managers were seeing five companies a day and were expected to provide helpful commentary to be fed back to the management teams, all to the greater good but of whom or what it wasn't entirely clear. It was mindless, but for now the constant activity provided a haven from the well-intentioned but draining sympathy of his colleagues.

He left the office the second the market closed and went

Chapter 54

straight home. He turned off his mobile phone, emptied a tin of tuna and a tin of sweetcorn into a bowl, put Donnie Brasco in the DVD player, and concentrated hard, trying to force himself to think about anything and everything apart from the only thing he could.

CHAPTER 55

On the Tuesday morning, Seb's direct line rang.

'Seb, Nigel. Signal Bio. Down five percent on no news. Down twenty percent year to date. Where are these deals you were so confident about?'

'They're overdue.'

Seb spat the words out of his mouth without censure. Nigel paused, waiting for some further explanation. It was not forthcoming.

'Sorry? Overdue? Is that all you can say?'

Nigel Stuart was a senior fund manager at Friends Investcorp. He was also a mid-ranking bully, too often tolerated.

'Well since you ask Nigel, no. I should add that you bought this company at the IPO from your best mates at UBS three years before I ever heard of it. The company's first two drugs failed two years ago, again, on UBS's watch, making the company pretty much worthless. You will recall that they had one half-decent drug candidate in the back of the cupboard that needed twenty-five million pounds to put it through Phase 2 trials, and you and the other whingeing shareholders needed me to find that money

Chapter 55

from new investors to save this basket case. Which I did. Third time lucky. Last month's readout was, as we know, as good as we could have hoped. Christ, the drug might even fucking work. So now we wait for the out-licensing deals to hit the screen. And they haven't yet, and the shares will drift until they do. But you own five percent of a two hundred and fifty million pound company, and you have invested six million to date, so more than doubled your money. You would have owned twenty percent of fuck all if I hadn't rescued this for you Nigel. That clear enough?'

And hung up.

Penny had overheard this conversation and span round on her chair.

'You, home, now. I'll explain to that lot. And I'll call that prick Nigel back and explain.'

Seb didn't protest. He grabbed his jacket off the back of his chair and walked off the trading floor. A dozen colleagues watched him leave the scene. As he went down the escalator to the main reception area, he heard his name shouted out from the top.

'Seb, hold up.'

Seb turned to see Paul Flynn hurrying down after him.

'Did Penny send you to babysit me?' asked Seb.

'Well, she said you might just need some company.'

Paul was one of the few blokes in the City that Seb had some affinity with.

'I'm going to the pub to get wasted. You're welcome to join me.'

'That'll do me just fine.'

They strode out into the dank Tuesday drizzle and were in the bowels of Balls Brothers subterranean restaurant five minutes later. They sat down at a corner table and without any discussion Seb ordered two steak sandwiches and a bottle of house red.

'We'll have two pints of Guinness as well, please, Jane.'

Paul had read the waitress's name tag, and judging from her blushes, had used it to some effect.

'Might as well do this properly. So, let's hear it. What did you say to Nigel Stuart?'

'A few home truths.'

'Nice. How did he take it?'

'Dunno. I hung up.'

'Even better. Cheers!'

The pints and wine had gone down before their food arrived, and they ordered a second bottle from the waitress delivering their sandwiches. They weren't ignoring the elephant in the room, but there was no point charging straight at it, even though the enormous collision was inevitable. It would find them when it found them.

Paul's diversionary tactic was to draw fire upon himself.

'So, you saw us then?'

'If you mean your lunchtime shag with Vicky, yes we did.'

'Jesus, she was mortified. It was a good thing actually. We've not done anything since then. She's shittin' herself that her fella finds out.'

'Her fiancé?'

Seb wasn't normally so pious.

'I know, it's not great. But it's all done now.'

'Paul, I couldn't give two shits. She's a big girl. She makes her own decisions. Bet it was quite fun.'

Paul's taut, contrite face relaxed.

'Now that would be telling,' said Paul, with a grin.

Seb was in a dark place. He launched into a monologue about Vicky being a spoilt princess and carried right on

Chapter 55

round the trading floor slagging off his colleagues one by one. It was fertile territory. He left nobody unscathed, even finding faults in O C-B and Penny that he felt needed airing. Paul just listened.

The room was now full of men in dark suits, all of whom had walked in out of the rain. The room carried the faint odour of stale, wet wool amplified by the airlessness of the subterranean cavern.

'Let's get out of here. This place is bloody depressing at the best of times, and this definitely isn't the best of times,' said Paul, sensing a change of scene was urgently needed.

They jumped in a cab and directed the driver to Chelsea, where they'd decided to entrench themselves in The Phene pub for the rest of the day. The traffic on Fleet Street and the Strand was moving at its usual pedestrian pace; the pedestrians were actually making more progress.

'Bollocks to this. Let's get out and find a pub in Covent Garden, preferably one with a pool table. I'm not going to sit listening to your miserable monologue for the next three hours,' said Paul.

'Fair enough. The Springbok has tables,' replied Seb blankly. 'And it'll be full of Aussie and Safa girls you can crack on to.'

Paul's eyes lit up.

CHAPTER 56

They strode into the South African themed bar and were met by the usual mix of Southern Hemisphere backpackers and miscellaneous youth. The wall mounted televisions were playing a provincial South African rugby match, a few devotees on the stools beneath them. Both the pool tables were in use, so Seb put two twenty pence coins on the side of one of them to register their place in the queue.

Paul ordered two pints from the bar, and they sat at a table, Seb watching the rugby and Paul scanning the room for signs that any of the girls had noticed him. The black ball was potted, and they walked over to the table to be met by the larger of the two, a shaven headed man in his mid-twenties dressed in loose fitting, plaster-stained jeans, white T-shirt and heavy labourers' boots.

'Which one of you am I playing?' said the builder.

'We're going to play each other if that's alright fella,' piped up Paul.

'It ain't. Winner stays on. My table. One of you plays me.'

Paul, a fair-sized former rugby player with a bit about him, was indisputably a lover not a fighter. He hesitated, and Seb stepped into the vacuum.

Chapter 56

'No. Our money, our game.'

Seb started to walk to the end of the pool table to put his twenty pence coins in the coin slots to release the balls, but the builder stepped into his path.

'I don't think you're hearing me,' he said, squaring up.

Paul could see where this was going.

'Easy fellas. Why don't I see what the manager has to say,' and he hurried over to the bar to find the publican.

'The paddy doing all the talking for you is he? Always the same with you lot. Bunch of fucking poofs. You can fuck right off out of 'ere.'

He span round, scooped Seb's coins off the table and released the balls, sniggering with his admiring sidekick.

'That was a mistake,' said Seb.

Without pause, the labourer grabbed a cue, rotated it in his hands and cocked it like a baseball player preparing for a pitch.

'I *said*, fuck off.'

Seb glanced up to the corner of the room saying, 'You stupid prick, you're on candid camera,' and used that brief moment of distraction to land two well placed punches and a kick.

The labourer fell backwards, his fall broken by the pool table, and slid to the floor with a guttural groan, his nose spewing blood, his broken jaw crunching agonisingly as he tried to speak. Paul rushed over, followed by the manager and the doorman. Unfortunately for Seb, they hadn't seen the raised pool cue, just the aftermath. Despite his size, the doorman was visibly wary of approaching him.

'I'll wait here while you call the police and an ambulance. I'm not going anywhere,' said Seb, and he sat down at a table in the corner of the room and carried on watching the rugby.

'What the fuck just happened?' asked Paul, in disbelief.

'He came at me with the pool cue. Not much else I could really do. It'll take a while to sort all this out but there should be enough witnesses and camera footage to demonstrate self-defence.'

There was a chilling stillness to Seb's tone.

'Fucking hell, Seb. They teach you that stuff in the Army?'

'I suppose so.'

The technique, he'd learnt in the Paras. The instinct to strike first, he'd been forced to learn as a teenage inmate.

The police arrived within minutes. Two young officers wandered in to assess the unusual scene. A badly injured lump of a site labourer being nursed by his similarly hefty mate, while a suited, unruffled 'city gent' sat calmly watching a rugby match at a corner table, with a twenty-stone doorman notionally standing guard.

'You sit tight there, sir, and we'll get to you in a minute,' said the ranking officer to Seb, who stayed put, calm and apparently oblivious.

The ambulance arrived minutes later, and paramedics tended to the injured party while the policemen took statements from the few remaining bystanders who'd hung around after the fight, if 'fight' was in any way an accurate description. The patient was loaded onto a trolley and into the ambulance, a dose of morphine administered to silence his whimpers. He would be interviewed in detail once his injuries had been dealt with, but his companion suddenly found his tongue.

'We was just giving 'im the cue and the bastard attacked Gary!'

'Alright, sir, calm down. We'll get this sorted.' said the

Chapter 56

younger officer, while his colleague walked over to Seb and sat down with his notepad flipped and primed. After taking his name, address and contact details, he moved on to the preliminary statement.

'Can you tell us what happened sir?'

Seb told them. An open-and-shut case of self-defence that would be confirmed by the CCTV footage as soon as the recordings were viewed.

'Just a couple more things sir, have you been drinking?'

'Yes, a bottle and a half of red wine I would guess, and two pints of Guinness.'

'And did you receive any blows from the injured party sir?'

'No, but I wasn't going to wait to have my skull caved in before I protected myself.'

The young officer approached his senior colleague and called him away for moment. They had a brief exchange and the ranking officer returned to Seb.

'Our records have you as a retired army officer. That correct sir?'

'Not retired, invalided out.'

'Understood. I have to ask, sir, did you have hand-to-hand combat training in the Army?'

'Of course.'

The officer shuffled forward on his stool. He felt he was on to something.

'Just one more thing. Did you declare your combat training to the victim before you assaulted him?'

'Victim?! That man was about to hit me over the head with a snooker cue!'

'So you say sir, but no one we've spoken to saw that. And you made quite a mess of him if I may say so. From the paramedics' initial assessment, the victim has sustained a broken nose, a broken jaw and has serious ligament damage to his right knee.'

'What? There must have been a dozen people in here when he came at me!'

'Seems that most left the scene sir, others probably don't want to get involved. Unreliable witnesses anyway as most had been drinking quite heavily.'

'What about the camera footage. It'll be as clear as day!'

'Well sir, that's the thing. The manager has informed us that the camera up there is broken. So, with no eyewitnesses to confirm your claim of self-defence, I must inform you that I am arresting you for the assault of Gary Shaw. I have to caution you that anything you say can and will be....'

Holy shit.

CHAPTER 57

'God this is ridiculous,' Seb muttered to himself as the elder policemen nervously led him out of the bar by the arm. It was a two-minute drive in the back of the patrol car to the station and Seb suggested that they walk, but the idea was swiftly rejected. A 'flight risk' apparently.

After having his rights explained to him by the custody officer, Seb handed over his wallet, keys, phone, watch, pen and the loose change in his pockets. He also surrendered his tie; had he not been wearing loafers, his laces would have gone too. Then he was taken down a long corridor to an open cell and told to step in. The steel door was locked as carefully as the evidently sympathetic officer could achieve, but the noise of the bolt was still deafening. And he sat, and he thought. No eye witnesses. No CCTV evidence. His word against two others. He sat on the concrete bench thinking of all the faces that he could remember in the bar, trying to make sense of it all.

His tangled thoughts were interrupted by the clunk of the door being unlocked. An attractive Anglo-Caribbean woman in her early thirties entered the cell.

'I'm Detective Inspector Chalmers. Mr Faber, is it?'

'Yes, it is.'

'As the custody sergeant will have explained, you have a right to a lawyer. If you do not have the private means to retain one, the state will provide you with a solicitor to act on your behalf.'

'I need to make a call.'

'I assumed as much. Here you go.'

And she produced the phone from her jacket pocket.

'One call. I'll be just outside.'

The situation had got very serious, very quickly. An hour ago, he was drinking beer and watching rugby with a colleague. Now he needed legal representation to keep him out of prison. He took a deep breath and called his sister.

'You're where? You did what?!'

He rattled off the story, barely drawing breath.

'Why didn't I grab some of the witnesses then and there? Stupid. There must be other cameras in a big place like that? There must be cameras in the street that could identify people leaving the scene? They could be traced, surely? Did the bloke definitely raise the cue above his head? I think so. No, he did. He definitely did! But the second punch, and the kick. He wasn't a threat after the nose went. They never are. The knee's a problem. He's a bloody labourer. He'll come after me with lawyers. ABH? GBH? Compensation for lost earnings. He has forty years of work ahead of him. I've done this before. I've been here before.'

It took a few minutes for him to pause and Emily's initial entirely human response to subside. Painful flashbacks of the past made her feel quite sick. They couldn't go back there again. Seb, just as desperate, made her swear to keep it from their mother, at least for now. She wouldn't cope, and she shouldn't have to.

Chapter 57

'Look, I know you're a civil barrister but please say you know a criminal lawyer who can help me….'

Her legal brain took over then, and she paused for thought.

'In fact, I do. You do too. Andrew Willington.'

'Are you serious?' Willington was Emily's Oxford beau. Then fiancé. Then her cheating bastard ex.

'I know. He's a wanker, but he's a bloody good barrister. And chances are he feels more than a little in my debt.'

'OK. But don't expect me to be nice to him.'

About an hour after the call his cell door was opened, and Andrew Willington strode in. Seb was already on his feet and was the first to speak, neither party offering a hand in greeting.

'I want you to know that I wasn't the one who asked for your help.'

'I know, and I know you never would, but I'm the only thing between you and an assault charge so let's bury the hatchet, even if only on a temporary basis.'

They eyeballed each other for a few seconds before Seb thrust his hand out.

'Agreed. Let's get on with it.'

'You'd better sit down to hear this Seb.'

'I'll stand, thanks. Go on.'

'OK. In the eyes of the law, you aren't deemed a normal civilian. Your combat training is analogous to the use of a weapon. It is very likely therefore that the most serious offence of grievous bodily harm is what they will charge you with. I don't want to scare you unduly, but you need to know that GBH carries a maximum penalty of life imprisonment.'

Seb was all too aware of the tariffs for assault. And

contrary to his words, Willington did want to scare Seb. He wanted to make the very most of this opportunity for redemption; the more Seb had to lose, the more there was to save.

'For fuck's sake! The room was half full. There must be people who saw a skinhead threaten to skull me with a pool cue! And what about other security cameras?'

'Being reviewed now. The police seem to think that none of them were pointing at the pool table, but they will at least provide information on who else was in the room. We can try to trace them and interview them under oath. Unfortunately, that will take too long to avoid the charge being brought forward, but it will be essential evidence for pre-trial hearing. And, of course, the trial.'

'The trial? Christ, I cannot believe this is happening. Cameras everywhere in London and the only time I need one it's fucking broken! Do we even know for sure that the others were working?'

'As I say, detectives are down there now. We'll know soon enough. Sit tight. I'll be back in an hour. Officer...'

The cell door was opened, and Andrew Willington swept out as he'd swept in. He'd always loved the theatre of his job, and he'd waited a long time for a chance to make amends for his treatment of Emily.

Seb lay on the bench and listened to the sounds of a Central London police station on a Tuesday afternoon. The reality was far more mundane than the television dramas would have you believe. He counted three people being taken from their cells. Two were silent, and from the chatter of the accompanying officers, they were being transferred to Wormwood Scrubs while on remand pending trial. The third departure was to freedom. A magnificently drunk

Chapter 57

woman whose aroma was so appalling that the occupants of the adjacent cells had all complained vehemently about the inhumane conditions they were being forced to suffer. The response was a full aerosol can of air freshener sprayed up and down the corridor. The combination of 'pine forest fresh' and stale urine was about the most appalling stench Seb had ever experienced. She was still drunk when she left, but they needed her out of the place to avoid a riot.

Dotty was evidently well known to all the local police officers, and a regular visitor to the station when her verbal abuse of the public became too much to tolerate. She swore with astonishing range and fluency, with the clarity of a public orator and the plummy tones of the English nobility. Seb asked about her when the custody sergeant next looked in on him. It turned out that despite her upper-class diction, she was, in fact, a train driver's daughter from Wembley. Swept up in the amateur dramatic society that her parents devoted all their spare time to, she used *My Fair Lady* as her template for speaking proper, and did very well from the illusion she created. She worked the door of several high-profile night clubs in the mid-sixties and made quite a name for herself as someone it was useful to know. Many young men did know her. She'd become pregnant by an Iranian businessman whom she'd only met once, a complete scandal and something she couldn't contemplate sharing with her parents, or the father of her child. Whether she was intending to kill herself as well as the baby was never established, but she survived. Her little girl was stillborn at 36 weeks. The hysterectomy that followed had saved Dotty's life, and ended it. She had been drunk every day since 12th September 1967 and had called the streets of London her home for almost all of that time.

He heard two more arrivals. One was shouting in an Eastern European language, Romanian Seb thought. He needed some encouragement to make his way to the cell, and the two officers offering support seemed to bounce off the walls and cell doors all the while keeping up a veneer of civility. He was a pimp, it later transpired. He deserved everything he'd get. The second man came in chatting to the custody officer like an old friend. A shoplifter who was so identifiable to local shopkeepers and security staff that he hadn't successfully stolen anything of any value for years. Seb imagined that was the point. The 'honest thief' had created a community for himself, and the countless arrests, trials and short prison sentences were the seasons of his life. The state fed him and clothed him and put a roof over his head. Sure, the doors were locked at night but if he'd never said boo to a goose, he'd always be accommodated in minimum security prisons from which he'd never attempt to abscond. Why on earth would he?

Seb's mind was dragged back to Sophia. She'd have had very little sympathy for his plight. She abhorred violence, always insisting that there was another path. She had once conceded that defence was the only justification for violence, but the definition of defence was something they'd had to agree to disagree about.

Shortly after five o'clock, multiple footsteps approached his cell. He could clearly hear the clippity clop of the blakeys on Willington's half brogues, an anachronistic prop that he was convinced helped his performance as a British barrister. The heavy lock opened with a clunk and the door opened to reveal Willington, Paul and DI Chalmers. They all stared at Seb as if waiting for a cue.

'Well, it's clearly bad news, so spit it out,' he snapped.

Chapter 57

Willington spoke first.

'All the cameras work, but none were recording when this happened. It turns out they only record from six pm to midnight because that is when almost all the problems arise.'

Seb heard him, but it was as if it were it happening to someone else.

'Detective Inspector Chalmers will now charge you with GBH. You will hear some technical terms but to cut to the chase you were initially going to being charged with the most serious offence under Section 18 of the Offence Against a Person Act, wounding with intent, which, as previously mentioned, carries a maximum sentence of life imprisonment.'

He paused for full effect.

'However, despite the hospital confirming that you broke his nose, his jaw and ruptured two ligaments in his right knee, your distinguished and more importantly, unblemished service record has worked in your favour, and they concede that in all likelihood you acted in self-defence. As such I have managed to get it commuted to the lesser charge of GBH which carries a maximum sentence of five years. Unfortunately, due to the perceived severity of the offence you haven't been granted police bail, despite the extenuating circumstances.'

Willington delivered this pronouncement while glaring pointedly at DI Chalmers, who was completely nonplussed.

'Extenuating circumstances?' enquired Seb.

'Extreme grief,' said Willington.

'Which implies that I was somehow not in control? The only pertinent extenuating circumstance was a pool cue in the hands of a drunken thug!'

'Seb, mate. It looks like you won't be at your desk tomorrow morning. Who do you want me to speak to?' asked Paul.

Seb sagged, burying his head in his hands.

'It doesn't matter who you speak to. I'm done. There's nothing anyone can do now. Tell anyone you like.'

'That's bollocks. You'll get through this sure enough, and then you'll need the job to go back to. So, who will it be?'

Paul's dispassionate kick up the arse was exactly what he needed, however unwelcome.

Seb ran his hand through his hair as he considered his options.

'Call Bathurst. He won't be able to keep it quiet for long but he'll do what he can, I think.'

'Ok. I'll get some fresh clothes from your flat.' He turned to DI Chalmers. 'Keys with the custody sergeant?'

'Yes. There's a form to fill in that Mr Faber needs to sign. Wait at the front desk. I'll be with you shortly.'

'Right, I'll go and prepare for tomorrow's hearing. First things first, we need to get you out of here. We can work on tracing the people in the bar once we have you out of custody,' said Willington.

The door was unlocked from the outside and the two men left DI Chalmers alone with Seb. She read out the charge and explained the likely schedule for the next twenty-four hours. The custody sergeant would shortly be offering him food and a shower, and they also had a change of clothes for him, a grey track suit and white cotton underwear which Seb was quick to decline. She left him alone with his thoughts. He lay on the bench and closed his eyes. The chaos of the last few hours had forced his grief to the corners of his mind, but now his loss came back in full force, competing with the horror of his immediate situation. He felt numb. It was a catastrophe and, more than that, it would drag his family back into the misery they'd spent so many years overcoming.

And Sophia was still dead.

CHAPTER 58

He lay back punishing himself with thoughts of court appearances and sentencing. The expressions on the faces of the people who loved him when they heard the news. The loss of job and status. Focusing on the grimness of the moment actually made him feel better. The clear and present danger was diverting his attention from the emotional amputation. The phantom pain from something that no longer exists. The total and absolute knowledge that Sophia was dead and nothing in this world or any other could bring them back together. Forever.

He thought about prison, how he would cope second time around, then mulled over his actions in the bar. Did he need to react with such force? That cue was probably never going to come down on him. He couldn't be certain of that, but he was certain he could have walked away. And the punch to the nose was more than enough to buy him time to get out of there. But that wasn't what he'd wanted to do. The clout to the jaw had neutralised any remaining threat when the cue dropped into the pool of fresh blood by his feet. The kick to the knee that followed it was therefore attack, not defence. He knew it, and so would a magistrate.

Chapter 58

He lay there questioning his actions and motives, playing out imaginary scenes in a courtroom drama to be staged the following day. His predicament was actually just a puzzle. A problem to solve. Nothing more. He closed his eyes, and by some divine grace, fell into the sanctuary of sleep.

* * *

He woke to more footsteps coming down the corridor. He had no idea how long he'd dozed off for, but it had been a blessed oasis of peace. The door unlocked and swung wide open. Willington, Paul and DI Chalmers filed in, all wearing smiles. Willington's was self-important, Paul's of unmistakable relief. DI Chalmers', unless Seb was wrong, benevolent. She was the one who delivered the news.

'The charges have been dropped, Mr Faber. New video evidence has come to light leaving us in no doubt that you acted in self-defence.'

Willington, who couldn't bear being out of the spotlight, jumped in.

'Yes. The camera mounted on the lamp post on the opposite side of the road pointed straight at the doors of the Springbok bar. Apparently took some technical people two hours to neutralise the reflection from the glass in the doors and enhance the image. But it's all there.'

Seb sat bolt upright in a state of utter confusion.

'Wow. Thank God. But hold on. The criminal charges may have been dropped, but he could still come after me in the civil courts, couldn't he?'

'That is correct, Mr Faber, he could,' said Chalmers, 'but the paramedics found three grams of cocaine in his jeans when they were cut off him in the ambulance. Not enough to get him on a dealing charge, but an open-and-shut possession collar. We came to an understanding. He won't be taking his complaint any further. Paperwork for personal use isn't worth the effort anyway. Best for everyone.'

She delivered the information dispassionately, but she was on his side, he could tell.

'Here you go, your keys Seb. I was halfway to your flat when Andrew called with the news.'

'Thanks Paul.'

'You can pick up your things from the desk on your way out Mr Faber. On behalf of The Metropolitan Police Force, I apologise for the inconvenience caused. You can get on your way.'

'Thank you, Detective Inspector.'

'Imogen'

'Thanks, Imogen. I hope we don't meet again.'

She laughed.

'They all say that.'

'I somehow doubt that very much.'

She smiled as he shook her hand and left the station, signing for his possessions with a cursory scribble, almost without breaking step. He stood on the steps of the station with Willington and Paul.

'Thanks, Andrew. I don't know what you did but it worked. And I acknowledge the gesture.'

'You are very welcome, Seb. I just asked the right questions. All fell into place better than I expected actually and...'

He paused and his expression softened.

'Well, I hope we can put history behind us.'

'What's done is done,' said Seb. 'If it's OK with you, Paul, I'm going to go straight home. Amazing how the prospect of

Chapter 58

life imprisonment sobers you up. I'll call Bathurst, though, and break the bad news that I'll be in tomorrow morning after all.'

They walked off in separate directions. Willington to a cab rank, Paul to Covent Garden tube station and Seb, finding that he couldn't resist the urge to return to the scene, made for the Springbok Bar. As he walked, he took out his phone to call Bathurst but before he could dial the number, the phone rang. It was Fletcher. His instinct was to let the call drop, but he had to know if Fletcher had been told what had happened. Better sooner than later.

'William.'

'Hello Seb. I have been apprised of recent events. Set upon by some neanderthal with a pool cue. You set him straight I hear.'

Bathurst had obviously sung like a canary but at least he'd got the messaging right.

'That's about it. But the bloody camera in the bar wasn't on so it all got a bit hairy for a few hours.'

'But the fact that you are speaking to me now suggests that the situation has improved somewhat.'

'Well, yes. It has. All the charges just dropped. They managed to get the CCTV images that confirmed my description of events. The idiot was carrying drugs too, so he's unlikely to have the appetite to come after me.'

'Jolly good.'

Seb detected absolutely no surprise in Fletcher's tone. Perhaps it was disinterest, but it felt more as if Fletcher already knew what he was being told.

'We'll see you in the morning then, Seb. And don't do it again please. Not becoming.'

'Got it William. See you tomorrow.'

Seb walked up to the glass double doors of the Springbok Bar and stood with his back to them. There was the camera across the street, pointing directly at the doors, but from a height of at least ten feet. Ten feet high and twenty feet from the doors. The pool table was at the back of the bar. The camera couldn't possibly have recorded the fight, much less the exchange leading up to it.

Two hours to 'enhance the image and neutralise the reflection.'

CHAPTER 59

Seb could conceivably have kept the incident from his mother, but since he had been completely exonerated, he chose not to.

'Darling, come home,' was his mother's briefly delivered response to his re-telling of the events.

He stuffed a bag with a few basics and drove home on Friday immediately after work.

No version of a story that involves alcohol, violence and the police can be spun without some level of shame from the storyteller. There were mitigating factors, it was not violence of his instigation, he hadn't started it. But he had most emphatically ended it. He grew increasingly anxious the closer he got to home. All too soon, he was turning down the single-track lane and pulling into the gravelled drive, past his childhood home to her tiny annexe. By the time he was out of the car, his mother was standing outside the front door with an expression that could be interpreted any number of ways. As he approached, she walked out to greet him. Seb wasn't a big crier, but he was hit by a wave of overwhelming emotion as she folded her arms around him. He took a deep breath and choked it back.

'Come on, let's get you inside.'

They sat in the kitchen and, it being after six o'clock, his mother had her first glass of white wine on the go.

'You'll have a beer?'

'I will. Thanks mum.'

He noticed immediately that the kitchen was full of cigarette smoke; in recent years his mum had only smoked heavily when troubled. But his overwhelming feelings on arrival were back under control and he braced himself for the compassionate exploration of his soul to come.

'Listen to me, Seb. Falling apart and lashing out physically does nothing to honour Sophia's memory. You learnt that the hard way when your father died. Bad things happen to us all, but you just have to go on, Seb. Life does just go on.'

This was not the shoulder to cry on he was expecting.

'To the best of my knowledge you have managed to get through ten years in the Army and a year in the City without getting dragged into a bar brawl,' she carried on. 'But perhaps I'm being naive?'

'No, you're right.'

'Listen, I know you're in despair, and I can't do anything about that. But as painful as it is you *have* to shoulder this burden with dignity. The alternative is no good. No good at all. Not for you, or for anyone else.'

Despite her irrefutable logic, Seb instinctively stood his ground. He hunched forward in his chair which brought his face close to his mother's, who didn't budge an inch.

'I was attacked. I defended myself, and eventually that was proved. Then I was released!'

Mary took a long drag on her cigarette.

'And did you need to put that man in hospital?'

Chapter 59

She looked directly into Seb's eyes through the dancing ribbon of smoke rising from her right hand. Seb had been held in this cool gaze many times before, always with the same outcome.

'I had to do something. Maybe not that. I don't know.

She didn't respond, just held his gaze.

'OK, I went too far.'

'That's what I thought, and as long as you know that, you can put it behind you. You can fool everyone but yourself.'

Seb finished his beer in silence with one long glug and went to the fridge for another. 'Truthfully? I enjoyed it,' said Seb.

His mother's face switched instantly from motherly concern to dismay.

'What did you enjoy?' she asked.

'I enjoyed hurting him. I enjoyed damaging him. Ever since Feltham I've turned the other cheek. Even when I was in the Army. Particularly when I was in the Army. Always the sensible choice. The right choice. In that bar, it felt good to see what the other choice feels like. God, Mum, the idiot was so surprised. It was the last thing in the world he expected when I punched him. The look is his eyes was pure astonishment.'

'One punch wasn't enough?'

'No it wasn't. I wanted to destroy him.'

His mother just listened. He'd expected her to be disgusted, but she wasn't.

'And how do you feel now?'

'I don't know. Part of me wanted to go to court, to be punished. And for an hour or so it made me forget about Sophia. God, she would have hated me for it.'

'She would know what I know, my darling. You are doing

your best.'

He looked back up at her, taken aback.

'But listen. I know you will have thought about this, but it needs to be said. Had things gone differently you would have lost your job and any prospect of a career anywhere in the City. Not to mention your freedom.'

A switch flicked in Seb.

'I *have* thought about it. My job, my so-called career, is a lot of bollocks. Selling mispriced hope. Always the same outcome. We get the money, the company spends it, the product fails. Repeat. An utter waste of time, time that is so *fucking* finite. I'm done with it.'

'Try to keep calm my love.'

He couldn't. He was purging his soul.

'Dad was a surgeon. All he ever wanted to be. He had purpose and value. I was a soldier and even I found my place in the world. But now I just sell crap to arrogant pricks all day. It would drive you insane, Mum.'

'All jobs are mostly repetitive and largely dull, Seb. Dad's was no exception.'

He shook his head in despair.

'You know I went to church, Mum. I'm such a fucking hypocrite.'

The pent-up tears began to run down his face. He never swore when he was with his mum, but she didn't flinch. Different rules for this. Seb's Catholicism had lapsed to the point of nonexistence. He had long ago lost faith in an afterlife, certainly the literal interpretation that gave comfort to the faithful.

'And I spoke to Father Dennis. Do you know what he said? He said that Sophia was in a better place. A better place. No she isn't. She fell on a rock and bled to death

Chapter 59

minutes after agreeing to marry me. Better place? Better than my arms now? Or on our wedding day? With our first baby? No. She's in a worse fucking place because she's dead. I want her so badly and I can't ever see her again. There's nothing that can ever change that, and I can't bear the fact that all I can hope for is the pain of her death fading. And that would only be because I start to forget her. I forget how her smile wrinkled her nose. The noise she made when she held back a sneeze. The taste of her lips. The way she held me. I have to lose her to feel less pain. And I don't want to. I want to feel this pain, this fucking agonising pain for the rest of my useless life because it's all I have left.'

His mother stood behind him with her arms clasped around his shoulders, her head bent to his.

'And when I stopped thinking about her for a few minutes it felt like life could be normal, could be OK. I even noticed the pretty police officer. I may even have flirted with her. What kind of a monster am I? And then Sophia's back. The things we were going to do. The places we were going to go. Then I feel like I've betrayed her for having a few minutes of normality. And the one person I want to talk to about this is her. Just her.'

His mother said nothing. She just held him and listened. She was there, and that was enough. After a while she gave him one more squeeze, walked over to the fridge and took out her duck liver paté, removed the clingfilm and sat it down on the table, handing Seb a corkscrew and a bottle of red wine.

'I think you'll be needing this.'

Seb opened the bottle and poured himself a glass.

'If the work is making you unhappy then you should make a change. You have an exceptional brain. You could do anything you like, but give it six months. You're in no state to make big decisions like that now and you won't be for a while yet. Above all, you need stability, so just sit tight and keep turning the pedals. If you feel the same in six months, then you can act. I know about this.'

Seb couldn't respond, but his silence was his tacit acceptance. His mother served the paté then raised her glass, looked briefly to the skies and gave a little nod.

'To absent friends.'

His grief wouldn't magically evaporate, but the crisis had passed. And as she'd promised, life would go on.

CHAPTER 60

Six months was what he promised, and he was good to his word. Six months later to the day, immediately after the morning meeting, Seb took his letter of resignation and put it on Bathurst's desk. Bathurst wasn't in the least surprised but took Seb into a meeting room anyway to see if there was anything he could do or say to reverse the decision. There wasn't. The news was passed swiftly up the chain, and within minutes Seb was summoned to Fletcher's office.

'Come and sit down Seb. Shut the door behind you.'

Seb had never been offered a seat before.

'I know you have your reasons, and I also know that you know your mind. I haven't asked you in here to beg you to stay or pretend that everything will be different in the future. This is equity broking, Seb. It is what it is. The reason I asked you in here was to tell you to clear your diary for the week of 13th December. I'm going on a site visit to FS Biotech and you're coming with me.'

'Can't Saki go? There's not much point in me doing the due diligence if I'm not going to be here to lead the IPO.'

'No he bloody well can't. The technical due diligence can be done from his desk and save me the air fare. I won't go into details now, but there will be some conversations with various interested parties that you're better suited to. I should also point out that your contract has a three-month notice period, so as long as I'm paying you, you'll do as you're asked.'

Now that he could see the light at the end of the tunnel, Seb found he was immune to Fletcher's brusque ways.

'Well, I'll look forward to it then, William. Better dig out my trunks.'

CHAPTER 61

They landed at Johannesburg Airport after an unremarkable night flight, stretched out in some comfort at the front of a 747. They'd been given window seats on opposite sides of the business class cabin when they boarded. Seb suspected that this was pre-ordained, but it suited him just fine.

They retrieved their bags, transferred to the domestic terminal and got into a rather tired looking twin propeller aircraft which took them on the final ninety minute leg into the Tswalu Game Reserve in the Northern Cape, the southern gateway to the Kalahari Desert. It was a five-star reservation, self-consciously understated, an extravagance justified by being the nearest suitable accommodation to the client's facility. The flight there took them over vast, empty swathes of northern South Africa. Yellow dusty plains peppered with acacia trees, punctuated by the occasional ramshackle farming settlement.

Fletcher took his backpack from the overhead compartment, pulled out a document and handed it to Seb. 'Read this before we land. It covers some of the background you need to know before we meet our hosts.'

Seb started to wade through the sixty-page report,

impossible to digest in the remaining fifteen minutes of the flight.

'Look, the most important thing you need to be aware of is that earlier this year the South African Council for Scientific and Industrial Research officially recognized the San's rights over Hoodia, allowing them to take a percentage of any profits from commercial products resulting from Hoodia Gordonii. The details were murky and the terms are negotiated on a case-by-case basis, so we have the whip hand and, make no mistake, our client is expecting us to use it.'

'But the San will have their own lawyers and financial advisors to stop people like us taking advantage of them?'

'Of course they will, but they're state funded lawyers and accountants. A little out of their depth. I don't anticipate any real resistance.'

'Why so easy? The rights of indigenous South Africans are front page news all over the world. Why would a couple of smart-talking London bankers be allowed to push them around?'

'That is precisely the point. Keeping the locals onside is a very necessary PR exercise. If Free State Biotech is to be attractive to a giant pharmaceutical company, they need to demonstrate impeccable social responsibility credentials. At the same time they have to avoid burdening the acquirer with an overly punitive on-going liability, more specifically, an enduring royalty payment directly linked to the ongoing sale of Hoodia products.'

'So, what remuneration has been put to them?'

'Barnard has proposed a single, one-off perpetual licence fee of ten million pounds, triggered by the first regulatory approval of H57 in the US or Europe. The San are a simple

Chapter 61

people. Ten million pounds is a hundred and sixty million rand. It's more money than they could need in a hundred lifetimes.'

Seb continued with his thread.

'But a little short of the fifty million pounds of annual royalties they could expect if Hoodia even delivers a fraction of its market potential.'

'Something like that, yes. The outline terms have been offered but not yet agreed. The single cash payment doesn't sit well with the San leadership. As self-anointed 'guardians of the Kalahari', they're motivated by long term sustainability. Money that could help them preserve the land and their ways in perpetuity. Barnard is facing a rising tide of disquiet and needs our help to clarify the benefits of the current arrangement to the San elders.'

It was all flooding back. The subterfuge at Sunningdale; everything he saw at Ickling Hall. Fletcher was in on this.

'Is this the right thing to do?' he persisted. 'FS Biotech could agree a lower one-off fee and a fair ongoing royalty payment, say five percent of in-market sales. That should keep everyone happy, shouldn't it?'

'No Seb, it wouldn't. Richard is our client and wants to avoid any ongoing royalty obligation, so that and only that is what will make *him* happy. Am I making myself clear?'

Seb sensed that this wasn't the time for a fight. Not yet. He nodded dutifully, picked up a pen and skim read the document, studiously underlining and circling key points to keep up the pretence of enthusiastic compliance.

CHAPTER 62

They touched down at Tswalu at eleven thirty where they were met by Richard Barnard, stepping out of a 'Tswalu Lodge', branded open top Land Rover, with the unmistakable frame of his giant manservant behind the wheel. Barnard was dressed head to toe in khaki safari clothing and looked the very image of a white hunter. The bulging profile of a handgun was clearly visible on Mandla's left flank, holstered beneath his tailored jacket. It was a precaution that seemed totally disproportionate to any threat Barnard might face, but doubtless made him feel important.

They were ushered to the car with grim-faced urgency.

'Please talk freely in front of Mandla, he neither speaks nor understands English'.

'Useful man to have in a scrap, I should imagine,' volunteered Fletcher.

'Now look here, South Africa is a land of millions of dispossessed poor people of colour, who feel that the white man must pay for the crimes of the past. That we should hand over the wealth that we have created from nothing. For those who want to try and take it with force, I have Mandla. For those who want to negotiate like gentlemen, I

Chapter 62

have my British bankers at my side.'

Barnard smirked, pleased with his little joke, and within minutes they were at the lodge and were shown to their rooms. Seb's room was dominated by a huge timber-framed bed with a mosquito net suspended above it. Animal skins decorated the polished concrete floors. Tribal paintings of Kalahari scenes hung on all the walls, dark wood and white linen the dominant colour scheme of the room. He kicked off his shoes, threw his jacket over a chair, lay on the bed and listened. Even before he took in any sounds, he breathed in the smell. A fragrance in the air that was, to his European nose, the scent of Africa. He lay in peaceful silence enjoying the subtle perfume carried in on the afternoon breeze and allowed his mind to wander. He would have liked his honeymoon to have included a safari, and how he would have loved to have Sophia by his side on these crisp white sheets.

He was jolted out of his daydream by the sound of leather soles on sprung wooden floors. Fletcher had left his room and was striding purposefully out of the lodge to the veranda. A second, more languid stride came a moment later. The scraping sound of iron-legged chairs being manoeuvred and then, silence. Almost. As Seb adjusted his senses to the quiet, the muffled tones of a hushed dialogue became audible. Fletcher and Barnard were having a conversation they didn't want overheard. So, he listened. The low rumble continued at a steady pace but the only word he was sure he could make out was 'Seb', and he heard it several times.

By now his curiosity had taken him from his bed to the window nearest the veranda. The shutters were closed, the window ajar. He carefully opened it and put his ear to the wooden vents.

'So, we're agreed, and we'll keep your boy Seb out of this. A decent chap but his decency is likely to get in the way here,' said Barnard.

'I think so. He's not quite ready. But he'll get there. We all do sooner or later. Now, how about a glass of that Groot Constantia Chardonnay you bang on about before we head out?' replied Fletcher, which Seb heard loud and clear.

CHAPTER 63

The forty-minute drive out to the facility was dusty and hot. The canvas roof had been put back up on the Land Rover to keep the worst of the mid-afternoon sun off them, but it was still oppressive for anyone unused to it. The last few miles of the journey were over a bumpy, dust road criss-crossed with deep channels gouged out after flash floods. Mandla weaved wildly to avoid the potholes, rarely entirely succeeding. Barnard, solidly installed upfront, was happy in the knowledge that Seb and Fletcher were being bounced and flung around in the back like ragdolls.

The FS Biotech facility consisted of thirty acres of cultivated desert in the lee of a rocky outcrop, and a half-acre greenhouse adjacent to a small, corrugated iron laboratory building. A dozen or so San women tended to the long parallel lines of Hoodia that were being drip fed through miles of black perforated rubber pipes snaking their way around the site.

The newcomers were met by the plant manager, a thick set, middle aged Afrikaner called Henke Strauss, and it soon became clear that Henke, a man of few words, deferred heavily to Barnard. As most men did.

'Henke is the man responsible for cultivation of the Hoodia, and the extraction and isolation of the active ingredient.'

'Kan ek terug na my werk nou gaan?'

'Yes Henke, don't let us distract you.'

Henke walked back to his lab with a grunt.

'Henke has no love of the English. He's a fifth generation Boer. He tolerates me because I pay his wages but I'm afraid the addition of two London investment bankers is more than his manners can cope with.'

They walked up and down a few rows of the fleshy, flower capped plants and were smiled at warmly by the San women, young and old, who were bent double harvesting them manually in the full desert heat of the day. Seb smiled back.

'That looks like brutal work, particularly in this heat,' said Seb, addressing Barnard directly.

'To your eyes, yes, but the women you see are not like yours at home. The San women are tough and are born to work in these conditions. Here they get an income, eight-minute breaks every two hours and all the water they need. You can see from their faces that they're happy, isn't that right Gloria?'

'Yes, Mr Barnard sir, oh yes sir.'

'Quite right. Now, come. I'll show you our controlled growing environment.'

He led them to the vast greenhouse. The vents in the glazing, he explained, were controlled diurnally with full venting during the heat of the day and drawn shut at dusk, at which point electric lamps illuminated the plants during the hours of darkness.

'This is a large-scale trial to assess growth and yield

Chapter 63

performance in a theoretical twenty-four-hour permanent growth cycle. If a Hoodia Gordonii derived pharmaceutical is to be even remotely successful, the issue of raw material supply will become paramount, and given the very particular conditions that the plant thrives in and the inaccessibility of the natural habitat, we're exploring all means of increasing yields. As it happens, from what we can see so far, the twenty-four-hour cycle marginally increases the rate of overall plant growth, but it also reduces the percentage of the key active ingredient.'

They had to get out. Even with all the windows set to full vent, it was like standing in an oven. Barnard ushered them into the air-conditioned comfort of the lab. It looked like little more than a large tin shack on the outside, but it was a fully functioning biopharmaceutical laboratory complete with centrifuges, HPLC machines, electrophoresis baths, electron spectroscopes and other associated bits of kit that allowed the raw plant fibre to be broken down to its components at a molecular level, then analysed by the characteristics and testing the pharmacology.

The tour was interrupted by the sound of Venetian blinds clattering against glass. The door to Henke's corner office was closed and the blinds were down and shut. It looked as if someone was being pushed up against the glass wall. Seb couldn't be sure, but through gaps in the contorted aluminium he thought he could make out the outline of a pair of white-coated shoulders. Moments later, Henke trotted out, slamming the door behind him. A manic smile was plastered across his face, quite unrecognizable from the open hostility they'd been met with just thirty minutes earlier.

'Sorry for the disturbance gentlemen. Office is a bloody

mess. Tripped and nearly went through that wall,' all delivered with an almost impenetrable Afrikaans accent.

'Here is a pack of information about our facility. Call me if you have any questions. My card is in the pack.'

He handed the folder directly and very deliberately to Seb.

'Any questions at all,' Henke reiterated with emphasis, and he trotted back into his office.

Site visits were all very worthy, but in Seb's experience, once you've seen one laboratory you've seen them all. He understood the subject matter and had certainly seen enough. Fletcher, who didn't understand a word of the science, had glazed over not long after getting out of the car. They had done what they needed to do. Shaken some hands. Confirmed the facility actually existed. Fletcher drew the visit to a close.

'Excellent set up. Really pleased we got the chance to see it.'

Barnard responded to the cue and led them up to his office on a mezzanine floor which looked out over the whole facility. On the table there were two six-inch-tall clear plastic 'tombstones', each with a Hoodia flower and a vial of H57 embedded within them.

'A memento from your trip to the Kalahari. The airlines won't let you take the live stuff, so this is something for your desks.'

'That's really great Richard,' lied Seb, and they all headed back to the car, where Mandla was waiting steadfastly at the wheel.

CHAPTER 64

They ate at dusk. Heralded as 'Dinner in the Desert', in a semi-permanent canvas construction set up a few miles into the bush from the lodge. Seb had been to South Africa before, but not the Africa of King Solomon's Mines, images indelibly planted in his head as a small boy. Very hot days, very cold nights. Dry, dusty and wild. Tswalu sat at the foot of the Korannaberg Mountains, rising up from vast grassland plains. It was full of game, large and small. And the world's rich paid astonishing amounts of money to enjoy it.

Seb would have much preferred the twenty minute walk it would take to get there, but Barnard insisted that they were driven out to the camp in a high-sided game vehicle.

'Nah look here, all sorts of animals that are scarce and docile in the heat of the day are very active at night. You don't want to run into any of them, or worse, tread on them while you're stumbling around in the dark.'

It sounded like overkill to impress, but he didn't protest and they arrived at the small torchlit camp at the foot of the mountain a few minutes later. Barnard drove, Mandla not having been seen since their return from the lab. There was a steel fire pit at the centre of the ring of torches, fifteen feet in diameter with two small tree trunks throwing up a five-foot blaze and plenty enough heat to offset the rapidly plunging temperature. The Lodge's head waiter, a very elegant, immaculately presented Xhosa man, showed them to a dining table set under a canvas gazebo. The table was dressed in white linen and a spectacular array of silver cutlery, with the full complement of crystal glasses: champagne, red wine, white wine and water tumbler. A similarly arrayed serving table held innumerable plates and dishes, a gas stove and a large metal ice bucket. The head waiter was accompanied by a chef, in full whites complete with a crisp new Toque Blanche, and a rather beautiful young San waitress, decked out like a Victorian lady's maid. They were served champagne, the only non-South African item on the menu, and some delicate guinea fowl egg appetizers, then left alone to enjoy the fading light of the African day.

Seb and Fletcher listened politely as their host described every aspect of what lay before them. Little of the flora and fauna of the Kalahari was left out of his self-appointed seminar, and while this was interesting to a point, Barnard reached that point remarkably quickly. Fletcher nonetheless affected intense interest in Barnard's every nugget of superior knowledge. Seb merely nodded his head a few times which was all his patience could muster. It was a relief when the waiting staff appeared to serve the starter and pour the white wine, and Fletcher leapt into the momentary silence as Barnard sipped his wine.

'Let's address tomorrow's meeting. We need to be sure of what we are trying to get the locals to agree to.'

'Indeed. I know what they want. And I know what they are going to get,' said Barnard, with a self-satisfied smirk.

Chapter 64

'I'm not sure they'll roll over as easily as you think. The elders and their advisors are bound to come prepared,' volunteered Seb.

'Then you had better have a good think about how you're going to approach it, my boy.'

Seb was gathering himself for an unguarded response when Fletcher shot a stare across the table as effective as a kick in the shins.

'We should be able to handle their objections, Richard. If a long-term income stream is what they're after they can put their windfall in a tax-shielded income fund and collect the interest til the end of time. After all, they didn't invent this plant, they were simply fortuitous enough to stumble upon it'.

'Now that sounds more like it. I knew I could rely on you William. I'm sure you will help your young buck here to see the bigger picture.'

Barnard stared out over the plain as he spoke as if Seb were not present at all.

'I'm over here, Richard,' said Seb, finally discarding the pretence of deference. Barnard and Fletcher both flinched.

'I will represent you and your company with all the enthusiasm of a trained seal, but I won't lie for you, or obscure the truth.' They stared at Seb, mouths open, united in disbelief. 'But as you would never ask that of us, of course, we're all good.'

Barnard took a theatrically long sip of his wine allowing himself time to compose a response.

'You are a spirited young man, Seb,' he said. 'On this occasion I will overlook your impudence, but I think you had better leave this discussion to us. Mandla will drive you back.'

And much like a shark rising from the deep, Mandla stepped out of the darkness where he must have been standing for some time. Seb drained his wine glass, put his napkin down and got up from the table.

'He needn't bother. I'll walk.'

This time Barnard offered no objection. Seb thanked the serving staff, even popping his head round the tent to include the chef, and headed out into the darkness. Not raging, but planning.

CHAPTER 65

The short walk back to the lodge was illuminated by a three-quarter moon. Mandla followed him on foot, making no attempt to disguise his presence. With Seb safely back in his room Mandla conspicuously dragged a chair into the hallway and took up watch, confirmed by Seb cracking the door to immediately lock eyes with his sentry.

Seb turned on the ceiling fan, stripped to his boxers and lay star-shaped on the bed, staring up at the slightly offset motion of the blades above him, turning like a clay pot that isn't perfectly centred on the wheel. He was hazily going over the events of the day when he was jolted out of his reflections by the memory of Henke urgently thrusting his information pack into his hand. He reached for the folder on his bedside table and pulled out Henke's business card. His mobile didn't work outside the EU so he carefully picked up the hotel phone on the table opposite his bed and took it into the bathroom, feeding the cable under the door so that it could close fully. Turning on the shower, he dialled the number. Henke picked up after one ring.

'Henke, this is Seb Faber, we met today.'
'What's that noise? I can barely hear you.'

'The shower, Mandla is sitting outside my room…'

'Ah shit man!'

The panic in Henke's voice was alarming.

'Listen, Henke, I need to speak to you but I can't talk on the phone. We're busy all day tomorrow and we leave for Johannesburg on Wednesday afternoon. Can you meet me in the early morning?'

Then Seb remembered Mandla.

'Wait a sec. I need to check something. Stay on the line.'

He walked up to the rear window of his room and tried to open it, but it was bolted shut and only opened a few inches. He'd need the key and he only had a day to get hold of it.

'OK. There's a way to get out of here without being seen. Wednesday morning, 5am, I'm going to cut through the back of the property out to the main road. I don't know if the front gate is manned twenty-four hours a day, but if it is, I don't want to be seen and I guess you won't want to be either. Pull off the road half a mile to the west, engine and lights off. What do you drive?'

'A white Toyota pickup.'

'OK. 5am sharp. This won't take long. Just please be there.'

CHAPTER 66

Tuesday started early. They were met by Moses, their driver and guide in reception at 5.15am for their morning game drive, ushered into the safari truck without exchanging more than a few words, and set off into the bush. Fletcher took a seat on a bench on the left side of the aisle, and Seb on the right, staring away from each other into the morning darkness. Barnard sat at the front, a rifle propped against his leg, lest anyone forget who was King of the Jungle.

'My father's Winchester Model 70. Greatest hunting rifle ever made.'

They weaved and bounced down the rutted, dust roads for half an hour until they reached the watering hole that promised the best game viewing of the morning. Three times on their way there Barnard halted the wagon to check for game that only he could detect. None of it materialised. Moses's fault, apparently.

As they reached the pool Moses slowed the vehicle to a crawl, and came to a stop on an elevated bank under the bow of a baobab tree, with a full view of the expanse of water. The sun was just beginning to rise, and it wasn't long before he drew their attention to the awakenings before them. A pair of hippo wallowing in the middle of the pond. Moments later a family of cheetah appeared; two cubs, guileless and dependent, padding down to the water to drink, their parents anxiously watching on. All around, birds of impossibly vivid colours alerted the world noisily to their presence. A sudden movement at the far end of the pond. A huge crocodile plodded towards the water and slid in silently. Cardinal birds in the nearby trees immediately took flight; the hippo couldn't have cared less. There were zebra, kudu, warthog, wildebeest. Everywhere he looked, life was emerging. A morning armistice in lives defined by ever present threats.

Moses pointed out the many birds and animals they hadn't noticed. Fletcher tried to photograph them with the new, but entirely inadequate, digital camera of which he was so proud. Seb just soaked it all up, but under the cloud of a single thought. Sophia would have loved to see this.

He was dragged back into the present by Barnard, impatient and needing to be back in control.

'That's all we're going to see here. Let's go Moses.'

Moses obliged, with a doleful look in Seb's direction.

They drove to more lakes and streams, to high vistas and across dusty plains, and at 10am, they pulled into a sheltered copse of acacia trees on the foothills of the Korannaberg. 'Do you hunt, Seb?'

Of course he didn't hunt, or stalk, or shoot, apart from his eventful day at Ickling Hall, but he could handle a rifle. And had.

'Not animals. But I'll try anything once.'

'Good. Moses, give the chaps their rifles. They both know how to use them.'

Moses retrieved two bolt action hunting rifles from

Chapter 66

a wooden trunk in the back of truck and handed them to Fletcher and Seb, who both checked them over swiftly and efficiently without conscious thought.

'What am I aiming at? I thought everything was protected in the reserve.'

'Not everything. We are going to take a kudu. Magnificent beast, best tasting meat you can eat. You can handle that can you?'

'I should think so, Richard. I guess we'll find out.'

Moses moved forward onto the tracker seat and Barnard took the wheel. They had to stay downwind of their target and make as little noise as possible. Kudu were a skittish quarry, and they could cover a lot of ground very quickly. Once spooked, they would be a kilometre away in a matter of minutes over ground the truck wouldn't be able to penetrate. Moses stared at the terrain a few metres in front of the truck, giving directional signals with a short stick in his outstretched hand. It was slow progress. An hour into the hunt they'd seen gemsbok, steenbok, springbok and impala, and as many zebra and wildebeest as Moses could point his stick at, but no kudu. Then, just as Barnard's faith in Moses's tracking skills had reached its limit, Moses raised his hand and signalled to stop. He stepped out of the seat, squatted down and pointed at something on the ground.

'Fresh kudu dung. From here, we must walk.'

They left the vehicle and set off in single file behind him. Fletcher was dressed for hunting game, sporting cargo pants and desert boots, and a wide brimmed hat. Seb wasn't so well prepared. His chinos and rolled up shirt sleeves were fine for watching wildlife from the back of a safari truck, less suited to tracking large game on foot. He clearly hadn't got the memo, or been sent it.

After a few minutes, Moses pointed at a solitary acacia tree on a small hill about a hundred metres ahead of them. There were a dozen kudu sheltering from the sun. One male, and the rest females and calves. Barnard took his Winchester off his shoulder and knelt by a fallen tree that made a perfect rest for the barrel of his rifle, but immediately stood up again.

'What am I thinking? You're yet to be blooded. You take the shot.'

He ushered Seb forward. Seb rejected the fallen trunk, choosing to brace himself up against a shepherd tree instead. He had a clear view of the herd, docile and static. Unsporting, unchallenging, sitting ducks. He could have taken any one of them, and the bullet would have killed it before it had even heard the shot. As he scanned the animals to identify the dominant male, the herd suddenly scattered. The kudu galloped away in every direction quickly hidden from view in the long grass. Seb kept his rifle trained on the open ground immediately in front of them. He saw nothing at first. No movement or sound. Then a terrified kudu calf burst out of the bush at speed. Seb held still.

'Now! Shoot it now!' yelled Barnard.

Seb waited.

'You have it?' asked Fletcher.

'Eyes on,' replied Seb.

The kudu dashed into the bush behind them without a shot being fired.

Barnard leapt up, "What the fuck…"

Seb fired, and, as an immediate reflex, reloaded.

The lioness giving chase was dead before it hit the ground inches from Barnard's feet.

A perfect shot between her shoulders.

Chapter 66

Moses spoke first.

'She's dead, but we are still in danger. There will be others.'

Seb and Fletcher instinctively worked as a team, scanning different sections of the bush, their eyes and rifles working as one as they retreated. Barnard darted back with Moses to retrieve the truck, his Winchester bouncing on his shoulder. They pulled up to Seb and Fletcher who stepped backwards into the vehicle, their eyes and weapons still scanning for threats.

As Moses pulled away, a second lion appeared from the vegetation.

'That is one of the male cubs. The dead lion is the mother.'

The young lion wasn't interested in the hunting party. It paced over to the body of its dead mother and licked her face. This was Barnard's moment.

'Stop the truck!'

'No sir. We must go now! There will be others.'

'If you want to keep your job you stop this vehicle now!'

Barnard meant every word of it, and Moses did as he was told. Barnard took aim. A shot rang out, but not from his rifle. From Fletcher's. An explosion of dust and earth erupted inches in front of the lion, and it squealed and dashed away into the safety of the undergrowth. Ex-forces or not, for a middle-aged stockbroker Fletcher was a consummate marksman.

'That animal was no threat. It didn't need to die today. Let's go Moses,' said Fletcher.

Moses looked at Barnard for confirmation, and Barnard meekly nodded his approval. He drove away at speed, leaving behind the corpse weeping blood into the iron red earth, the vultures already circling high above.

Fletcher offered no apology and Barnard made no complaint. The hierarchy had somehow reversed. Fletcher was the alpha male now.

CHAPTER 67

Seb didn't see Fletcher again until they met at four o'clock in the conference room at the Lodge for the negotiation with the San elders. Seb was the first there, arriving fifteen minutes before the scheduled start as requested.

'You're early. Good,' said Fletcher, getting straight down to business with no mention of the events just two hours earlier. 'You'll have read the document I gave you, so you know what we're up against. Despite there only being about ten thousand of these people in the Southern Kalahari, they have a tribal and now a federally ratified claim to the use of Hoodia in pharmaceutical products. The details of exactly how they should benefit are rather nebulous, so this is how we play this. Richard will introduce us, and I'll do a short introduction on the Bank and our history of working with indigenous communities in emerging markets. That's your cue to speak to our record in the healthcare sector. Richard will then confirm his cash offer and open the table to questions. At that point you will say precisely nothing. Richard and I will handle any questions or objections they may have. Got it?'

He shrugged his shoulders.

'I think I can manage that.'

'Don't be glib, Seb. Just do your job.'

Seb scowled at him, tilting his head to one side, his brow furrowed, his expression relaying 'fuck you' every bit as well as if he'd said the actual words.

Barnard stepped into the room, and the moment passed.

'They're here, and they've come mob handed. Two San and three lawyers. I recognise the fat one. He is a partner at Strauss & Venter. Second-rate firm. This is going to be pretty straightforward.'

The visitors filed into the room, the lawyers first then their clients. The two San representatives were impassive, apart from their obvious discomfort at being there at all. The visitors took seats on the opposite side of the large oval table to the FS Biotech team, and Barnard kicked off with the introductions. The senior San representative spoke no English. The younger man, who looked to be in his fifties, was the spokesman and translator, though his deference to his elder made it clear he wasn't the decision maker.

The process of translation dictated the pace of the discussion, and encouraged an efficiency of debate that Seb found refreshing. No obsequious small talk, not a wasted word. The introductions were soon over, and Barnard handed a copy of the offer document across the table to Francois Steyn, the senior counsel. It was a twenty-page document, but Steyn scanned it for the essential content in under a minute. He then passed it to his most junior colleague to analyse as he spoke.

'Thank you, Mr Barnard. And thank you for the advance notice of the outline terms, which as far as I can see, are substantially unchanged from the draft you sent us last week.'

Chapter 67

He spoke with a heavy Afrikaans accent. English was evidently his second language.

'I have discussed your offer with my clients, and they wish to thank you for your time and interest in the potential of Hoodia in a pharmaceutical context but they cannot agree to the terms.'

And that was it. No counter offer. No alternative solution. The rebuff wasn't translated into Khoisan as all the previous dialogue had been. This was rehearsed; there was no need.

For a minute or two both sides looked at each other, neither party ready to blink first.

'Well, if that is all,' said Steyn, rising from his seat.

'Oh sit down, man,' snapped Barnard, glaring at him as he gathered his papers from the table. 'We've all come a long way to get this done, so why don't you start earning your money and help us get something sensible agreed!'

'We are happy to review any new offer you may have, Mr Barnard.'

Barnard stood up abruptly.

'William? Gentlemen, you'll excuse us for a few minutes.'

'Of course. Take all the time you need,' said Steyn.

Seb was conspicuously left in the room while his boss and client decided on their next move, and looked across the table at Steyn's plump face and wide grin. He had most of the cards, and he was having fun playing them.

He considered the two San. The elder's eyes were fixed on him. Neither of them looked away. After a pause that should have been uncomfortably long, but wasn't, the old man said a few words in his native Khoisan tongue, a language more clicked than spoken, and his fellow tribesman translated.

'There is a sadness in your eyes.'

Seb was dumbstruck. The words bore the wisdom of

ages. His thoughts leapt to Sophia, then to his family, to his father, to the essence of right and wrong. Something stirred in him, and he turned to the lawyer.

'Mr Steyn, they'll come back in any second now and offer a larger one-off payment. Please advise your clients to decline it. After that, they'll suggest a way of investing that money to give you a long-term income stream. It will sound attractive, but you should turn that down too.'

Steyn had his pen in his hand and was about to ask Seb a question when the door opened, and Barnard and Fletcher returned to their seats. It was Fletcher's turn to earn his money.

'Sorry for the delay gentlemen. We have discussed the maximum we feel we can offer, and subject to board approval, we would like to increase the offer by fifty percent. We will pay you fifteen million pounds, paid thirty days after the first approval of H57 in the US or Europe. The offer, however, only lasts for the duration of this meeting, so please consider your response and take the time you need to discuss with your legal counsel.'

The lawyers had a quick-fire discussion amongst themselves in Afrikaans, a language the San also understood without the need for translation. Steyn responded.

'For absolute clarity, if my clients agree to the payment, they forgo the rights to any pharmaceutical products derived from Hoodia Gordonii in perpetuity. Correct?'

This was Fletcher's big moment.

'Not necessarily. We know that long term preservation of your way of life is paramount, and that an ongoing income stream derived from Hoodia is your primary goal. To that end, we have created a tax-exempt financial instrument that provides an annual yield of nine percent. It is shielded from inflation and exposed to a portfolio of stable, low volatility assets that will give modest but compounding capital growth over and above the dividend income. In essence, you will receive one point five million pounds a year for as long as you wish. The money will be paid to you irrespective of whether H57, or any future Hoodia derived ethical pharmaceuticals, actually sell in any volume or not. I think you'll agree, a very robust long-term solution.'

The way Fletcher presented it, his solution did sound very attractive, unless of course you were reminded that at the point of approval, the drug would have proven beyond doubt that it was both safe and efficacious. That would make H57 a multi-billion-dollar product overnight. Which would give the San in the region of a billion pounds in royalties in the fifteen years that remained on the patent. Seb knew that, but he was confident that the men on the other side of the table didn't.

As each sentence was translated, Seb could see the San leader struggling to cope with the new information contained in Fletcher's structure, seemingly quite dazzled by it. He looked at Seb, and Seb gazed steadily back at him.

The San leader responded. His kinsman turned to Steyn and whispered the translation, which Steyn communicated crisply.

'My clients would like to thank you for the offer but will have to decline. Our information indicates that the fair value for the rights to commercialise the knowledge and resources of the indigenous people of the Kalahari is way in excess of this figure, and we would like to conclude our discussions until a more appropriate compensation package is presented to us.'

For the second time, the legal team gathered their

things and started to lead their clients out of the room. The meeting had taken months to arrange; without the Hoodia licence agreed, FS Biotech's deal with Zencor Pharma was in serious jeopardy.

'Fifteen million pounds plus a two and a half percent royalty. That's the last offer I'll make.'

Seb couldn't believe it. He knew that Barnard needed a deal but didn't expect him to fold quite so quickly. Just as surprisingly, Steyn responded almost without pause.

'Fifteen million pounds up front and a four percent royalty.'

Seb had given them the spine to get there and, whether Steyn knew it or not, that was about the right price.

'No! Absolutely not!' roared Barnard. 'I said that was my last offer.'

But he stayed put, and his presence meant he was still negotiating. Steyn, now brimming with confidence, tucked his pen back into his jacket for the third time.

'Oh God. Alright! Three and half percent.'

Steyn didn't break his step and was halfway out the door with his colleagues and clients when the capitulation rang out.

'You win!'

Steyn turned around, for the first time revealing the huge gap between his front teeth, his moustache dancing on his top lip.

'Excellent. I'll amend the documentation and send it over first thing tomorrow morning.'

The San and their legal team left the building and got straight into their waiting minibus. Barnard had skulked off to sulk in some corner of the lodge. Fletcher was polite but perfunctory, and left Seb to walk the visitors to their transportation. As the elder was about to climb into the minibus, he turned to Seb and remained still for a moment.

'You are a kind man, Mr Faber. Good things come to kind men.'

He spoke with perfect English, and his words found a place in Seb's soul he thought was long gone.

CHAPTER 68

If there was any form of dinner that evening, Seb wasn't invited to it. No matter: he wasn't remotely hungry. All his focus was on the task in hand. The window. Housekeeping unbolted the windows in the mornings and bolted them at dusk. The bolt key was on a ring with a dozen other keys in the housekeeper's pocket.

It wasn't a particularly sophisticated locking system. All he needed was a solid object that could be wedged tightly into the square aperture of the bolt, with enough of a handle to be able to unscrew it. His first idea was the end of the teaspoon, jammed in corner to corner. Too small. He wedged a pencil into the bolt, but that just burred when he twisted it. He checked the bathroom. His razor handle was a good fit, but despite being notched for enhanced grip in the wet, being round it offered barely any traction. And both ends of his toothbrush were too wide to fit. He sat down on his bed with his razor in his right hand and his toothbrush in his left. It could work. His attempt to shave the hard plastic of the toothbrush handle shot the razor blade three feet across the room, no impact on it whatsoever. As he was picking the blade up there was a gentle knock on the door.

Chapter 68

'Housekeeping, sir.'

'Come in,' said Seb.

The maid's routine was to turn down the bed and bolt the windows. Seb tugged at the corner of the bedding and, as she stepped forward to straighten it, held up the bladeless handle of his razor.

'Don't worry about the bed, but I need your help. I'm afraid I've broken my razor. Is there any chance you might be able to find me another one, Sylvia?'

The name badge on her dress helped.

'Oh yes, sir. I'll just do the windows then ask reception.'

She took the keys out of her pocket and made towards the first of the three windows.

'I'm sorry but I'm in a bit of a rush. I need to tidy up for dinner. Why don't I sort out the windows for you while you hunt down a razor?'

She looked anxious. He offered her a generous smile by way of compensation.

'Yes sir, but the keys must stay with me. My boss says keys must always be with me, sir.'

'Of course. I'll just take the window key if that's OK. I'm Seb, by the way.'

She hesitated, then smiled, and took the window key off the chain and handed it to him, putting the heavy bunch of door keys safely in her pocket before she hurried out of the door.

Seb quickly bolted the two windows at the front, then lowered the window at the back of the room to the correct height and wedged his toothbrush with all his might into the sliding mechanism on the right side of the window, then gave the bolts on either side one turn onto their host threads. Easily removed, even with a damaged pencil.

The maid wasn't much more than five feet tall and was very unlikely to see the red toothbrush stuck into the edge of the window a foot above Seb's head. He decided not to risk it, and turned off the main light, leaving only his bedside lamp on.

He gave the window a firm tug. It was stuck fast, but the left side, the un-wedged side, had a centimetre of play. It wouldn't move at all if it was properly bolted. He made for his bedside table where he had left his razor handle and blade but before he could do anything more there was a knock on the door. Seb invited Sylvia back into the room.

'All done,' said Seb.

He walked away from the rear window towards her, stopping her in her tracks.

'Here you go. All done.'

She took the key and handed him a pack of disposable razors.

'Perfect. Very kind Sylvia. Right. Better jump in the shower.'

'Oh yes, but first I need to do my check.'

'You don't trust me?' said Seb, pretending to be shocked.

'No, no, Mr Seb, sir. I don't know you. But it's my job.'

She went to the two front windows and give them a sharp upward tug to make sure they were fast. As she approached the rear window Seb walked with her and stood to her left looking out into the near darkness.

'Anything I should be worried about out there Sylvia?'

She could only lift the right hand side of the window. Seb occupied the left, and strong as she was, the makeshift toothbrush wedge did its job.

'Nothing to worry about out there Mr Seb, sir, just be careful of the man you see looking back at you.'

Chapter 68

Seb refocused his eyes on his reflection as she left him alone with his thoughts.

CHAPTER 69

Seb was already awake and dressed when his alarm went off under his pillow at 04.50. He pulled his toothbrush out of the window and used the handle to gently remove the bolts with a quarter anti-clockwise rotation. Henke had done exactly as he was instructed and was waiting for Seb in his bakkie by the roadside. He looked scared out of his mind, ushering Seb into his vehicle with a frantic wave of his arm and pulling away in second gear as quietly as possible to avoid any unwelcome attention.

'Thanks for meeting me, Henke. I need to ask some questions about your boss. I noticed you looked very uncomfortable when we saw you at the facility. And you seemed to have a run in with Mandla.'

'Anything I say to you now could get me killed if it gets to Barnard, you hear!'

Seb frowned.

'Isn't that a bit dramatic? He's an aging corporate executive, not a bloody assassin!'

'Have you asked him what he did before he came to FS Biotech. Before he came into this industry?'

'I haven't. He was some sort of advisor to the SA

government, wasn't he?'

'He certainly worked for the SA government. But not as a business advisor.'

'So, he was some form of contract killer? Listen to yourself Henke. He's an arrogant prick and far too used to getting his own way, but apart from that giant mute he has in tow, he's harmless.'

'That's bullshit, man. He's a total bastard. And very dangerous. But that's just part of it. The data we're about to publish is fake.'

'What do you mean, fake?'

'Fake man. Total fraud. Pure untreated Hoodia extract was used to dose the volunteers in our Phase 2 trial, not H57. God knows Hoodia extract works. It has done for thousands of years. We don't know how, but it does. The big problem for Barnard is that the isolated ingredient that we believed to be the active agent, the one we call H57 and have global rights to, is inferior to the whole plant extract in its natural form. It actually works slightly less well than the placebo. And we ran the trial three times.'

'When did you discover this?'

'Six months ago.'

'Jesus Christ! Who knows?'

'Barnard, me and now you'

'Mandla?'

'Mandla?! No! No, he has no brain for such things.'

'So, the fraudulent Phase 2 trial is almost certainly going to have a positive read out.'

'It *is* positive. It has met the primary endpoint of equal to or greater than a fifteen percent reduction in calorific intake over the twenty-one-day trial period.'

'Hoodia works, but your very expensive patented

product doesn't.'

'Correct.'

'And the shares will triple when you announce the fraudulent data. Zencor will trigger their licence option and inject fifty million dollars into a massive Phase 3 trial, using actual H57, which will almost certainly fail.'

'No. Will definitely fail.'

'But the world will shrug its shoulders because drug trials fail all the time, often for no identifiable reason. By which time Barnard will be long retired having most likely sold his shares for more than a hundred million dollars.'

The sun had just started to illuminate the desert scrub. There was enough light now to see. And to be seen. Henke had been glancing at the rear-view mirror from the start of the journey but now he did a violent double take. He could see a small dot in his rear horizon. A very small dot that was growing fast.

'Ah shit, they have me,' he whispered in despair.

Seb span round and saw Barnard's powerful 4x4 approaching at an alarming speed.

'Just pull over. I'll say I wanted another look at the facility, and I didn't want to disturb anyone or waste anyone's time.'

'At five in the fucking morning! They won't believe you! Oh my God.'

Henke was gripped with terror. Seb's own fight or flight impulses were racing, but he'd trained for this, he could control his instincts.

'Look, we can't outrun them in this, so we have no choice. Don't worry. I'll do the talking.'

They pulled over and Seb got out, leaving Henke with a frozen grin in the driver's seat. Mandla, as always, was driving, Barnard, imperious as ever, riding shotgun.

Chapter 69

Seb walked boldly up to Barnard who had opened the door but remained seated with his left leg resting on the running board.

'Morning Richard. I hope we didn't wake you? I wanted to take another look…'

The last thing Seb heard was a horrified gasp from Henke, then nothing. The short wooden truncheon struck his head with calculated precision.

CHAPTER 70

He came to in a small wooden hut with a corrugated iron roof. From the unbearable heat and the angle of the light coming through the slatted timbers, he guessed it was the middle of the day.

The pain from the back of his head was like the worst hangover he'd ever had. Just like a hangover, he had a dangerously dry mouth and was desperately thirsty. He would have got up to do something about it had he not been bound fast to a chair, his wrists lashed to the wooden arms with multiple loops of garden twine, his ankles bound to the legs. His watch had been removed from his wrist. His phone was in his jacket, left behind in Henke's bakkie.

He wasn't gagged. No need. From what he could glean from the gaps in the walls and the smells wafting in from outside, he was in a hut on the outer edge of the Hoodia plantation, well out of earshot of the main building. Nothing but desert rodents to hear any cry for help.

'This is fucking absurd,' he said loudly.

He found he was as surprised by his predicament as he was frightened. He'd become ever more certain that Fletcher was caught up in some sort of financial crime, but

Chapter 70

he'd never truly believed he was in any real peril. Now he had to accept the logical conclusion that he probably was.

The thing most in his favour was the fact that he wasn't dead; they must still have need of him. On the other hand, he'd left a game lodge without alerting anyone to his movements. It would be very easy indeed to concoct a perfectly plausible cause of death. Murdered for the fifty rand in his pocket and the clothes on his back. Stung by a scorpion, or a snake bite perhaps, although that would take quite some organising. No, much simpler to mock up a car crash. An alcohol-related traffic accident, so commonplace that it wouldn't draw any particular attention from the authorities.

Fear began to creep into his consciousness. He acknowledged it but wouldn't let it take its grip, not yet. But if Barnard was some sort of 'operative', as ridiculous as it seemed, he knew he would be more than willing to protect his position and his fortune, and he had the mountainous Mandla at his beck and call to help.

He thought about his family, he thought about Sophia. But mostly he thought about how to get out of this situation alive.

Hours went by, and the pain in his buttocks, arms and legs morphed to numbness. He wasn't at all sure he'd be able to trust his limbs by now even if he were freed.

Muffled sounds came from beyond the timber walls of his makeshift cell. Footsteps, someone with a long stride, approached the hut, then stopped. The beam of sunlight coming though one of the larger gaps in the timbers was obscured as a dark-skinned face pressed against the opening. Seb was sure he saw a flash of white as a broad grin broke out across Mandla's face. He couldn't fail to hear the deep guttural laughter.

'Mandla. Listen to me. Tell Barnard that I am happy to talk.'

No response. Instead, Mandla drew his enormous frame up and strolled away, in absolutely no hurry.

More time passed, perhaps two hours. Seb tried to sleep, but his thirst wouldn't allow it. He distracted himself from the pain and discomfort by taking in every detail of his environment and rehearsing scenarios over and over in his head. Then a commotion, someone being dragged towards the hut, petrified, gibbering. It was Henke, pleading. He was pleading to Barnard. The sound of a car door slamming in the far distance.

Footsteps approached. The clunk of a padlock being unlocked and removed. The door swung open, and a few metres beyond it Seb saw a badly disfigured Henke, as limp as a scarecrow, being held upright by Mandla.

'Bag him, please, Mandla,' said the unseen Barnard.

Mandla produced a hessian sac and put it over Henke's head. Still pleading in Afrikaans, he was too weak to offer any resistance. Barnard, in his standard khaki uniform, strode into the shack until he stood a foot in front of Seb.

They looked at each other in silence. Seb cocked an eyebrow.

'This is all a bit unnecessary, isn't it, Richard? Why don't you just tell me what you want?'

'How's your head? Not too bad, I hope. Mandla has hit many heads, broken most. Yours we did not want to break.'

'It's fine. Thanks for asking.'

'I suspect you would like a little water,'

'No thanks, I'll have a beer when I get back to the Lodge.'

'Oh, very good Seb. Ever the unflappable British Army

Chapter 70

officer. Yes, we can drink beer together, but first I have a question for you.'

He paused and tilted his head.

'Are you with me or against me?'

'I'm not sure I understand the question. We're here to act for you, so I'd say we're with you.' said Seb, squinting up at him as a sliver of sunlight momentarily blinded him.

'But you don't agree with my ways, and you don't like me much, do you?' said Barnard. 'That's OK. I don't seek admiration, and I have no need of friends. I do demand respect, however.'

With that, Barnard slowly raised his right hand with his index finger extended.

'Thank you, Mandla.'

He stepped to one side to give Seb a clear view of Henke and Mandla outside his cell. Mandla pulled out the handgun from the holster under his jacket and held it to Henke's bagged head. The noise was deafening. The exit wound exploded blood, brain matter and skull fragments onto the parched earth. Henke wasn't whimpering any more. His legs twisted in the ghastly contortion that only a lifeless body could achieve. This was unexpected.

'What the fuck have you done?' said Seb steadily. 'You won't get away with that, you crazy old bastard. William saw that scuffle in Henke's office, and he'll send the police straight to your door.'

'Oh yes. William. He might suspect something I suppose. Why don't we ask him?'

Footsteps approached from nearby, and a pair of fawn desert boots stepped over Henke's partially decapitated body. Fletcher strode into the shack, unmoved.

'Hi Seb. Look what a mess you've made.'

'What the...'

'A bit confusing I'll grant you. No time for that now. Richard and I need to ask you an important question. Listen carefully and think before you answer. Are you with us or against us?'

'What have you done? What are you doing?'

Seb searched Fletcher's eyes, stunned.

'Don't be so bloody oversensitive, Seb. We have the chance to make hundreds of millions of dollars for Richard's shareholders, a very generous windfall for the San community and, yes, a little bit for ourselves. The only losers will be Zencor, and God knows they can cope with a little setback.'

'But Zencor aren't mugs! They'll investigate the fake trial and prosecute the FS Biotech directors and advisors. They've got billions of dollars to spend on lawyers. You won't have long to enjoy any money you make out of this,' said Seb.

Barnard cut in.

'No risk of that. The way Henke prepared the trial material there's no way any wrongdoing can be proven. And, of course, the poor chap takes that information with him.'

'And I just go back to London and carry on as normal?'

'No, much more than that. We want you to work with us on our next projects,' said Fletcher, still chillingly unaffected by the cold-blooded murder he'd been complicit in. 'You have skills we value, Sebastian. And there's always plenty of opportunity to use those skills to give our partners a head start. Improve the odds shall we say,' said Fletcher.

'And what do I get out of this arrangement?' asked Seb.

'More money than you could ever dream of earning,'

Chapter 70

said Barnard. 'But more immediately, you get to keep your life. And so, for the final time, are you with us or against us Sebastian?'

This was about survival.

Seb paused, weighing up his options.

'Well, that's some offer, and I was getting bored of broking anyway. OK, I'll do it.'

'Very wise. I thought you would see sense,' said Barnard. 'But of course, you'll do whatever you need to do to save yourself. You'll go to the authorities with your story the moment you are free, so we have taken some extra precautions. You have a twin sister don't you Sebastian?'

He froze.

'Living at 17 Sterndale Road, Brook Green, and a brother living at Apt 308, 150 Bleaker Street, New York. And of course, your widowed mother lives in that little house in the countryside. Have you not been responsible for enough tragedy, already Sebastian?'

This was the test. He had lived with the guilt of his father's death most of his life, but no one had ever suggested that he was even a bit responsible for Sophia's death, however much he believed it himself. He strained at the twine with such force that it embedded itself into his flesh. But blind fury was what they wanted. He forced himself to ease back and took some deep breaths.

'To be entirely clear with you, if either one of us is taken into custody,' continued Barnard, 'I will instruct your brother's execution. Him first. He has no family, and I'm not a barbarian, Sebastian. However, if you fail to retract the charges after that, I will give the order for the execution of your sister, and none of us wants to leave your niece and nephew motherless. We are businessmen. We take no pleasure in this, but as poor Henke found out, we do value loyalty.'

Seb was trapped. It would be his word against theirs, and their threats weren't idle. Henke's corpse, already swarming with flies, made that all too clear.

'There's no choice to make. I'm with you. So, I think there's no more need for all this?' he said, looking down at his bindings.

'Nothing silly now. Mandla seems to have a taste for blood today, and I can't always control him,' said Barnard. He produced a small penknife from his shirt's breast pocket, opened the blade and handed it to Fletcher. 'I think we can trust him now, don't you?'

They couldn't of course, but Fletcher was a former SBS commando and had done a lot more with a blade than cut string. And could again if he needed to.

Seb had been scanning the room for anything he could possibly use to his benefit. Six inches from his right foot was a flat, oval shaped stone, about four inches long and three wide. Fletcher cut the wrist bindings; right hand then left. As he went down on one knee to cut his right leg free, Seb leant forward and grabbed the stone from the dirt floor, concealing it in his palm. Fletcher turned his attention to Seb's left leg and the moment the tie was cut, Seb lurched clumsily out of the chair and took him to the ground. Within seconds Mandla was in the hut, hoisting Seb up and dumping him violently back onto the chair. Fletcher picked himself off the floor and dusted himself down, instinctively tapping his hip pocket to confirm that his phone was where it should be. He felt the solid mass of the stone, his Nokia now concealed in Seb's left sock.

'Now you've got that out of your system let's get on, shall we?'

Chapter 70

Their shared training session, months ago, on their brand-new phones had given Seb two pertinent facts. The first that Fletcher's password was the foundation year of The Royal Marines, 1755. The second that this device had a voice recorder.

'Take your time Seb, we'll be outside clearing up your bloody mess,' said Fletcher. 'We'll need you too, Mandla,' he called as he and Barnard walked out of the hut into the searing afternoon heat.

Seb grabbed the phone out of his sock, concealing it in the palm of his hand, and walked unsteadily to the front right corner of the shack. In a matter of seconds, he had unlocked the phone, activated the voice recorder, and slipped it back into his sock. Thirty seconds of recording time that ended with a distinctive ping. No signal. He slumped back in the chair and started counting in his head.

'Guys, I need help here. I can't move.'

Fletcher first, then Barnard, stooped into the shack once again.

'You do look a bit of a wreck, I must say, Sebastian. Mandla, come and give our new comrade some assistance,' said Barnard.

Mandla's mass completely filled the door frame as he bent almost double to get through it. He stood behind Seb, put his hands under his arms and raised him to his feet with astonishing ease.

'You really didn't need to kill Henke. He was shit scared. He'd have done anything you wanted.'

9 seconds

'He came to you, so he would go to others. Simple risk management,' said Barnard.

'And you, William? Twelve years in the Marines and the

SBS, is this really what you got out of it?'

'Oh, for heaven's sake don't be so bloody sanctimonious! We've both served our country, it's only right that we get some sort of payback.'

17 seconds

'And Mandla does all the dirty work?'

'When we want to keep our hands clean. Sometimes we don't. It's what we all trained for Seb. You're no different.'

Ping.

He'd planned to cover the chime with a cough, but he'd misjudged the thirty seconds. Fletcher, puzzled, recognised the tone and hastily tapped his left hip pocket. Seb had one chance. With two outstretched arms, he burst for the door only just evading Mandla's bid to grab him from behind. Barnard and Fletcher were still in his path, but his swift, ferocious hand-offs knocked them both off balance, Fletcher back-pedalling into the timber wall and Barnard onto his back.

Henke's body had been removed, but the evidence of his execution was clear to see as Seb sprinted past the bloody mess.

He'd seen Fletcher use his mobile phone in the laboratory building the day before. There was a signal there then.

He tore down the dusty pathway between two Hoodia fields towards the main building. The phone was riding up his sock with every stride, and he bent to grab it before it ended up in the plantation. He barely missed a step, but as he looked over his shoulder, he could see the triathlete frame of Fletcher and the surprisingly fleet of foot Mandla bearing down on him, just ten yards behind. There was no sign of Barnard. With the phone now in his hand, he powered forward with all the strength he could muster in his taut aching limbs.

A hundred yards to the building. No plan for when he got there. The closer he got, the shorter his advantage became. With fifty yards to go, his lead was reduced to eight yards. Twenty yards from the building, and Mandla and Fletcher were just five yards behind him. His legs were giving up, slowing him down. Still, he didn't break stride as he approached the locked door. He charged at it with his good shoulder. The lock exploded in the timber frame, and he careered into the building.

He made straight for Henke's office and found the door ajar. He ran to the far side of the desk, dropped his body to a forty-five-degree angle and pumped his legs, driving it across the room and flush to the door. Seconds later Fletcher and Mandla arrived at the blockade, and stopped behind it to draw breath and consider their options.

Seb started scrolling through the menu on the Nokia.

Email
Attachment
Audio file
To: uksales@blountandco.com
Send
Sending mail...

By the time he looked up again, Mandla had a photocopier above his head and was hurling it through the glass wall. Seb stood his ground as Mandla unhurriedly enlarged the glass aperture so that he could step though unscathed. He glanced down at the phone and read from the screen.

'Mail sent,' Seb said loudly for all to hear.

He looked up to address his enemies.

'The office has now been appraised of today's events. Funny, I remember you thought that audio recording function would come in handy one day, didn't you, William.'

It hadn't sent. The office hadn't been told. The phone kept on stubbornly displaying 'SENDING MESSAGE', and had been for far too long. Fletcher looked at the phone and tapped his left hip pocket once again. With growing confusion, he put his hand in his pocket, pulling out the stone with a look of reluctant admiration breaking across his face. Mandla stepped through the hole in the glazing and towards a retreating Seb, but was checked by Barnard's shouting.

'For Christ's sake unblock the door will you. I'm too old to be crawling through broken glass.'

Mandla pulled the desk away from the door and slid it halfway across the room. Barnard stepped into Henke's office, wearily mopping his brow. He gestured to Mandla with his long bony index finger.

'Why don't you introduce yourself properly?'

Mandla looked at Seb steadily, a grin washing across his oversized face with the preternatural look of a hunter that has cornered its prey. Seb picked up the only thing that came close to being a weapon, a polished stone paperweight, assumed a defensive stance and raised it above his head.

CHAPTER 71

A female voice cut across them, calmly but firmly.

'That's enough.'

It was unmistakably an order, and they all froze as she strode authoritatively into Henke's office. It was her, the same woman he'd seen outside Fletcher's office, and leaving Ickling Hall.

'Hello Seb. I think we've seen enough. Unwise to get in a scuffle with Mandla with that shoulder of yours.'

Seb stayed where he was, the paperweight at the ready.

'Who *are* you? And what the *fuck* is going on?'

'My name is Lucy Mannings. I think you've met everyone else here.'

Mandla spoke, for the first time to Seb's knowledge.

'Whoa, Seb. Put that down before you hurt someone.'

Seb glared at him, lowering the paperweight but not letting it go. Barnard broke the silence.

'Sebastian, allow me to introduce you to Mandla Solomon William Barnard, my youngest son.'

Mandla extended his right hand. Seb put the paperweight down, and accepted it expressionlessly. A door opened in the distance and footsteps, faintly familiar, approached. Henke, alive and well, and grinning all over his moustachioed face. Seb gawped at him.

'But I watched your head being blown off five minutes ago!'

'Oh, it got better, thanks,' said Henke, laughing uproariously.

There was a buzzing sound and a green light came from Seb's left hand.

MESSAGE SENT

'That message has gone,' he said fiercely, as he tossed the phone over to Fletcher.

'You clever sod. I'd better get this unravelled pronto.'

He pressed a number on speed dial and gave terse instructions to someone on the end of the line to delete the message from Blounts' email server and report back immediately if anyone had opened it. What would happen then wasn't discussed.

Lucy Mannings was now standing directly in front of Seb.

'The events of the past year, culminating in the last few days, will be explained in due course Seb, but what you need to know now is that I head up a specialist unit of the British Secret Intelligence Service, and William, Richard and Mandla here are among my colleagues. We have observed you unobtrusively for over two years and, though you were unaware of it, you have been in an intense process of trials and observation for the whole of the last year. As a selection process, it's every bit as exacting as the one you've already experienced, but unlike that one, this is a process that the candidates are unaware that they're participating in. Unless of course they pass, and less than one percent does. Congratulations, Seb. If you want it, your new life starts now.'

CHAPTER 72

She left the scene as quickly as she had appeared. A large Mercedes was waiting for her in the car park, a burly man in an ill-fitting suit holding the door. Seb went back to the lodge with Barnard, Fletcher and Mandla. This time, Barnard took the wheel. Seb sat in the back with Mandla, too exhausted to speak.

They were at the Lodge in less than forty minutes, and Seb had only one thing on his mind as Barnard pulled up outside reception.

'If anyone wants to tell me what the hell just happened, I'll be in the bar.'

Fletcher span round in the front passenger seat and did something completely unexpected. He smiled.

'The drinks are on me.'

That was all. No lengthy exposition, no apology. But it was all Seb needed; they were on the same side.

All four men went to the bar, Fletcher ordering a round of beers and ushering them to a table on the veranda bathed in the last golden light of the day. Seb cast his eyes around the table. Barnard was discussing travel plans with Mandla, while Fletcher was fielding a call from the IT department.

Five people had opened the email, Seb gathered, but the audio file was too muffled to understand. Judging from the relief on Fletcher's face, the matter was now closed. As he put his hard-working Nokia back in his left hip pocket, the four ice-cold draft Windhoek lagers were brought to the table. Fletcher picked up his glass.

'A toast. Whatever happens from now on, you handled yourself with honour. Well done, Seb.'

He clinked his glass tankard against Seb's.

'To Seb Faber, in whom we have great expectations.'

They all drank to Seb, and Seb drank to himself. He had so many questions that he didn't know where to start.

'You all work for that woman, Lucy Mannings?'

'From time to time,' replied Fletcher.

'And Richard, I don't have a small fortune to make getting your IPO away at some ridiculously inflated price?'

'Sorry to disappoint you, Sebastian. The company is a real entity, but I stepped in when the previous CEO retired early after the first trial for H57 failed. It was a good place for me to operate and Lucy thought it would give us a chance to have a good look at you.'

Seb momentarily felt ill-used, confusingly mixed with pride.

'And Henke. That was some performance!'

'I'm glad you appreciated it,' said Fletcher. 'It wasn't easy procuring a fresh corpse that matched Henke's physical dimensions and ethnicity. The body was three inches taller and thirty kilos lighter than Henke, so we had to get it out of the way before you had a chance to get in an eagle-eyed look!'

'What about the San? Were they all in on it?'

Barnard responded.

'No. The San will find out about the failure of H57 with

Chapter 72

the rest of the world when we publish the real results next week. They won't get a financial windfall, but on the other hand they won't have to battle against the exploitation of their lands had it worked. No harm done in the end.'

Barnard sounded only marginally less self-satisfied than the character he'd been portraying, but in a world of small margins, it was the difference between a cast-iron prick and a charismatic rogue.

'Now Mandla and I must go. We have a new assignment and a plane to catch.'

Seb had wanted more time with Mandla, who he guessed was roughly his own age.

'You are one big, scary bastard, Mandla,' he said.

'I didn't scare you, though, did I?'

Fletcher was also on his feet.

'I need a quick chat, Richard, I'll walk out with you. Seb, I'll meet you at eight o'clock for dinner. We can finish our debrief then.'

As they walked off, Barnard suddenly paused and half turned to face Seb and offered a reluctant grin.

'You can shoot.' Miserly gratitude for saving his life, but it was all that Seb was going to get.

Seb was left alone on the veranda. He sat in a rattan armchair staring out towards the plain, but his mind was elsewhere. He was looking back over his tracks, thinking about everything that had happened to him that might have been manufactured or observed. He was so absorbed in his thoughts he didn't see the waitress standing there.

'Another drink sir?'

'Yes please. A large glass of your very best white wine please. Would you put it on my tab? The name is Fletcher, William Fletcher.'

CHAPTER 73

Despite having a shower, which took some of the edge off, Seb was still feeling a bit drunk and proportionately bold when he joined Fletcher for dinner. He needed some answers.

'Have you been watching me ever since I joined the bank?'

'Before you joined the bank, actually. Why do you think you got the interview in the first place?'

'Err... ability?'

Fletcher let that thought hang in the air.

'And Richard. Who *is* he? I know he was CEO of another healthcare company that took investment from a shady Finn. Then they both disappeared, completely. My contact said he considered him a very dangerous man.'

'Well, he was. South African Special Forces Brigade. Very capable outfit.'

'Then what happened?'

'His wife died, leaving him with five children to support, two of them being Mandla and his younger sister. Mandla's parents worked for Richard on his farm in Natal, you see. They were murdered in their home by a white police officer,

Chapter 73

'resisting arrest' being the 'just cause'. The officer was, in point of fact, raping Mandla's mother when her husband returned from work. He shot Mandla's father, and then their mother, in front of Mandla and his sister. Mandla's facial scars aren't tribal. They're the marks left by the officer's sjambok as he tried to get him off his mother. Richard and his wife took them in as their own at the ages of nine and five.'

'And the policeman got away with it?'

'No. He died before he got to trial. Shot in a robbery was the story, but no one was arrested for the crime.'

'I see.'

'Yes, I think you probably do. After that everything was going OK for Richard and his family, then he lost his wife to cancer. An army salary couldn't pay for all the childcare so he left and started taking private security work for anyone who could pay the right money.'

'A mercenary?'

'Something between a mercenary and an assassin. And that eventually led him to the Russian mafia. Ivo Karvonen, your Finn, was the front man for one of the big Moscow mob families, and his job was to wash money though the financial markets. He needed a complicit CEO to place into a company that needed investment badly, and Sanderson Medical was that company.'

'And the disappearing act? What happened to Karvonen?'

'Our security services were watching him, and after the investment was made, they took him and Barnard in. Vauxhall Cross knew the mob would be after them both for the lost money, and that they'd never stop looking. Lucy saw long term value in Barnard, less so in Karvonen, so she did a deal.'

'She gave them Karvonen in return for Barnard.'

'That's right, Seb. And that was her first recruit.'

'And she wants me to be her next recruit. What is this unit, William?'

'For now, all you need know is that the group you've been selected for is lawful, ethical and works under the umbrella of Her Majesty's Secret Intelligence Service. As to the nature of the work, it involves the disruption of large-scale organised crime. All major crime needs to be funded, and the proceeds of the criminal activity needs to be washed. Much of that activity is in the big global financial hubs and, right now, none more so than London. From time to time, we're called upon to gather information and, on occasion, intervene. But don't get excited: James Bond you won't be. Neither am I for that matter. There'll be a folder in your safe when you return to your room. Open it, read it, but then leave it 'til the morning. Hand it back to me at the airport and not before.'

'OK, William, I think I can manage that.'

'But by far the most important thing you need to do now is precisely nothing. You go back to your desk and do the same job with the same pragmatic efficiency as you did before.'

'Yes Sir!' replied Seb, aping military respect for rank.

'And none of that 'Sir' stuff either. Even in jest.'

'Got it. But can I ask you one question?'

'One.'

'At the risk of appearing vain, why me?'

Fletcher was quick with his answer.

'Honesty. You tell the truth, and more importantly everyone knows it. You do what you say you'll do. You say

Chapter 73

what you see, and you don't seem to give much of a shit who cares. And that is how it will continue until we call upon you, if indeed you choose this path. Now help me finish this bottle, and then I'm off to bed.'

Fletcher emptied the rest of the bottle into their glasses, and they sat in silence as Seb began to process everything that had happened. After a while, Fletcher drained his and flagged down the waitress to sign for the bill. Seb wasn't quite finished.

'Did you rig that bar fight? Was that another test?'

'No, it damn well wasn't. You nearly cocked the whole thing up as it happens. We had to pull in more favours than we wanted to get you out of that one.'

'I knew it. The camera.'

'Indeed. And the cocaine in his back pocket was a bit of extra insurance. My idea actually.'

Fletcher, allowing himself a little self-indulgent smile, signed for the bill with a flourish and stood up to leave.

'Don't do that again, Seb. We can't get you out of every scrape you get yourself into.'

CHAPTER 74

Once in his room he opened the safe, wondering how they'd managed to guess his four-digit code. He pulled out a folder with 'S Faber - FS Biotech Briefing Document' written in black marker pen. The only security was a solitary rubber band.

Official Secrets Act 1989

Be it enacted by the Queen's most Excellent Majesty by and with the advice and consent of the Lords Spiritual and Temporal, and Commons, in the present Parliament assembled, and by the authority of the same, as follows....

A strong start, but as he leafed through the fourteen-pages, his initial fascination for the legendary document in his hands swiftly dissipated; the language was so cloying it made every clause and subclause a conundrum. The final page was the one for his signature. His full name, address and date of birth were already printed there. The date was also printed in anticipation. He felt a flash of irritation that he'd been so easy to predict.

Chapter 74

Still. Pretty sure that he wasn't going to be permitted to amend the content of the Official Secrets Act to suit his own ends, he took a pen from his jacket pocket and signed it. He put the document back in the folder, resealed it with the rubber band and put it in his backpack.

He lay on the bed, hands clasped behind his head. He was in sensory overload but with the help of the wine and the companionship of the gently wobbling and whirring ceiling fan, he was soon sucked into his deepest sleep for many months.

CHAPTER 75

Seb and Fletcher said little to each other at the Airport before taking their separate flights; Fletcher's to London, Seb to Geneva via Zurich. Seb handed Fletcher the folder in the international departures hall.

'I'm in,' said Seb.

'Good,' replied Fletcher. 'Just one more thing. You haven't asked, but that episode in the kitchen at Ickling was entirely choreographed. Phoebe helps us test young men's weaknesses from time to time. Most capitulate.'

'I can well imagine they do,' said Seb, careful not to overstep the mark, relieved when Fletcher smiled.

'Good luck tomorrow. I'll see you in the office on Monday.'

That was all that was said. Fletcher knew what was occupying Seb's mind. And he understood.

CHAPTER 76

Seb landed at Geneva Airport at 4pm and transferred to a crowded minibus filled with over-excited children and exhausted parents for the last leg of the journey to the resort. He took a seat at the very front and did his best to sleep during the hour-long shuttle. He didn't succeed, but at least avoided any interaction with the other passengers.

He checked into the same hotel and requested the same room. He had expected to be overwhelmed by a torrent of grief, but he felt calm. In control. Empowered by facing his fear and facing down the horror. He'd been so unbearably sad, so pissed off for so long and he was weary of his hamster wheel of misery. He lay on the bed for a while, staring out of the window towards Mont Blanc, now shrouded in darkness, its very permanence continually drawing people to try to conquer it for no other reason than that it was there. Eventually he stood up, walked over to the window and swung both sides open, leaning on his folded arms as he breathed in the freezing night air. A few unsteady twenty-somethings wandered down the road below and a muffled drumbeat could just about be heard from the subterranean night club in the middle of town. And he was OK.

After a while the cold forced him to close the window, and galloping fatigue drove him to bed. He slept a dreamless sleep, empty of the demons he'd grown so used to battling day and night since that day.

He rose with the light and met his guide at the bottom of the Aiguille du Midi cable car at 08.30 sharp. He was a short, bird-like man in his early fifties whose every day on earth was etched into his deeply furrowed face.

'Sebastian, no? I am Phillipe. Welcome to my mountain.'

He had enough English to communicate perfectly well but not quite enough to stop him sounding like an extra from *'Allo 'Allo*.

Mountain communities are small, and news always travels fast. Phillipe hadn't been on the Vallée Blanche that day, but he knew of the tragedy of the beautiful young girl within half an hour of it happening. The whole of Chamonix knew about it within the day, and Seb's return to the town hadn't gone unnoticed. The hotel staff knew. The mountain rescue team knew. The guiding community knew. Clients booked Phillipe a full season in advance, but he had volunteered himself the moment the call came in. A group of Russians had been bumped to the afternoon to release him. It would do them no harm, he felt.

He chatted away in the cable car and Seb was politely responsive. They carefully avoided direct reference to Sophia until they were in the granite tunnel at the top station, two kilometres above the valley floor, when he took Seb to one side.

'You show me where you need to go. Then follow me. I will keep you safe.'

It was a glorious day. Not a cloud in the sky, and nothing more than a fresh breeze to contend with. Seb was roped to

Chapter 76

Phillipe as they descended the arête on foot, time Phillipe filled with commentary on the birds circling high above them, the direction of the wind rising from the glacier, and the condition of the snow. Nothing that required more than a grunt of acknowledgement from Seb but still diverted his attention from the precipice just a few feet to his left. They put their skis on at the usual place. The group of Swedes ahead of them set off left to tackle one of the more technically challenging routes. The group behind were motionless halfway down the southern path. One of their party was frozen to the spot with terror at the point where you can see exactly what will happen if you lose your footing. She was safe, but they'd all be getting very cold talking her off the cliff.

Phillipe followed the 'Route Classique' as Seb and Sophia had done the previous Spring, although he soon diverted from the tracked-out path with a freedom born of his knowledge and instinctive feel for the mountain. Seb called out to him.

'Phillipe.'

Phillipe made three bouncy turns in the foot-deep powder and came to a gentle stop. Seb pointed to a spot further to the side with his ski pole.

'I need to stop over there. Is it safe do you think?'

'Yes, I think, but I go first then you follow my tracks. Yes?'

'Thanks Phillipe.'

He peeled off to the right and stopped twenty metres away, at the spot Seb had identified.

'Snow is good.'

He beckoned Seb down with a wave of his ski pole and Seb made his way towards him. Seb planted his poles, took off his gloves, reached into his jacket and took out a photograph and a large aluminium cigar case.

'I will be down there. Just follow my tracks when you are ready,' said Phillipe, and skied off to leave Seb alone.

Seb looked at the photograph one of their exuberant witnesses had taken at that very spot. Their engagement photograph. They'd been so filled with happiness in that moment, their future together infinite. He stared at it for a few minutes more, lifted his head and drew in a deep lungful of air.

'I loved you so much, Sophia. I still do. Always will.'

He kissed her picture, gently rolled it up into a scroll, removed the lid of the cigar case and slowly pushed it in, firmly resealing it with the screw top lid. He took off his backpack and set it down carefully on the uphill side of the slope, flopped down next to it, his skis still on, grabbed his shovel and, from his prone position, dug a hole about a metre deep. Then he took the cigar case, pushed it deep into the firmer snow at the bottom and refilled the hole, compacting it so that the case was secure, and safe from the skis and boards that would pass above it for millennia. He levelled the area off, first with his hands, then with his skis, re-secured the shovel to his backpack, put his now frozen hands back into his gloves and pushed off towards Phillipe. He stopped next to him, his eyes glassy, his face composed and determined.

'Happy to continue, Sebastian?'

'Happy to continue, Phillipe.'

'Bon. We go. Stay close.'

They set off, weaving down mile after mile of alpine wilderness. After forty minutes they came off the glacier and entered the moraine field, the path snaking down

Chapter 76

between granite boulders as they had done before. Phillipe knew where Sophia had died. All the locals did. As he approached the spot, he slowed down and looked back at Seb.

'We stop?'

Seb raised his right hand and pointed down the mountain.

'No Phillipe, we go on. We go on.'

THE END

FACT: *Hoodia gordonii* does indeed exist and is a cactus indigenous to Botswana, Namibia and South Africa, where it has traditionally been used as an appetite suppressant. Over the last twenty-five years a number of clinical trials have been undertaken to see whether a safe and effective standardised extract of the plant could be developed commercially as a pharmaceutical product. In 2002, the San peoples' rights were officially recognised, allowing them a percentage of any profits and spin-offs resulting from the marketing of *hoodia*.

FICTION: Beyond these basic facts, this is a work of fiction. Names, characters, businesses, places and events are either the products of the author's imagination or used in a fictitious manner. Any resemblance to actual persons, living or dead, or real events is purely coincidental.

The Last Cut

The turf now softened,
Garden tools in the hut,
The grass's last gasp effort,
This will be the last cut.

The air now feels heavy,
So fresh and so still,
So subtle, yet so absolute,
And ushers that thrill.

Where are my boots
And the rest of my kit?
A new gum-shield to buy,
To mould, and to fit.

Enough training, am I ready,
Did I drink too much beer?
Will the coach pick me,
Will this be my year?

Triggers, my memories
I will never forget,
But, for others, now
My time past, and yet.

I can still run fast,
I am still strong,
My passing still straight,
My kicking still long.

Brave in the tackle,
In the ruck and the maul,
Robust in defence,
And under the high ball.

But no, these dreams
Are from an old fool,
The moment will pass,
The ardour will cool.

My hamstrings too tight,
Too weak of the knee,
My stamina waning,
I must accept the new me.

My boots long hung up,
A generation has passed,
Those days, so honest,
The longings, they last.

So I sit on my mower
For the last time this year,
And I yearn for the battle,
The contest, the fear.

The apples are ripening,
Leaves fall from the trees,
That's what my eyes view,
But not what my heart sees.

Metal studs tap the concrete
On the changing room floor,
Deep Heat is the scent
As we charge out the door.

Memories, such memories,
Buried deep in my soul,
Such happiness, some sadness,
But content in my role.

But look yonder, it's my boy
new boots on his feet,
New season, new team,
New challenges to meet.

He can tackle, he can pass,
He can dart, he can weave,
He can ruck, he can maul,
He has made me believe.

Believe in the seasons,
Faith that all is not lost,
Hope that all will be well,
Long after the first frost.

This is the last cut,
Last cut of the year,
But I have hope in my heart,
In nothing I fear.

Go well, my son,
Give of your best,
You carry me with you,
With you I am blessed.

H. C. Kingsmill Moore